WHEN WE WERE FRIENDS

SAMANTHA TONGE

Boldwood

First published in Great Britain in 2023 by Boldwood Books Ltd.

Cover Design by Head Design Ltd

Cover Illustration: Shutterstock

A CIP catalogue record for this book is available from the British Library.

Paperback ISBN 978-1-80415-438-0

Large Print ISBN 978-1-80415-437-3

Hardback ISBN 978-1-80415-436-6

Ebook ISBN 978-1-80415-439-7

Kindle ISBN 978-1-80415-440-3

Audio CD ISBN 978-1-80415-431-1

MP3 CD ISBN 978-1-80415-432-8

Digital audio download ISBN 978-1-80415-435-9

Boldwood Books Ltd
23 Bowerdean Street
London SW6 3TN
www.boldwoodbooks.com

For Clare Wallace, the best kind of publishing industry friend. As the girls would say, she's got my back — and my front.

PROLOGUE
JUNE 2004

Having checked that no one had followed her there, Morgan stood at the back end of Dailsworth High, by the hazel tree that grew next to the hidden basement door. To her mother's horror, no-frills Morgan had insisted on wearing a tux to the prom. She adjusted the bow tie her dad had fastened and glanced down at the smart, black jacket. Morgan was more used to seeing the vertical rows of metallic school achievement badges down her bottle-green blazer's lapels when she stood on the school grounds.

Untended plants sprawled across the ground and climbed the cracked windows of the disused science lab. Glad to never have to suffer the stuffiness of classrooms again, she breathed in the smell of woody soil. A sprig of her spiky, short hair stuck defiantly in the air as she consulted the clock on her mum's old flip phone.

With her confident stride, Paige was the first friend to arrive, her rusty-red salon hair stylishly covering the top of her slinky, white, halter-neck dress. The silky material almost reached the ground and was cut to show off her bare upper back. The two girls gave each other a side hug.

Next, Emily appeared like a rabbit from the undergrowth, paused, moved forwards and then stopped again. Morgan and her friends had gone shopping to Debenhams in Manchester to buy their outfits for the prom.

Their mums had joined them, apart from Emily's who'd been ill for over a year and wasn't up to it. Emily loved knitting and the girls had teased that she'd make her own woolly outfit. However, she fell in love with a baby-blue dress, it had polka dots and was retro fifties style, going down to her knees. She'd ignored her outgoing mother's advice to get something that showed off her legs and cleavage. Morgan drew Emily in for an embrace whilst Paige playfully pulled on her high ponytail. The four of them had been looking forward to the prom for weeks, getting dressed up, seeing how their teachers danced, and the sleepover at Paige's afterwards. Yesterday, Morgan, Emily and Tiff had dropped off their overnight bags at her house.

Tiff turned up last, running as her cheeks billowed in and out with puffs of humid air. Her pace slowed and she sashayed up the last steps, almost tripping as she bowed to imaginary fans at her sides. Tiff's mum insisted her daughter went full-blown Hollywood, convinced that her one and only child was going to be a world-renowned actress. She almost passed out with delight when Tiff's curves fitted into the silver, long fishtail covered in sequins. It was purple and matched her glasses. Tiff blew the other three girls kisses, sparkly pink lip gloss marks left on her fingers.

Together, they brushed aside strategically placed branches on the ground to reveal the hidden door. Due to a mini heatwave over the last week, the ground and fallen leaves were bone dry so the girls ran no risk of dirtying their fancy clothes. Paige and Tiff heaved it up. Emily checked around before following the others in.

Climbing down, the four of them chatted about the evening ahead and whether anyone would sneak in alcohol. Emily closed the door behind herself as Morgan switched on the torch they always left by the bottom of the steps. The school's old basement, run down and forgotten, smelt of mould and crawled with spiders that didn't scare these teenagers.

'The last meeting ever of The Secret Gift Society,' said Morgan, her voice sounding full and unexpectedly trembling.

'It's been a lifesaver,' said Emily. 'I don't know how I'd have got through this last year without you four.' Her face was tinged pink. 'You're the best. More like sisters.'

'I wish we were all going to the same sixth form,' mumbled Tiff. 'It's scary, the thought of having to make new friends, right? It's hard to imagine another group of girls understanding me like you lot do.'

'But we'll still see each other out of lessons,' said Morgan, back to her usual steady self. She did breaststroke in the air and the others smiled and followed the gesture. It was inspired by *Finding Nemo*, one of their favourite movies even though the target audience was much younger. In it, Dory the fish said to keep on swimming however tough life became.

'Something tells me we'll never lose our friendship, it'll always be there, like a favourite book, even if we lose touch on and off,' said Paige and she laid her head on Morgan's shoulder.

'Love you guys,' said Tiff. 'Here's to a great night – until I get home, that is. I spotted a plastic tiara Mum's bought. I overheard her saying to Dad that when I get home, she's going to crown me prom queen. It's so cringey. You know, she bumped into—' Tiff stopped abruptly.

'What?' asked Emily.

'It doesn't matter.'

'Tiff!' the other girls chorused.

Red blotches appeared on Tiff's neck. 'It's nothing, just that Mum bumped into Hugo's dad. He was boasting about how his son is bound to be voted prom king...'

Silence fell. Morgan's friends all looked uncomfortable, but then Hugo was the boy the four of them hated with a passion.

Paige consulted her watch. 'Come on, let's do this, for the very last time, for old time's sake.'

With a shy look, Emily was the first to stretch out her arms, dark rings under her eyes. The girls stood in a circle and linked hands, fingers intertwined, Morgan clenching the torch under one arm. As the words came out, loud and proud, their voices synched and sent echoes along the dingy walls of the basement.

> 'The Secret Gift Society swears through its blood,
> To only act for the good,
> Its four powers to serve those in need of defence.
> All hail...'

As the last line of their oath listed each of their gifts, it also reached the smirk of the smartly dressed boy hiding behind the hazel tree.

'These losers have no idea I'm going to tear apart their so-called friendship at the prom tonight,' he muttered. 'They're gonna get everything they deserve.'

1

MORGAN

Morgan sat at the kitchen table, in pyjamas, unaware she was shivering. The heating had gone off hours ago. When she'd gone up to bed, the door of his room had been left ajar. Olly must have slipped out after their argument. *And breathe*, she told herself. He'd only been missing a matter of hours. Yet it was three in the morning and this was unprecedented behaviour.

She'd just picked up her phone to ring the police when the front door clicked. Morgan jumped up and ran into the hallway, heady relief making her stumble at the sight of the sticky up, chestnut hair she herself had had at his age, and at the lean frame that was so like his grandfather's.

'Why haven't you picked up my calls? Where were you?'

'Out,' he replied, with a deadpan face.

'Olly...' Her voice broke. 'It's freezing outside.'

'I was at a friend's house, okay?' he muttered. 'Vikram's coming over after physics tomorrow. Don't say anything embarrassing.'

Arms open, she moved towards him but he stepped away.

'You can't go off like that, love, not answering your phone. Let's talk about it.'

'What's the point, Mum, when you won't even give me his name?'

Still this. 'Like I said, you're better off without your dad in your life. I don't know what I ever saw in him. Anyway, he left Dailsworth before you were born and could be anywhere in the world by now.'

'You never even told him you were pregnant.'

'I was sixteen. I didn't know myself until it was too late to find him. I did try but he'd already moved away.' She reached out and touched Olly's arm.

He shook her off. 'It's taken me so long to... understand and... come to terms with who I am, to feel that sense of calm and relief.' The words came out of his mouth with a tremble. 'But there's still this, the final piece of the puzzle. To know myself completely, I need to know my dad. It's *shit*, you refusing to tell me, still treating me like a child.'

'Don't speak to me like that, young man.'

Olly kicked of his muddy boots. 'Yes, I'll officially be a man in February when I turn eighteen, yet you won't even trust me with the smallest detail about him. Have you ever thought about how your silence affects me? Like my sense of shame because you hate the person who made the other half of me, as if there must be something wrong with me too?'

'There is *nothing* wrong with you, don't ever think that. I just...'

'It's a shame I've carried my whole life, with teachers and friends asking about my father, it looking as if I'm worthless for having a dad who didn't want to stick around.' His voice faltered. 'When I was little, I couldn't understand why I didn't have one like my best friends did. I'd pretend mine was an astronaut. I'd say he was away, busy discovering new planets. I almost believed it myself. Yet in bed at night, I'd ask myself, what if he *did* know about me, after all? What if Mum's lying, and I was really rejected, a son who wasn't good enough for his own father?' He threw his hands in the air. 'I'm sick of all these questions flying around my head and I intend to get answers, one way or another.' He shouted the last sentence.

A lump rose in Morgan's throat. If she told Olly his dad's name, that would be the beginning, not the end. There'd be more and more questions, she'd have to relive that terrible time, and then there was the matter of protecting her son. Who knew what sort of person his cruel, conniving father had turned into?

Olly had demanded to know, two years ago, in a much more determined way than he ever had before. A girl in his year had got pregnant. She was sixteen, like Morgan had been. It brought it all back and she'd wondered if

Olly heard her sobbing in her bedroom, after their argument, as he hadn't mentioned the subject of his father again, so forcefully, until now.

'Keep your voice down, Olly, you'll wake the neighbours.'

'I don't care,' he hollered.

'You're practically a grown up now, act like it,' she snapped.

'Why won't you tell me then?' he said and glared. 'I've a right to know and if you don't tell me, I'll be able to do what I want to find out, as soon as my next birthday is here.'

She opened her mouth and closed it again.

'Do you know what it's been like to have been born on Valentine's Day?' he said. 'It's as if the universe is laughing at me every year, what with my parents' romance being over before I was even born.'

Her eyes pricked. Yes, she'd always felt that and had always hoped that her son hadn't. Olly stormed upstairs, leaving her standing in the hallway, feeling numb.

'Olly's back, that's the main thing,' she whispered to herself as she walked into the kitchen and slumped into one of the wooden slat back chairs. Since her son had come out to her about his sexuality, she'd hoped they'd become closer again. On Bonfire Night, when he'd got back from a night with his friends, he'd blurted it out and the two of them had sat on the sofa until dawn, talking in a way they hadn't for ages, about love and boys and his fears and hopes for the future. But instead, the opposite had happened and now Olly hardly spoke to her. His bedroom door slammed and a framed photo toppled over on the scratched Welsh dresser, onto her *Best Employee of the Month* certificate. She'd often received them and had lost count of the times management had asked her to become a supervisor. It would mean more pay, more responsibility – but less time to dedicate to Olly.

Morgan picked up the photo of the two of them on a beach. He was six. They'd made a stick man in the sand, out of washed-up driftwood, and as if it were an Olympic torch, he proudly held an ice cream with a chocolate flake in the top. She ran her thumb over his little face.

Had that boy felt rejected, despite the love she'd smothered him with? A sunny June day came to mind, when he'd been in primary school. Every year, the teachers organised a Father's Day event. Olly's grandfather,

Morgan's dad, couldn't get the day off work, so his great granddad, in his late sixties, went in instead. When they got home, Olly was very quiet. He opened up to Morgan later – he did in those days. Everyone else's dad had played in the football match, but what with his bad hip, Olly's great granddad couldn't. Oh, they had fun crafting, but Olly had wanted to play football. It hadn't helped when one of the boys teased that he'd done a girls' activity.

Morgan switched off the lights and trudged upstairs. She pulled open the bottom drawer by the side of her bed, rummaging before she took out a sheaf of homemade cards, with misshapen flowers and hearts drawn on the front, with phrases such as *best friend Mummy* and *love you more than Teddy*. When he wasn't slamming doors, Olly was a reliable, caring lad who visited his grandparents and helped with the washing up. He mowed the small lawn out the back without being asked and never forgot his mum's birthday.

She went to the window and gazed up at the moon. It had been full the night Olly was born. Mum had held her hand throughout the labour, unaware Morgan wished it was her three best friends Paige, Emily and Tiff who were there. They would have made jokes, said Morgan deserved an achievement badge to go with her others. Emily would have knitted clothes for the baby. Morgan shook her head as she recalled the horrible words the four of them had shouted at each other when the shocking truths came out, at the end of Year Eleven, when Morgan was in the early stages of pregnancy without knowing it.

Yet the hurtful comments hadn't stopped her wishing they'd been there to talk to. Not just on the day she had Olly, but also on that rainy afternoon in a dirty public toilet, in Manchester, when she'd done a pregnancy test. Even now, Morgan still missed the other three, especially at Christmas. Paige's parents used to throw a fancy party and the four of them would laugh at the word 'amuse-bouche' before scoffing far too many. And, even though she never won, because the others liked board games, Emily would organise a festive-themed session, which made Scrabble take even longer than usual. Tiff always landed a role in the school play, partly to please her parents, and also because she enjoyed the buzz of the stage. The other three would cheer loudly at the sidelines. Whereas Morgan would make them each a bag of fudge, classic plain for Paige, candy cane with sprinkles for Emily, and for Tiff, chocolate peanut butter.

Her phone pinged and she tapped into her emails. No, she didn't want to enter a prize draw to win a five-million-pound house, gambling was a mug's game. A second new email caught her eye, this one from Dailsworth High. The subject line said:

Last call for alumni news

Today was Friday 15 December. In exactly one month's time, the yearly email newsletter from her old school would arrive. It always came in the middle of January and contained a summary of the previous twelve months, along with hopes for those coming. She and her best friends hadn't been bothered about receiving it, but a few weeks before the prom, their English teacher had insisted the whole class sign up, said they'd be glad when they were older. Every January since leaving, Morgan had read up on the changes and achievements at her much-loved school. The deaths of favourite teachers, a new library built, the successes of sports teams, a report on an alumni get-together every summer, although she never attended it. Of course – unlike for Paige, Emily and Tiff – not all the news would be new to Morgan, as she'd stayed in Dailsworth and her son had attended their old high school until he'd gone to sixth form college nearly two years ago.

Letting go of her phone, Morgan dozed. Her stomach took its time to unfurl after Olly's return. At thirty-five years old now, surely Paige, Emily and Tiff wouldn't still hold a grudge? Her anger against them had mellowed a long time ago and now and then she'd been tempted to reach out. She'd even searched for them on social media once, but with no luck. Perhaps they used married names now. They were just silly teenagers at the time of their spectacular argument, the summer before Olly was born. Nineteen years later, she'd love to meet them, a wish that had magnified since October, one weekend when Olly was away on a field trip. She'd had to call out an ambulance in the middle of the night, with acute chest pains – to her embarrassment, a bad case of indigestion. She'd got back from hospital before he arrived the next day and was going to tell him about it, but he'd returned in such a black mood. When Olly opened up on Bonfire Night, she found out he and his friends had played Truth or Dare on that October trip, and he'd been teased by his friends for avoiding the opportunity to kiss one of the girls. So, at that point, she'd decided not to open up to Olly about the night in A&E that had pushed her one step closer to accepting he needed to be in touch with his dad, because if something happened to her, he'd be left without a parent. But more than that, what if Olly disappeared again? Despite the years that had passed, Paige, Emily and Tiff were the only people she could think of, in the world, who could help her find her son's dad. Olly might run away and *not* come back, go on some madcap mission to find his father himself. Her stomach knotted again at the thought. The Secret Gift Society was her only hope.

That A&E visit had also made her think about the rift at high school and how badly such important friendships had ended. How the four of them might laugh affectionately now about the secret society they'd formed that had tracked down lost calculators, revealed bullies to teachers, found out which pupil was stealing dinner money. They never could resist a challenge. Now more than ever, she wanted those three friends back in her life. Oh, she went bowling or out to eat, thanks to work, and met other mums for drinks, but she'd never built friendships like those three at school. What if something happened to one of them before they all made up?

What if one of them had already passed?

Morgan sat up and reached for her bedside water. Was there any chance they could become friends again, re-form the society and solve the mystery of Olly's father's whereabouts? Could she send a message to them in the next newsletter?

No.

Stupid idea.

A fantasy.

Yet...

Arranging to meet her old friends, digging up the past: some might say neither of those ideas were *sensible*. However, Morgan had become sick of that word, after so much of her youth had been spent changing nappies and missing nights out, doing a job that didn't inspire her, never getting hungover. This once it wouldn't hurt for her to do something wild... would it? Her bus to work drove past Dailsworth High every day and on Saturday mornings she saw parents standing in the field, cheering on their children playing football. The four friends – former friends – could easily slip past and head to the old science block, to their old secret meeting place. It might remind the others of the fun times they once shared.

Morgan put down the glass and tapped into her phone. Her first weekend day off, after the newsletter would go out in January, was a Saturday in February, not long after Olly turned eighteen. She exhaled. Would his questions wait until then? With mock exams looming, she had to hope he'd be too wrapped up with studies to focus on finding his dad, and meeting the others in February might bring answers quickly enough. The four of them always used to work so well together.

At seven, Morgan showered, got dressed into her lime-green supermarket uniform and set about making her packed lunch that every day consisted of a sandwich cut in half, one apple and a multi-pack chocolate wafer. Order, routine: such had been her life since giving birth. Sequencing was important in maths to get the correct answer, in life too, she used to reckon. Teenage Morgan had her sequence all worked out; she'd achieve her goal of leaving behind her life in Dailsworth, would go to university and then travel, before settling down as a maths teacher – a far cry away from the life of her cashier and warehouse manager parents who'd unexpectedly had her in their teens. Yet here Morgan was, working in the same supermarket as her mum, still on the council estate where she'd grown up. The sequence of her life had simply echoed that of her parents. She gave a wry smile. Teenage Morgan often used to make comparisons to maths, the other three would tease her about it.

'Shall I make your favourite tonight, love, for you and Vikram?' Morgan asked in a bright voice, as Olly stood in the hallway with his rucksack. 'I can thaw out some chicken. Or how about pizza? The supermarket has got a special offer on for staff at the moment and—'

'Stop fussing, Mum, we'll sort ourselves out,' he said, with a rare shot of eye contact.

Morgan stiffened as she placed a halved sandwich in her lunch box. After the front door had closed, she went to the kitchen window. Oh, Olly had grown in height and needed to shave now, and very often only answered with a grunt, but he still went down the street with that enthusiastic bounce, still smiled at strangers, she could tell by their faces as they walked past him. Olly was a good lad. He deserved every happiness. He wasn't going to grow out of needing to know his dad, like he'd grown out of the Harry Potter fancy dress outfit she'd saved up ages for.

She went back onto her phone and into the email about the last call for alumni news, fingers poised to start typing. However, instead, she washed up the breakfast dishes, cleaned her teeth and put on her coat. The others probably felt exactly like her. What idiots they'd been to fall out because of that creep Hugo Black. She imagined her friends living in big, detached houses, enjoying holidays abroad and shopping trips without a budget, in some fancy market town or by the coast. They must have all moved away because she'd never bumped into them during all this time. However, she wouldn't swap Dailsworth for Dubai if having a fancy life had meant she'd never had Olly. Morgan's phone pinged.

Pizza sounds good.

Olly's way of saying sorry.

She'd never taken Olly to Disneyland, his laptop wasn't as flash as his friends' and his sports trainers came from the bargain store. When he was younger, none of these things mattered, he'd had a happy childhood, her love filled the gaps. But things were different now. The days had gone when a hug and episode of *Scooby-Doo* would wave away his problems. Morgan went back to the email and tapped on reply. After several moments' thought, she typed out the sentence she wanted included in the next newsletter:

TSGS. Meet at the usual place. 10 a.m. 25th February

Hopefully, her old friends would see it. Her breath hitched. They had to...

She went to a kitchen cupboard, took out her recipe book and turned to the first page, dated in the 2000s, reminding herself of the ingredients she'd use nearer the time of meeting up – of course, butter, sugar, condensed milk... A smile crossed her lips. Her friends were going to be so surprised! She grabbed her phone, pressed send and as the email went off, gave a little jig, as if three bags of soft fudge could easily sweeten nineteen hardboiled years apart.

2

PAIGE, EMILY, TIFF

Paige breathed in the subtle fragrance of cotton fresh pot-pourri from the low, oblong table, and balanced the laptop on her knees. She opened her inbox before reaching for her coffee. In a pin-striped trouser suit, she was perched on the white leather sofa and lifted her head to gaze through the windows at February clouds, across the wide balcony and to the morning Manchester skyline. As usual, her husband, Felix, had left for work early, leaving her a period of quiet before her first client arrived after the rush hour. She worked hard, they both did, to maintain their luxury penthouse flat in the Castlefield area of Manchester. They'd bought it outright using his savings and the trust fund Paige's parents set up. She'd not had access to it until she turned thirty. Her mum and dad prioritised securing their daughter's future, but felt she needed to find her passions, her own way, first. They'd always had strong views about their daughter following her own destiny, and going to state school like they had, not private, mixing with pupils from all walks of life, about experiencing the satisfaction of reaching goals through hard work, not by being given leg-ups.

Her eyes swept over the solid oak laminate floor and walls painted a shade called Digital Grey. It suited the curtains that – along with the lighting, thermostat, and security cameras – could all be controlled remotely, by smartphone. The two bedrooms were generously sized and the kitchen was open plan, with a vase of giant, white daisies on one of the units. The ultimate luxury was a hot tub on the balcony, a much-loved feature of Paige's.

To check that she hadn't missed anything important, Paige scrolled back through emails from the last few weeks.

Dailsworth High.

She hadn't opened those newsletters for years. Her old teachers had probably left. With money from the local council or lottery funding, the school would have no doubt been made over beyond recognition. Paige didn't need details about any class reunions. She'd never go in case she ran into those three. Yet... something told her to open this one. Paige put a manicured hand up to cover a yawn and half-heartedly read its first news item.

No! It couldn't be true.

Jasmine White was the new head teacher? She sat bolt upright and an ache grew inside. As if they'd seen each other yesterday, she could picture her best friends' faces, Morgan rolling her eyes at this revelation, Emily doing her best to find the positives and Tiff's over-dramatic arms flailing in the air.

Surrounded by her bitchy clique, popular Jasmine would follow them around at break, making kissing noises and asking if they'd ever had a boyfriend. They were mean to other pupils too who didn't look up to the popular crew, but Jasmine especially enjoyed being cruel to Paige and her friends, perhaps because they succeeded in rarely showing that the insults bothered them. She said Morgan smelt like the sports' changing rooms and Emily had bat ears, and every time they passed Tiff, she'd give a really loud oink. As for Paige, Jasmine would say she was a stuck-up cow who thought she was better than everyone else. In Year Seven, Jasmine had actually tried to make friends with Paige but listening to her parents' stories, Paige had picked up how to spot people more interested in money than genuine friendship. So she'd ignored Jasmine's fawning comments about her clothes, her house, her parents' new car.

Paige's eye swept over the rest of the newsletter and she was about to close her inbox when a sentence caught her eye, mentioning a date in

February. Paige focused intently on each word and was still transfixed half an hour later when her first client rang the doorbell. She gave the sentence one last glance.

Good grief. Good God. She got up and opened the door. 'Good morning, so very nice to see you.'

* * *

Emily snuggled into her wearable hooded blanket that smelt like it hadn't been washed since forever, making it even more appealing to her tortoiseshell cat, Smudge, who slept on her lap. Scrolling down her phone, she saw the email from Dailsworth High. Curled up on the sofa, she glugged her mug of wine, hoping it would drown out the teenage boys outside throwing bang snaps. Even though it was now seven in the evening, she'd not been up long, having handed in her notice on New Year's Eve. She'd spent the days since catching up with the last couple of years' missed sleep – and Netflix too, plenty of takeout and a lifetime's worth of hangovers. She'd only just started checking emails again; it was the middle of February and six weeks since she'd been signed off ill. The emergency care matron had phoned her the day after she'd left and insisted she take back her resignation. Emily had humoured her, for the sick pay. Her first counselling session was due at the beginning of March. Waste of bloody time.

She prepared to do the usual – skim the school news and then delete. However, this time, a name caught her eye and Emily gasped. Jasmine White in charge? Back in her schooldays, Emily had done her best to find the good in the pupil every girl wanted to be, with her model figure and string of boyfriends, with her pinches, shoves, and words that stung sharper than the nettles at the bottom of the sports field, away from the eyes and ears of teachers. Smudge listened as Emily told him all about her and the other three's old nemesis.

Younger, naïve Emily and scheming Jasmine: stupid cows, the pair of them.

Unable to stop herself, Emily read the whole article and studied the photo. The thin eyebrows had grown more straggly, the lips shone less brightly, the flowing mane of wavy hair was severely tied back. Smudge yawned. Emily couldn't leave it; who'd have ever guessed Jasmine would lose her glamour? A warm sensation infused Emily, not because of the wine. She'd gone through a phase in Year Ten of having bad acne, and Jasmine would always offer her concealer really loudly. Young Emily told herself she was just being helpful, despite Jasmine's laughter – despite Emily's own secret tears in the toilets.

Emily sat very still as an acronym jumped into view. TSGS. *What the...?* Was this a joke? Her heart pounded and she couldn't breathe for a moment until out of nowhere, a sob catapulted from her chest. Smudge jumped up and looked at her curiously. Wine tipped over the edge of her mug and onto the sleeve of the old, stained jumper she'd knitted in happier times, sticking out from under her hooded blanket. Tears ran down her face as her whole body shuddered and memories fought their way through a haze of cheap Chardonnay. How she and her three friends used to practice kissing on pillows during sleepovers. Paige would give the others tips, as she'd actually had experience, and Tiff was always the most enthusiastic, saying she'd need a good technique for her acting career. Then there was the silly dance they'd do to 'Hey Ya' by OutKast, shakey-shaking their bottoms. It was rare for them all to like the same piece of music. How they'd do baking at Morgan's and lick out the bowl, fighting over the wooden spoon, giggling as cake batter ended up in their hair. Best of all, the excitement in the pit of Emily' stomach as they'd creep into the school basement and plan another investigation. The Secret Gift Society had offered a total escape from her difficult mother, from bullies, from the general angst of adolescence.

But then Hugo's image arrived, his smirking mouth telling everyone at the prom to be quiet, then as hush fell, he pointed to her, Morgan, Paige and Tiff. As his explosive revelations rang out, the girls turned angrily on each other. She'd never forgotten the humiliation dripping over her like a bottle of poisonous venom, soaking into every pore as all the pupils gazed, jaws dropped, at the four of them. It wasn't as if she could go home and be comforted by her mother, so Emily had stuffed her emotions down, deep inside.

Emily pushed the memories down again. She had enough problems in her current life without reliving ones from the past. A message for The

Secret Gift Society? She could do without Morgan's razor-sharp brain working out what a failure Emily had become, or Paige, who was no doubt a millionaire by now with a luxury lifestyle and successful husband to match, smugly sympathising with Emily for her recent marriage break-up. As for Tiff, with her aspirations of fame and glamour, Emily's life couldn't be more diametric. Whichever of the others had called this stupid meeting in two weeks, they could eff right off.

* * *

Friday 24 February and Tiff paced up and down in her old teenage bedroom. The discussion in her head wouldn't quieten down. A meeting had been called for tomorrow, at her old school, in that grotty basement. She'd read the Dailsworth High newsletter weeks ago and was still confused. To reunite or not reunite – a Shakespearian tragedy in the making.

She was in between acting jobs and home from London, visiting her parents. Shortly after the terrible events at the school prom in 2004, her mum and dad had received an inheritance and moved from Dailsworth to fancy Wilmslow. She'd forgotten Manchester's nip in the winter months and had let Mum make her a hot water bottle to take to bed last night.

Tiff rolled up her sleeves and sifted through paperwork, doing her best to focus and prepare for her next project starting in the middle of April. However, a magazine caught her attention, placed prominently on the dressing table, 'Tiff' on the front in a sparkly dress. Her parents couldn't be prouder of the way her career had taken off. Both felt they hadn't had opportunities. Her dad had always wanted to be a jazz singer and her mum's fantasy had been to be a member of the *Top of the Pops* dance troupe, Pan's People. Since the day Tiff could walk, they'd signed her up for extra-curricular lessons they could barely afford. Along with their genes, Tiff had inherited their dreams.

What would Tiff's old friends think of her now? She lay on her bed, turned on her Spotify playlist and rolled onto her front, legs raised from the knee down and kicking in the air in time to the music, as if time had spun back nineteen years and she wasn't in her thirties. 'If I Ain't Got You' by

Alicia Keys had come on the radio, one day not long after the girls split. She'd danced to it, alone, crying in her bedroom, missing the others like crazy, realising how difficult it was going to be to shake off their friendship, laughing through tears at how the others would have raced to turn off the slushy track. Emily preferred boy band McFly on repeat, Morgan, The Killers, and Paige, her parents' favourite: The Beatles.

Perhaps the newsletter message had been planted by an admirer of Tiff's career, who'd found out about her childhood club and was using it as bait to meet up: a scenario as likely as any of the other girls wanting to meet up after what Hugo did. Disgust flooded through her body. Hugo had reduced the four of them to a bunch of disloyal hypocrites. Everyone at the prom had sneered, even those pupils The Secret Gift Society had helped. Sympathy arrived in the form of their French teacher Mlle Vachon, who'd also been their personal tutor for the entire five years of high school. She'd be in her mid-seventies now. On the quiet, they affectionately called her Miss Moo Moo, as the word *vache* meant cow. She'd ushered the four of them into a classroom and did her best to mediate. It lasted all of a few minutes before one by one the girls ran away, each declaring they never wanted to see the others again. To Tiff's surprise, gentle Emily had been the one who'd bolted first.

Tiff sat up, head in her hands. She wouldn't recall that prom night. She wouldn't. But like a jeering member in a theatre audience, the memory she'd suppressed for most of the years since got bigger, got louder, it wouldn't go away...

It was 2004. A warm June evening. The four girls had danced, holding hands, having just been to their last ever secret society meeting in the basement. But then Hugo had started talking after the track 'She Bangs' stopped playing. Despite everything that had happened, Tiff still loved Ricky Martin. The head had just been about to announce the prom king and queen. As his voice got louder, pupils gathered around, fascinated by his talk of The Secret Gift Society. Tiff and Emily, Morgan and Paige had exchanged bewildered glances, disbelief etched across their faces. Then they'd cowered as he'd revealed far more personal secrets than the fact they'd formed a private club. A student being sick at the back of the hall had distracted supervisors from hearing the commotion Hugo was creating.

He'd ended his tirade with a smirk and the words, 'Don't blame me, girlies, you're the ones who'd sworn an allegiance to each other. Now everyone knows why your stupid society means nothing, like the lies it made up about me.' Tiff shivered as she remembered how Paige had dropped her drink, the glass smashing and red punch splashing up her white dress.

Then Paige had turned on Morgan as soon as Hugo stopped talking. 'But you hate boys,' she'd said incredulously. 'I assumed you were gay.'

Bigger laughs from the crowd and jeers of *lezzie*, caused angry tears to glisten. How Tiff had stared at Morgan, the only one out of the other three she'd never seen cry before. 'How could you know me so badly?' Morgan had replied, flinching as the crowd jeered. 'What about you... Princess Paige? According to Hugo, you've been getting close to someone who's always mocked the very sight of us, even though their parents don't own a Porsche or go clay pigeon shooting. What a come down for a precious, spoilt brat.'

Paige's chin had trembled and her head gave a slow, disbelieving shake in Morgan's direction.

'Poor shy little Emily, what a front you've put on,' Tiff had spat. 'They say it's the shy ones you should watch. After what Hugo's said, it's clear you're nothing but a two-faced slut.'

Emily had jumped, cheeks burning as the room sniggered. 'What makes you think you're any better than me?' she'd whimpered. 'Better a phony than... a fatty. It's like being friends with... Jabba the Hutt.'

Adult Tiff's face puckered behind her hands, as an image from that evening came into her head, of the crowd laughing and pointing at the four friends, of how Emily's hand had shot up to her own mouth, as if trying, too late, to stop the insult.

Then Hugo had started the chant that went on and on. Despite the teachers' protestations, all the other pupils joined in...

'Lezzie. Princess. Slut. Jabba...'

Tiff sat very still for a moment, gripped by the horror of that night in 2004. Then she sniffed and let her hands fall away. She straightened her shoulders, stood up and checked her make-up in the mirror. What did one of the girls – women now – want to gain by calling this meeting? Or... perhaps it was Hugo taking the piss. Maybe the new head, Jasmine White, had left the message as a joke. At one time, she was such a bitch to Tiff, shouting, 'Oink, oink, oink,' and getting her cronies to join in.

'Tiffy, sweetheart, tea's ready,' hollered up a voice.

She got to her feet, clenched her jaw and deleted the Dailsworth High email.

3

MORGAN

Morgan had hardly slept last night, her mood swinging up and down as she buzzed at the thought of meeting her old friends today – and worried about Olly. Even though more than two months had passed since their big row. They'd agreed to put it behind them for the festive season. After that, Olly had been busy with his studies. Then it had been Valentine's Day and his birthday. He hadn't wanted a party, so she'd taken him out to his favourite pizza restaurant for lunch, her mum and dad went as well. The chat had flowed between her and Olly and for the first time in weeks, their usual warmth came back. He'd been looking forward to going clubbing with friends that evening, taking photos with the new phone Morgan had saved to buy him. It has been worth every hour of overtime to watch him excitedly test out its camera.

A father might have taken him out for his first legal drink, or was that some urban myth? Morgan's sleep had suffered since he turned eighteen, she'd wake in a panic and would creep into his bedroom and check that the human shape in bed wasn't a pile of carefully constructed cushions. The fear of him walking away, never speaking to her again, hung around, and her trip to the emergency department back in October still danced in the shadows when she hit the pillows and closed her eyes. Sweat-dripping bad dreams veered between Olly leaving her or her leaving him.

She couldn't wait for Paige, Emily and Tiff to meet her son. They were bound to turn up today. It has been so long. Her three friends had always been open, warm-hearted, not the types to carry a grudge for eternity. Perhaps they were parents too by now. Was Tiff an actress? Unable to settle, Morgan turned on her bedside light, rummaged around in the bottom of her wardrobe and pulled out an old shoe box. She got back under the duvet and, leaning against the headboard, sifted through the old photos until she came to the notebook.

A broad smile lit up Morgan's tired face as she mused over the sense of importance The Secret Gift Society used to possess. On the front, in bold letters, they'd written:

TOP SECRET

Closed Cases

It was a record of their successful investigations. She flicked through: *The Case of the Unkind Valentine Card, The Case of the Spiked Punch, The Case of the Stolen Packed Lunches.* The investigations were innocent enough at first. By Year Eleven, the content had changed, with *The Case of the Two-Timing Girlfriend* and *The Case of the Online Bully.* Word spread and pupils in their year would ask the girls for help with their troubles.

Morgan hugged her knees. On the very first day of high school, they'd been allotted the same personal tutor, Mlle Vachon. They ended up sitting together every morning, despite their obvious differences, what with Morgan's practical, no-nonsense attitude, Paige's understated maturity, Emily's selfless, quiet nature and Tiff's loud clumsiness. During the following years, they became aware that each of them had a particular strength that they called a 'gift'. Common ground was reading and their favourite all-time books included the Enid Blyton's *Famous Five* and *Secret Seven* novels, and classic Agatha Christies. Inspiration struck after they inadvertently worked as a team to help a girl in their class find out who was stealing her stationery, and in Year Nine, with earnest intentions, they set up The Secret Gift Society.

Morgan turned the page and pain shot through her chest. *The Case of…*

It was Hugo's and the investigation that had blown apart the four girls' friendship. She snapped the notebook shut and covered it once more with photos, before shoving the shoe box back in the wardrobe. She hurried into the bathroom and took a hot shower, forcing herself to sing a cheerful tune, the bad memories evaporating in the steam.

The kitchen clock turned to half past nine. Dailsworth High was only a fifteen-minute walk away. Morgan hadn't told Olly about meeting her old friends; she didn't want to get his hopes up about finding his dad. But she had tried to broach the subject of starting to look a few days after he'd scared her so much.

'Come and sit down for a moment,' she'd said when he got in from school, and she'd patted the space on the sofa next to her, moving a hammer she'd been using to put up a new bookshelf. He'd shrugged and collapsed into the armchair opposite. Trouble was, she couldn't find the words.

'I've decided... I'm sorry that...'

Olly had stood up. 'I've got homework.'

It was no good. She couldn't bring herself to tell him that she would help him find his dad, worried that he'd be crushed if they failed. Life had shown her that disappointments left a scar that never properly healed, even small ones – like how Morgan had always been ahead with maths at primary school, but then the use of calculators at Dailsworth High evened out the playing field – if only a little. Maths was the one thing in life she got completely.

Instead, Morgan did try to find out more by herself. The school secretary was adamant she couldn't give out alumni details or confirm if Hugo was listed, but said if he was, she'd email and ask if he was happy for Morgan to get in touch. With a deep breath, Morgan had given the go-ahead, but it was weeks now with no comeback.

She brushed her teeth and stood in front of the bathroom mirror, the narrow ledge beneath it always a mess since Olly started shaving. The woman who stared back was a far cry from the girl last seen by Paige, Emily and Tiff. Years of looking after a child who didn't sleep well had etched black semi-circles under her eyes. The short hair that used to stand defiantly upright lay limp and flat. Yet high school Morgan would probably have liked the sleeveless jumper and plain shirt that she was wearing with simple, straight trousers. She was still the same person underneath: older now, wiser, okay, perhaps a little jaded. But surely the others would recognise their old friend, like she would them?

Morgan pulled on her anorak and headed out the front door, leaves swirling in the wind like the butterflies in her stomach. An urge to skip almost overwhelming her, she made do with whistling.

Dailsworth High had also changed since that fateful prom. The L-shape building was now more like a U with an extra wing that housed the new library and two large computer rooms, along with an extended pastoral care centre for staff and pupils. Occasionally, over the years, Morgan turned up early for parents evening and took a walk first, past the old basement, the still-disused science lab, the hazel tree still standing proud. As if about to attend her first ever rock concert, adrenaline rushed through Morgan with every step that way. Despite the clouds, the night showers had stopped. Being outdoors always lifted her mood. When she was young, Morgan often helped her granddad, a landscape gardener, and as she got older, he paid her to work at weekends, come rain or shine. In the summer, she'd do her homework in the back garden and would take a walk in the local park if she needed to clear her head.

Morgan passed the basement's horizontal door and went around the back. With her anorak sleeve, she rubbed the window of the science lab. It was still filled with dilapidated desks and chairs, still overgrown with straggly branches. For a moment, she was right back in 2004, holding hands with Paige, Emily and Tiff, that last time they chanted in the dingy basement just before Hugo blew up their friendship.

The clouds darkened and she walked back around to the basement door, stopping dead by the hazel tree.

'Hello, Morgan.' A tone crisper than it used to be. The red hair swished back into a ponytail now hung as a sleek bob, the hint of ginger darker now. Paige still wore a blazer but instead of being plain bottle green, it bore a Burberry check.

Stomach fizzing, Morgan waved and hurried over. She'd waited so long for this moment. 'Paige. Wow. You look great! How are you keeping?' Her old friend was here, she really was, with that same mole above her lip, that same sophisticated presence no other pupil had. 'Have you had to come far?'

'Castlefield. Did you call this meeting?' she replied in a detached tone.

Morgan's arms fell to her sides. Oh. But at least Paige had turned up. That had to be a good sign.

Footsteps. A snapped twig. Another woman appeared, hair tousled, odd socks on underneath worn jeans. Morgan grinned. Dear Emily. But a sneer crossed the new arrival's face.

'Morgan, Paige. Which one of you called this shitshow?'

Morgan stepped backwards. The word *damn* used to be Emily's worst expletive. The others teased her about it. She dug her hands into her coat pockets and crossed her fingers. *Please, don't let this be happening.* Her heart pounded.

'Not guilty,' Paige replied in a tone as smooth as her hair.

'Me neither,' said a fourth woman appearing from the wooded area, the smell of strong perfume arriving before her.

Morgan's eyes narrowed as the figure neared. She gasped, along with Paige and Emily. Not one of the three found the words to say hello. As if owning the catwalk, the woman strutted over, with prominent cheekbones, a belt wrapped around a small waist, with previous mousey curls now brunette and straight, the purple glasses gone and clothes looking more expensive than Paige's. A woman with... a certain grace.

'Tiff?' said Morgan. 'You look so... so... different.'

Paige tilted her head. Emily couldn't stop staring.

'Thank you. I have to work very hard to keep off those extra pounds I used to carry around. First impressions are so important. That frumpy little girl would have really struggled to make it.'

Overweight? Frumpy? Back in the day, Tiff never used to entertain such notions, bouncing insults back if anyone said them. She'd even brazen out the oinks from Jasmine and her gang.

'You always looked great, Tiff,' said Morgan.

The others' faces softened, just for a second, a stranger wouldn't have noticed.

'I called the meeting. Thanks everyone, for turning up. I'm really grateful. It's so great to see you all again.' Morgan reached into her mini rucksack and pulled out three bags of fudge. 'Plain for you Paige,' she said and nervously held it out.

Paige hesitated before dropping it into her handbag. 'Thank you. I'll give it to my husband.'

Right. Morgan swallowed.

'Candy cane for you, Emily.'

Emily shrugged, opened the bag and stuffed a chunk into her mouth.

'Chocolate peanut butter for you, Tiff,' said Morgan, feeling more foolish by the minute.

Tiff took the fudge as if it were in a dog poop bag. 'Thanks. Not that I eat anything that sweet these days.'

Face flooded with heat, Morgan zipped up her rucksack.

'I only came out of curiosity,' said Emily and she put another chunk in her mouth.

'Me too,' said Paige.

'Same,' said Tiff.

'Or perhaps our friendship still means something?' said Morgan in a questioning tone. She longed for the camaraderie of their school years, how in their company, she liked herself more than when with anyone else. 'It's been so long... What happened at the end of Year Eleven – we were only kids. God, I've missed you guys.'

Emily kicked a stone. 'Or is it rather that you want something from us? Go on, spit it out.'

Emily used to be so gently spoken, she'd hang in the background, she'd bolster, she'd comfort.

Tiff looked at her watch. 'I'm expecting a call, Morgan. Any chance we could get on?'

'A bit drastic, wasn't it, calling us together here?' asked Paige, still in that smooth voice, formal, distant. 'You could have chosen a café for the meeting place.'

Tears threatened. They didn't do that often. Morgan always tried to be the strong one.

'I... just really wanted to see you all again, hoped the school grounds might remind us of...'

'Of how our friendship ended? Mission accomplished,' said Emily and an ugly look crossed her features.

Morgan twisted her hands. 'But also... I need the society's help.'

'The society?' Emily mimicked and she burst out laughing and the other two quietly joined in. Morgan winced and the smile dropped from Emily's face. 'Look... sorry, but really? Are you mad? We aren't kids any more.'

'Emily's right. You want to revive a teenage club that hasn't been up and running for nineteen years?' said Paige and she tightened her cream scarf. 'I've got a business, marriage, I don't have time for playing at being a detective.'

'We don't look a day older, if you ask me,' said Tiff and primped her hair, a smile showing off whitened teeth. 'But agreed, life is busy enough. I'm surprised you thought we'd be interested, Morgan. Out of all the people in your life, why ask us for help?'

You're my besties. My partners in solving crime. Her throat caught. *And complete strangers.*

Emily turned to go. 'You three enjoy chatting about your lives, your journeys to this point may be gilded with gold, and I'm happy for you, I am, despite our falling-out...' Her voice sounded strained. 'But mine's been potholes all the way.'

'I've got a son,' Morgan blurted out. 'Olly hates bluebottles but won't kill them, he could spend hours staring at a night sky, his favourite meal is chicken curry, as long as it's served with an onion bhaji, he refuses to wear belts and used to bite his nails and once he likes a song, he plays it eternally on repeat.' She stopped for breath. 'He's about to go to college. I need to find his dad. Olly is desperate to know who he is. He doesn't even know his name.'

Those last words echoed in Morgan's ears. Saying them out loud made it sound even more unfair on her son.

The other three stood stock still. 'College?' asked Paige finally. 'He's a teenager? That means...'

'Blood and sand. You had a kid that young?' Emily let out a long whistle and gave Morgan a curious look.

'Must have been hard,' said Tiff, giving Morgan her full attention for a minute.

Morgan paused and then did breaststroke in the air. Dory said to keep on swimming if things got tough. However, the others didn't acknowledge the gesture from their teenage years, let alone replicate it. Cheeks burning again, her arms dropped. She ran a hand across her forehead. 'Olly's the best thing that ever happened to me. His dad left Dailsworth before I could tell him I was pregnant. Olly and I have managed fine on our own, but...' Her voice broke. 'Things have come to a head. If my lad starts college without me helping him connect with his dad finally, I might lose him forever. He'll grow up fast there and I worry that if that independence is full of resentment... I urgently need to find his dad. Things have come to a crisis point.'

'But you presumably had this baby a couple of years after we lost contact,' said Paige. 'Why not ask your friends from that time, or I'm sure you can find him on the internet? Failing that, hire a proper detective.'

'Right, because we've all got as much money as you, Paige,' said Emily and she shook her head.

Paige flinched.

'I didn't have any friends. Not like you three,' said Morgan. 'The four of us used to be like dice, each side different, yes, but with similarities, like the way two sides of a dice always add up to seven. I've never found that synchronicity with anyone else.'

'You're still obsessed with maths, then,' muttered Paige.

Morgan stared at her, and then the others. They didn't want to get involved? Of course not. How could Morgan have been so foolish, believing that nineteen years would have salved the hurt and resentment, that they would still have things in common?

Tiff looked into the distance, at the school grounds. 'They still have no sixth form here? Which college is your son going to, then?'

Morgan breathed in, and then exhaled slowly as the wind lifted and clouds darkened further. 'They do have a sixth form here now. But by college, I mean... university. Olly's just turned eighteen. He'll be leaving home soon. He's keen on a course in Bristol.'

'Eighteen?' said Tiff, face looking like it used to when she worked on a case – she'd roll her lips together and not blink for a while. The others would joke that she never concentrated as hard in lessons as she did for the work of the society.

'I had no idea at the time, but...' It was as if the years had wound back and Morgan was breaking the news to her parents, the doctor, the neighbours... Her voice shook. 'I was pregnant at the prom.'

For a moment, the only noise was the caw of a crow.

'Holy shit,' said Emily.

'You can't have been...' said Paige, cheeks pale.

'But you always swore you'd never end up like your parents,' said Tiff. 'You're messing with us, right? This is some a prank?'

'Who is the father, then?' asked Paige. 'Why haven't you ever told Olly his name? It's not...' Her voice became unsteady. 'Was he in one of our classes?'

Morgan bit on her fist. 'In the end, you all knew him better than you wanted to. In the end, he knew too much about us too.'

Rain started to fall as bit by bit, drop by drop, faster and faster, horror stormed over the other three's faces.

4

MORGAN

'You *slept* with Hugo?' asked Tiff and her phone fell to the ground.

'You want us to find *him*?' asked Paige faintly. '*He's* Olly's father?' She staggered backwards and Morgan rushed over to prop her up but Paige put up her hand, regained her balance, and recovered her calm.

Emily picked up Tiff's phone and passed it to her, hardly taking her eyes off Morgan. 'You want us to help you track down that utter *bastard*?' Her hand covered her nose and mouth.

Morgan wished Paige would speak some more. They'd always been especially close, despite the differences on the surface, such as Morgan's down-to-earth dress sense compared to Paige's precocious elegance. However, she remained silent and looked like she used to when they drank too many ciders: as if she daren't open her mouth because she'd say something she'd regret later.

'Are you *sure* it's him?' continued Emily. 'Hugo made it clear at the prom just how much he detested us. Surely, he couldn't have hidden that hatred just to... to—'

'Get laid? Are you trying to ask if I'm making it up?' asked Morgan, her fist still clenched. Yet she understood the disbelief. Such intimacy seemed unlikely after his humiliating revelations that cut through the four of them. She could still picture his mouth, how it fell on one side, a flaw in an otherwise perfectly symmetrical facade, with the upper body V shape and strong brow, those eyes so blue and wide enough apart to trust him... So much for that. Morgan should have followed her gut instinct from the years before that told her he was a bully, a brown noser. Instead, she learnt the hard way that intuition can be swayed by the most popular boy in the school showing an interest.

Paige still hadn't moved an inch. Morgan got it. She'd sat on the floor of the public toilets for an hour after seeing the positive pregnancy test. An old woman had come in, peed and then asked her what the matter was. When Morgan told her, the woman called her a poor cow and left.

'Talk about a plot twist. It took me months to get over your three's betrayal.' Tiff threw her arms into the air. 'I'm not diving into that cesspool again and I'm certainly not interested in finding *him*.'

'*Our* betrayal?' said Paige finally, in a quiet, steady voice, looking more like her old self. 'You'd been as deceitful as us. Let's face it, we were a bunch of silly girls who should have known better. But look, we've clearly all made it on our own.'

Emily snorted. 'I imagine your mummy and daddy set you up for life, Paige.'

'Let's not be unkind to each other. It was a long time ago,' Morgan pleaded.

'And not talk about the fact that *you* actually *slept* with Hugo Black? You had his kid? Christ, there's me thinking *my* life was screwed up.' Emily's voice wavered. 'This has got to be the biggest pothole ever.' Unexpectedly, a tear ran down her face and angrily, she wiped it away. Tiff went to touch her but Emily shook her head vigorously. Back in the day, the two of them had such a strong bond. *Buzz and Woody* they'd call each other, both being fans of the two unlikely friends from the *Toy Story* franchise. Tiff was the astronaut with delusions of grandeur above being a toy, whereas Emily had her feet firmly planted on the ground, expecting far less from her life than Hollywood-chasing Tiff.

A man and woman approached. He carried a clipboard, she grasped an umbrella.

'It's about time the school made use of its derelict buildings,' the woman was saying, in a familiar tone. She wore a smart jacket and skirt, and practical loafers. 'They were run down like this when I was a pupil here. Well, no more. The old science lab would make a great art studio, and this overgrown outdoor area could...' The sentence petered out as the four gaping women caught her attention. A straggly eyebrow shot up. 'Do go around the back,' she said to the man, 'see what you think to my suspicions there might be signs of subsidence. I'll catch you up.' The man disappeared around the corner.

'Hello Jasmine,' said Tiff and her ears turned red.

'What's this? The Secret Gift Society still meets up?' Eyes flickering with humour, Jasmine focused on Morgan. 'Your son attended here, didn't he? I do hope your teenage pregnancy hasn't held you back.'

'Not at all and parenthood has brought me more joy than I could imagine,' Morgan said in a strained tone. No one needed to know that the one thing she regretted was not following her dream, but university would have been impossible with a baby. She'd told herself her time would come, perhaps when she hit her twenties, but she and Olly were so close and she treasured dropping him off at school and always collecting him. Her boss was good about things like that, and thank goodness, because there was no money for after-school clubs. Her parents wouldn't have been able to help out with college costs either. Like her, they both worked hard just to pay the bills. Over time, she grew to fear losing the certainty of her life as a single mum. She had regular money coming in, a roof over their heads and any spare money went into Olly's university fund, rather than one for her. Morgan's chin quivered.

Emily stared at Morgan and then turned to Jasmine. 'Weren't you going to be a flight attendant, Jasmine?'

'Yes and actually I passed my interviews for it before deciding it wasn't for me. Not everyone has got the right appearance but apparently, I ticked all their boxes,' she said and gave Emily a look up and down.

A blush spread across Emily's cheeks and Paige turned from her to face the headteacher. 'Yet here you are, not even one mile away, back at Dailsworth High.'

Jasmine gave a bright smile. 'Exploit your brains, not your beauty, for everlasting financial security. I had a fantastic time at university in London.

I'm very surprised to see you here in humble Manchester, Paige, and not living it up in somewhere like Paris or Milan.'

'Not that I consider Manchester humble, but as a matter of fact, my husband's off to Dubai soon on business. I may well join him.'

Jasmine's bottom lip jutted out and she turned her attention to Tiff, was about to speak, but then changed her mind. Why did Tiff get off so lightly?

The man reappeared. 'Lovely to see you four again,' said Jasmine and she gave a polite smile. 'But please don't be here when I come back. The governing board and I take trespassing very seriously.' She waved at the man and looked upwards. 'Coming! I've got the key for the old lab. We might need to shelter for a while.'

Navigating pools of muddy water, Jasmine vanished out of sight. In unison, the four women muttered, 'Creep, creep,' and exchanged embarrassed glances with each other. Before Morgan could smile, the others turned away and reverted to their stern expressions. They used to say, 'Creep, creep,' under their breaths every time Jasmine walked away after being mean. Whilst helping out her landscaper granddad, Morgan had learnt that the jasmine plant was a vine. Rather than growing straight and tall, it crept – creep, creep, just like Jasmine's insidious, toxic comments. Comments that deeply hurt her friends, especially Emily. She'd stopped tying her hair back, paranoid about the clique's *bat ears* insults.

Rain fell heavily now. Morgan put up her hood, looking at the ground where Jasmine had stood. So not everyone had changed. She took a deep breath, reached into her anorak pocket and pulled out three scraps of paper with her mobile phone number scrawled on. Morgan pushed one into each of the hands of the others. 'Please think about helping me. I'd be so grateful. Even if you don't want to be friends again. I've hidden the truth from Olly all these years. I genuinely had no idea where Hugo was and that made it easier. But if I'm honest, I was also scared that if he ever turned up, Hugo would hurt Olly like he once hurt the four of us. But that's a risk I have to take now.'

Tiff studied the scrap of paper and ran a thumb over the writing. 'It's like the notes we used to leave in each other's lockers, to call a meeting.' Back then, Emily wasn't allowed a mobile phone, so secret communications between the four had to be old-school style. Tiff's phone gave her a jolt as it rang and she shoved the piece of paper into her pocket. 'But you could offer me a date with Ryan Gosling, Morgan, and I still wouldn't cross paths with Hugo again. Wish I could help but it's a hard no from me. Good luck.' She gave the other two a cursory wave before heading towards the football match and car park.

Emily screwed the piece of paper into a tight ball and tossed it onto the ground. 'That's what I think of Hugo.' For a second, an earnest expression crossed her face and her voice became less harsh. 'Your son's better off without him, Morgan. I'm sorry you're having a tough time but bringing his slimeball dad into your life might make things even worse.' Emily left.

'What did you expect?' Paige asked quietly, before putting her umbrella up. She went to say something else. Tried several times. 'It's a lot to get your head around,' she eventually muttered in a numb tone, folded the paper carefully and put it in her handbag, then walked away without saying another word.

Cheeks slashed by torrents of rain, Morgan stood in a puddle as the best friends she'd ever had hurried off, feeling like a little girl left in the playground all alone. A random maths fact came to mind, the sort that would have made the others laugh affectionately, back in the day. Nine was widely seen as a magic number because if you multiplied any number by it, the sum of the digits of the new figure would always add up to nine. However, for obvious reasons, the girls always believed the number four was the most special, and it was also the only number that has the same number of letters as its value. But now one, plus one, plus one, plus one, didn't come to four.

It came to nothing. The Secret Gift Society had lost its magic.

5

PAIGE, EMILY, TIFF

Sodden umbrella at her feet, Paige sat in the café at the end of the precinct where a pedestrianised area stretched as far as the eye could see, towards the Tesco and multi-storey car park.

She pushed away her mug of green tea.

Morgan had got pregnant as a teenager. She had a son. By *Hugo*.

Independent, never-getting-married, never-having-kids Morgan was a mother.

And yet Paige shouldn't have been so surprised. The week or two before the prom, Paige's friend had seemed different. She'd looked more tired, lost her bounce, went off the snacks they'd buy from the corner shop near the school. Paige had got a feeling something wasn't right. Morgan wasn't one to suffer from exam stress. Then after the prom, she'd put it down to Hugo's revelations.

After the meeting with the others, in a daze, Paige had walked down into the town that hadn't changed much in all this time. She passed the shops, needing something that could warm the coldness that had taken hold inside. When she was a teenager, the town's box-shaped buildings and uninspiring high street shops didn't seem boring. In fact, she and her friends had loved Dailsworth, a ten-minute walk from school, down Rowan Hill, with Boots for toiletries, River Island for clothes, and the supermar-

ket's passport picture photo booth. They'd hang out at the café where Paige
now sat, although the leather-buttoned booths had gone, along with the
simpler menu. Now the counter paraded a row of syrup bottles and
toppings. A group of schoolgirls came in and ordered toffee nut lattes. They
looked about sixteen and Paige's heart raced as an image from the past
forced its way into her head.

The evening of the prom, Paige rang her dad and sobbed all the way
home. He was supposed to be bringing her friends back too, for the sleepover, but Paige cried even harder when he suggested looking for them. So
he rang their parents, explained that the four girls had fallen out, said he'd
drop off their overnight bags tomorrow. Paige had sat on the sofa in her
mother's arms. She didn't pry, or try to get Paige to talk, she simply held her
tight. Her mum had always been good like that.

In the early hours, Paige lay in bed, staring at the three overnight bags
on her carpet. Emily's was partly open and Paige squinted. A knitted mortar
board stuck out. She couldn't help zipping the bag open to take a look. Four
of them lay on Emily's pyjamas. One had a knitted lipstick sewn on top –
Tiff loved experimenting with make-up. The next had a big daisy on it,
Paige's favourite flower; she loved making daisy chains. A pen sat on the
third – Morgan's head was always in a puzzle book – and on the fourth was
a knitted cat. Emily dreamt of owning one; her mum wouldn't allow pets.

Paige had taken the little daisy mortar board to bed, carefully putting it
back in Emily's bag the next morning.

As if it had happened yesterday, not in a different decade, Paige's hand
shook as she lifted her green tea. After a sip, she texted Felix, told him she'd
be late back. But another drink later, Paige still couldn't face returning.
Felix had his work trip coming up and was so excited, she didn't want to
dampen his spirits. She'd done that enough in recent months. How
sensible the two of them had thought it was, not to get married until they
were financially rock solid, with a mortgage, decent cars, money for holidays abroad. Yet part of her envied Morgan, thrown into pregnancy at the
deep end before responsibilities held her back.

Tiff had undergone such a transformation and for different reasons,
Emily too, whose soft heart seemed to have turned to rock, like liquid sugar
burned to bitter caramel. As for Morgan, a sense of ill-ease had crept over

Paige ever since her old friend had talked about the society re-forming. Paige couldn't explain her hunch that there was more to all this than Morgan simply wanting to find her son's father.

Morgan, Emily, Tiff. For a fleeting second, her spirits lifted. Paige had lost count of the times, in the past, that she'd wanted to phone them to share good or bad news. She pulled Morgan's phone number out of her handbag and went to add it to her list of contacts. Paige had something monumental to tell her old friend. She could do it. But then a toddler walked past the café's window wearing a princess costume. Paige pushed the piece of paper into her pocket, paid for her drink and hurried in the direction of the train station. A man called from behind her, something about a forgotten umbrella. Memories flooded back about how the four of them used to giggle if one of their umbrellas ever turned inside out, in the wind. They'd grab each other's hands, pretending they were about to take off into the air, like Mary Poppins. However, Paige ignored the man's voice. Nothing would make her go back again.

* * *

After an untidy search, Emily found her car keys behind a cushion on the sofa. She gripped them tightly, on a mission. She had to get back to Dailsworth High as soon as possible. It was Saturday night. She'd collapsed onto the floor, back leant against an armchair. Smudge eyed her as he strode in and settled on her knee. Disco-like lights cheerfully lit up the room, but they came from a police car zooming past her small, terraced house, siren on. Getting on the property ladder had meant compromising on location, you wouldn't walk through Crouchden alone after dark. Yet it had been a safe haven all those years ago, after nursing college, when Emily found she could afford to rent a flat here, twenty miles away from Dailsworth – twenty miles away from her childhood home, from memories of her mother.

She hadn't knocked back a drop of alcohol since the shot of Dutch courage she'd swallowed before this morning's meeting with the other three at their old high school. For the first time in months, she wasn't drinking wine all evening to the point of passing out. She told Smudge all about it: Morgan had a child, a boy – by Hugo. It still didn't compute. Morgan had always been the sensible one – she didn't date, never had a romantic interest – yet Hugo's jubilant revelations had disproved this. Being a single parent must have been hard enough, let alone from such a young age.

Paige had changed the least and was still her old, poised self, but Emily had honestly found it difficult to even recognise Tiff. Back in the day, she'd felt sorry for her friend; now and then, Tiff's mum would hint that her daughter should go on a diet. She'd give her melon for breakfast, salad for lunch, hence the secret binge of sweets on the way back home. A twinge of sadness reverberated across Emily's chest. Mothers could really screw you over. For Emily, despite the challenges, it would have been a blessing to only have ever had one parent.

She ran her finger over a line of fudge crumbs on the carpet. Morgan was making a huge mistake trying to track Hugo down. All of Emily's relationships had fallen apart during her twenties – until she met her husband, paramedic Lewis, who gave her trust in people again after everything with her mum shattered her confidence. Well, ex-husband now, she supposed. He'd moved out three months ago, not long after Halloween. They'd both worked a strenuous shift, as was always the way on 31 October, due to knife injuries whilst cutting pumpkins, people tripping over their costumes, allergic reactions to face paints, and drunken parties. Their argument had scared her more than any ghost because she was forced to admit, for the first time, that her marriage was in serious trouble. The signs had been there for about six months previous: the arguments, the accusations of not understanding each other. Their sex life had fizzled out. Lewis spent more and more time with mates from work whilst she'd escape into Netflix's latest offering.

Emily picked a large crumb of fudge off the carpet and put it in her mouth. Gently, she lifted Smudge up and reassured him she wouldn't be long.

Thirty minutes later, she parked up outside Dailsworth High School. The gates were locked. She walked to the far-right corner of the front of the school's grounds. The oak tree still stood there, with that low branch at the front that meant you could easily climb over the railings. The girls would use this way in if a meeting was ever called at the weekend. Heaving herself up, Emily gripped onto the bark. She swung a leg over and fell to the ground on the other side, giving a yelp. Back in the day, the others would have laughed, having made sure first that she wasn't hurt. As Emily limped across the field, mud splashed up her grey joggers. On reaching the hidden door to the disused basement, by the tree, she took out her phone and switched on the torch app.

For fifteen minutes, she scoured the ground. It had to be there. Ten minutes later, she still hadn't found it amongst the soil and grass. About to leave, Emily kicked a nearby patch of nettles. They parted to reveal a small ball of white paper, perfectly dry. Fumbling, she unrolled it. Morgan's mobile phone number. Hugo might really mess Olly up. Some people should never have children – she knew that better than anyone. Morgan's son was an innocent party in all this. He deserved to be protected from worse heartache, the kind that had ruined Emily's life. Carefully, she pocketed the piece of paper, rehearsing in her head what she'd say to Morgan.

* * *

Walking down Wilmslow High Street, Tiff stole a look in a shop window. Still slim. Thank God. Time hadn't turned back permanently to the dumpy girl with mousy curls who the popular girls laughed at and the boys ignored. Since last weekend's visit to her old high school, painful comments from other pupils had flooded back, mostly from Jasmine's clique who used to tease her, until they didn't. *You're dumpy, clumsy, you'll never lose your virginity.* Over the years, Tiff had fantasised about going to one of the reunions, with her flat stomach and thighs that no longer rubbed together. That would shut them up. Not that she had ever broken down in front of the bullies. Tiff Anderson was happy with the way she looked, she *was*, and everyone else could do one.

Tiff sauntered into the bar, all gilt and shaded glass, each table lit by a flickering, white candle, an elegant ambiance typical of Wilmslow. It was early evening and most seats were full, but then it was Friday. She found her reservation and ordered a glass of prosecco. Two young women, in front of cocktails, stared at her from the corner of the room. They looked at each other, then tapped on their phones. Tiff gave them ten seconds. Five passed and they came over.

'Are you...?'

Tiff smiled broadly for the selfies. She never used to get recognised, but the last TV show had started to change that. Now it happened about once a week, so she never went out in messy clothes or without make-up. Unlike her former friends. Emily had let herself go and what was with that attitude? As for Morgan, she'd clearly messed up her life big time, whilst Paige was as together as ever, just a bit of an ice queen. Tiff wondered about her husband. It was crazy to think that Paige was married. What about the love lives of the other two? Thank goodness they hadn't asked about Tiff's. Magazines had only recently taken an interest and Tiff told them what she told her parents: that she was far too ambitious to settle down. The slightest whiff of a romance and her mum would have gone out and bought a hat.

At Dailsworth High School, Tiff had been the geek who was a bit overweight, but that didn't stop her pulling on a sparkly hair bobble in the hope that her latest crush would notice. Seeing Jasmine again reminded her of a secret Tiff had kept in a desperate attempt to be liked. Thank goodness Jasmine hadn't told the others all these years later. They'd have seen it as such a betrayal. The shame still came back whenever Tiff thought about those days. The new headmistress looked more content with herself now. Way back, Jasmine was always refreshing her lip gloss or primping her hair, as if she feared she might become as unpopular as Tiff if she didn't. Perhaps that insecurity was why she used to be so mean. Once, her clique called Tiff 'Eddie', after Eddie Murphy in the movie *The Nutty Professor* where he dreamt he was so fat that he exploded, just because she had curves. Morgan, Paige and Emily would moan they hadn't got boobs as good as Tiff's. They reckoned Jasmine was jealous.

Tiff consulted her watch and cut the conversation short with the young women, not wanting them around when her date arrived. He would be here any minute. The prospect filled her with emptiness, even though he was charming, attractive, witty and intelligent. She reached into her bag to fish out her compact mirror when her fingers touched a piece of paper. She pulled it out. Morgan's phone number. She sipped a mouthful of wine before holding the note in the candle's flame, letting go as it turned to ashes.

A tall, well-dressed man strode over. Tiff stood up and extended her hand. He kissed it.

'Lovely to see you again, Carter,' she said.

'The pleasure's all mine, Tiffany.'

6

MORGAN

Morgan threw down her rucksack, glad Olly was out, went into her room and without turning on the lights, fell face first onto the bed, tears streaming down her cheeks. She'd always been the least emotional member of The Secret Gift Society. Tiff used to say that's why she liked her so much. Morgan could be relied on to bring her down from the latest crisis. But she'd had another bad day at work, a week of bad days, following on from last weekend's disastrous reunion with the girls. Particularly challenging work shifts had started in 2020 and when retail was still recovering from that particular world crisis, the cost of living one hit and customers continued to take it out on the workers. Today, an elderly woman had berated her over the price of eggs, and another customer almost succeeded in shoplifting and threatened to punch Morgan when she confronted him. Security got there just in time. Life in the supermarket never used to feel like being on the frontline.

Olly had a Saturday job in the local garden centre and always got in just after her. He'd easily got hired, having picked up snippets of knowledge over the years, from Morgan and his great grandfather. She'd almost applied for a position there once, but the pay was less and hours not as flexible as her job at the supermarket, and frequently the end-of-day food items, reduced for staff, had helped Morgan feed the two of them.

Her nails dug into the duvet. If she and her three friends had never fallen out, she could have rung Paige, Emily or Tiff, gone for a drink and laughed off the stress. Friends had come and gone during the last nineteen years, but her day-to-day life rarely matched theirs, with often no partner and no progressing career. Her pregnancy had come well before everyone else's too.

Morgan sat up, wiped her nose and flicked on her bedside lamp, exotic looking with its colourful pewter base. Den had bought it, the only man she'd had a long-term relationship with. It lasted for five years, from her late twenties to early thirties. He wanted kids, but Morgan didn't want another. She knew how much hard work and money having another child would be. And she still harboured a dream that, one day, she'd become a teacher. She did her maths A-level on an evening course at the local tech as soon as Olly was old enough to leave at home for a couple of hours. The next year, she did further maths. Den didn't understand. He had a good job as a car salesman, they could get married, have babies, holidays abroad, without her needing to have a career. Morgan's parents didn't get it either, wanting her to enjoy a marriage like theirs.

Teacher? What a dunce she was. As if Morgan would ever be able to afford to put both herself and Olly through university. But what did she have without dreams? A son about to leave home, a rented terraced house with a miniscule garden, a job where she was insulted and snapped at...

She shook herself. Had a shower. Grabbed a plate of beans on toast and then sat in the kitchen, in front of her laptop. Neither Paige, Emily nor Tiff had contacted her since last Saturday. Morgan gritted her teeth. No matter, she'd try again to find Hugo Black herself. She drew up a list of potential online places to check and investigated them one by one. Facebook? Nothing. She searched on Instagram, Twitter, TikTok, LinkedIn, then simply put his name into Google. Perhaps Paige was right, she should hire a private detective. She searched on websites, finally found one that listed prices. Her eyebrows shot up. Their hourly charge was more than her daily pay.

Her phone pinged. Morgan ignored it as the front door clicked and Olly lolloped in. His bag fell onto the floor and he came into the kitchen. He drank a glass of water, despite there being a large bottle of Coke in the fridge, his favourite brand – Morgan bought it occasionally for a treat.

He stared at her face. 'All right?' he asked, with his familiar teenage mumble.

'Never better,' she said brightly. 'Saturday night, I've got a date with Ant and Dec, a packet of chocolate digestives and that book you gave me for Christmas about cool maths facts.'

'Isn't it Samira from your work's birthday drinks?'

'Did you know that in Thailand, teenagers text each other the numbers five-five-five to indicate something is funny, because the word five sounds like ha in Thai, so they're actually texting ha, ha, ha?'

'Mum. Don't change the subject.'

Yes, everyone was going out for Samira's birthday. A meal at a fancy restaurant in Spinningfields, but Olly needed new trainers.

'I'm worn out, love. What about you? Clubbing? The pub?'

'It's because of money you're not going, isn't it?'

'Olly. You know what it's like, working with the public these days. I've had a really bad shift, that's all. I'm not in the mood for going out. Anyway, I can live vicariously through you and expect all the gossip when you get back. I'll be asking "what's the tea?" Isn't that what youngsters say these days?' She didn't get why. Tea was clear, strong, reliable – honest.

He focused on his glass.

'What is it?'

He spoke to the glass. 'Do you ever regret having me?'

Her chair scraped back and she stood up. 'Are you serious? What's brought this on?'

His eyes met hers that were still red and blotchy. 'You've not had it easy.'

'Who does?'

'Vikram's parents both have jobs they enjoy. They share the housework. Still go on dates. They're going on holiday to Spain this summer.'

'But I've got what no one else has – the best son in the world. Even when he beats me at Wordle.' She slipped an arm around his shoulder and squeezed tight.

He shook her off. 'It's obvious I was a mistake. No one chooses to have a baby so young. At least your mum and dad had each other. Just think, if we found Dad, he could help pay for stuff. You could go on holiday. Maybe even change jobs.' He slammed the glass down on the kitchen worktop. 'I can tell you've been crying, I'm not stupid, Mum. There are lots of reasons we need to find my dad. It's not only about me.' He stormed off.

She left him for thirty minutes to cool off then went upstairs. Morgan knocked on his bedroom door. Eventually, he pulled it open.

'I suppose you want a shirt ironing?' she said gently.

'I can do it myself.'

'Indeed. You ironed that shirt so quickly last weekend, it had more creases than Elmer the Patchwork Elephant.'

His frown lines relaxed a little. As he handed her his current favourite going-out top, she passed him a twenty-pound note. 'Here, take this for tonight, not that I imagine it will buy more than a couple of drinks.'

'I've got my job, Mum, you don't need to…'

She held up her hand. 'I'm earning brownie points, for when you become the physicist who works out what came before the Big Bang. I'm counting on that house you're going to buy me in Malibu.'

'Five-five-five,' he muttered.

His phone rang and he closed the door again. Morgan plugged in the iron, hating the fact she couldn't give him more. But they loved each other and that was all that mattered. It was.

Her phone pinged again. Samira could be persistent. Morgan went over to the table, sat down. Two texts from… Emily?

Don't look for Hugo, Morgan. Take it from me. Not all parents make kids happy.

Followed by:

I'm in Manchester tomorrow. If you want to chat, meet me in Marks café at eleven o'clock.

7

MORGAN

Morgan travelled up the escalator and stood outside the café entrance. Marks & Spencer had always been one of her favourite shops. The others used to call her middle-aged before her time. She'd steadfastly defend her corner, raving about their reliable underwear – actually all she could really afford to buy there, apart from occasional cheaper treats from the luxury food store. It was a forty-minute train journey into Manchester from Dailsworth. With the rail fare and cost of a lunchtime coffee and sandwich, these days, Morgan balked at going in too often. She surveyed the shop floor for Emily, whose appearance had never stood out, despite her soft blonde hair, the shower of freckles across her nose and those transparent, blue eyes. Emily had always preferred to keep herself in the background, whereas Paige had been easy to spot, gliding down school corridors, as if her feet weren't moving and, instead, an aura of self-belief simply powered her along. You couldn't miss Tiff, either, because of that expressive face, the gesticulating arms, the sparkly accessories that broke the rules, her bumbling loud bursts of laughter that embarrassed Tiff more than anyone else.

Five to eleven. When they were young, Morgan always was early, Paige right on time, Emily never liked to be the first and Tiff was one for dramatic entrances. Finally, Emily appeared, body hidden inside a voluminous parka. She lifted the hood that had been firmly pulled down over her fore-head, even though it wasn't raining outside. Morgan made an awkward movement as if to hug her but Emily's arms didn't reciprocate.

'Let me get the drinks,' said Morgan.

'Oh. Cheers. Mine's a latte,' said Emily. 'I'll find a table.'

Ten minutes later, Morgan sat in an upholstered booth, opposite Emily, who still had her coat on, zipped right up the top. She didn't touch her drink.

'Don't look for Hugo,' she blurted out and her nose wrinkled. 'My life was miserable because of my mother. Hugo was intimidating enough back in the day. He's a dangerous, unknown entity now, as a father.'

Morgan stopped stirring her drink and the teaspoon fell onto the saucer. Emily had grimaced when she'd said the word *mother*, a mother who'd suffered so much. 'Okay... and I appreciate your concern, Emily, but... *dangerous*? Isn't that a bit extreme?'

Emily raised an eyebrow. 'Don't you remember anything about what he was like, back then? We knew him for what... five long years? He had muscles when the other boys still thought triceps were dinosaurs. And yes, he had that natural charisma – everyone in the school knew his name – and he was good at sport as well. But he was also devious, he sucked up to the teachers and could easily charm his way into – or out of – anything. He clutched onto his status as if his life depended on it, mistreating everyone who didn't look up to him. What about the time he shoved David Smith's head down the loos because he dared share a joke with Hugo's girlfriend. Or how Patsy – remember her from our biology class? – wouldn't let him copy her homework so he spread rumours that he'd spotted her buying a pregnancy test.' Beads of perspiration formed on Emily's brow and she took off her coat. 'Despite being an evil bastard, he cast a spell over so many people. That kind of boy doesn't grow up into an honest, loyal, good-hearted man. And Olly is still at an impressionable age.'

'It's true,' said Morgan quietly, 'but everyone needs to connect with where they came from and that includes Olly, whatever his father was like all those years ago. Maybe Hugo hasn't changed, maybe he has, but either way, meeting him will at least answer my son's questions.'

Everything Emily was saying was true. But Morgan knew she had also seen a different side to Hugo in those final weeks before the prom. Glimpses of a less cocky lad who actually admitted he struggled with studies.

She'd always walked the same way home after leaving the girls in Crowley Road. One afternoon, she was about to turn into her street when she spotted him, sitting on the pavement, head in his hands... He'd been waiting for her. Said she had a perfect right to tell him to get lost, but if he didn't pass his maths GCSE, he was going to get in so much trouble at home. He offered to pay her to help him. She'd carried on walking but... a funny noise, like a suppressed sob, stopped Morgan in her tracks.

Hugo? A sensitive side? She always had been a sucker for a puzzle and seeing him express heartfelt emotion shed a different light on the boy she'd always believed she'd hated. As she got to know him better, Morgan came to really care for him, to the point where sex, eventually, felt just... right. Kissing Hugo, touching intimate places, gave her such a rush of sensations, like being on a rollercoaster, once you passed a certain point, you were horrified, yet thrilled – a rollercoaster that you couldn't get off. That's what it had been like the one time they slept together. Hugo had kept asking if she was sure, if she was okay. The only time in her life that logic abandoned her, Morgan had replied by tugging down his underpants.

Had it been an act, on his part; had she been under a spell? Olly had such a good heart, his father couldn't lack goodness completely. Yet the prom... his self-satisfied laugh... his sneers...

Slowly, Morgan stirred her drink again. 'Are these doubts also because your mum... how it ended... you're worried Hugo might be ill, and Olly will only meet him to lose him again?'

Emily shuffled in her seat but didn't reply.

'You looked after her so well.' Her mum had been given a terminal diagnosis in Year Ten. Emily had done everything for her from that point on, even though they were never close. But even before she got ill, her mum had often gone down the pub with friends during the week, leaving Emily to babysit her younger brother, whilst their lorry driver dad was away. The Secret Gift Society had meant everything to Emily: her one escape from the sadness.

'She's been gone for nineteen years now, but the effects of that time of my life have hung around like... like a warplane, over my head, biding its time to drop a bomb, a bomb that has finally dropped in recent months and blown everything I've worked for apart.'

What did Emily mean? 'Your mum wasn't a like a normal parent. I mean... she always came across as so much fun. That Christmas she let us taste all the drinks in your family's drink cabinet and didn't mind if we put on eighteen-rated DVDs. I didn't sleep for days after that zombie movie. I've never been able to be that chilled with Olly.'

'Normal would have been nice sometimes.'

There had been nothing normal about being fifteen and nursing your mother through terminal cancer, about giving her bed baths after rounds of chemo, about cutting her nails – and painting them too, Emily's mum would insist. She also fed her meals, cooking whatever her mum wished for, anything to get her better. On top of that was the laundry for the household, of comforting her younger brother when Emily was barely more than a child herself, and keeping cheerful for her dad when he came home from a tiring week on the road. Although Emily's mum kept her sense of humour, and if the girls ever went around she'd often be laughing on the phone to a friend or watching television. She'd never let Emily go to the hospital with her, said it was important she didn't miss lessons. Emily once told Morgan that secretly, she was glad. Nine till four, at school, was precious time for herself.

'Mum was always such a wildcard,' Emily muttered.

Morgan, Paige and Tiff admired how she dressed in the latest fashions. She'd let them read her magazines if they went around and always bought takeout for tea. She was an oracle when it came to celebrity gossip. Emily preferred books, her knitting, she liked nature, and on the rare weekends he was home, she'd often go hiking with her dad. Back in the day, Emily and her mum couldn't have been more different. A bit like Olly and Hugo.

'How did your dad cope?'

She grimaced. 'It took him a long time to get over what happened, but he's retired now. Remarried. Gina's good for him. Used to be a care assistant.'

'You and her have that in common then. Looking back through grown-up eyes, I can see how selfless you were, looking after your mum, missing nights out with us, school events, all so that you could be there for her. I... wish I'd helped more.'

'It wouldn't have changed the fact that Mum *ruined* my life.'

What *had* happened? 'I'm so sorry to hear that.'

Emily got up. 'I don't need your pity... even though I don't have a high-falutin career like being a maths teacher, a solid future cut out and all sorted.'

'High-falutin? I work in a supermarket, live on the estate where I grew up, and still buy my undies from Marks.'

Emily stopped dead. Sat down again. 'You didn't go to uni? But you always wanted to and when it came to maths, were the brightest in our year.'

'How could I? Olly had to come first.'

'Of course he did,' she said, for the first time sounding like the Emily from high school.

'Please, Emily, help me find Hugo. We don't have to stay in touch afterwards. I just need to get this right or I'm scared I'm going to lose my lad. I would never say this to him, but... Olly's all I've got.'

'No partner?'

She shook her head. 'Just a job I hate. Some days, I wonder how I've managed to stick at it.'

Emily caught her eye, hesitated and then raised her arms and did breaststroke in the air. The two women exchanged a brief smile and Emily quickly dropped her arms, but not before a warm sensation had filled Morgan's chest.

'Mum and Dad living around the corner... In some ways, I feel like I've never grown up,' she continued. 'Apart from when it comes to Olly. He's the one thing I'm so proud of.'

Emily's tired face softened, and as if sensing a need for them to change the subject, she ran a finger around the rim of her cup and said, 'Tiff looked different, didn't she?'

'I still can't believe it, and what about Jasmine? She must have really upped her game at sixth form college.'

'She's still a bitch, though. See, some people can't change.'

'But the four of us have.'

Emily took another mouthful. 'Not Paige so much, apart from being a bit stand-offish. I wonder what she does now. Do you think Tiff's on one of those Hollywood diets, all cabbage and farts?'

'Remember that sulphur experiment in chemistry when you threw up because of the stink? Your breakfast landed on Jasmine's new shoes.'

Morgan had forgotten what a toothy smile Emily had. Tiff used to be jealous, said it was celebrity perfect.

'What about that five-mile cross country? One mile in and Tiff pretended to faint.' Emily shook her head. 'The teacher got his car and drove her back to school.'

'We always knew that one day she'd be a great performer,' said Morgan. 'We were good at lying when we had to be. Like Paige wearing her mum's pale foundation to school, pleading illness as the reason she hadn't done her homework.'

The laughter left Emily's face. 'Yes. We were. Great liars. Even to each other. Prom night proved that.'

Shit.

Emily stood up, slipped into her coat and zipped it right up again. She pulled up the hood. 'One thing life has taught me is that lies hurt. Lies have consequences. It's because of that we can't ever be proper friends again.'

Morgan stood up and held out her hand. 'Thanks for coming anyway. I really appreciate it.' Emily paused and then slipped her hand into Morgan's. The years fell away, leaving them in the dark, unused school basement, fingers intertwined, chanting their oath.

'You're absolutely convinced it's the right thing to do, aren't you?'

Morgan hesitated. 'A few months ago Olly came out to me, as gay. He's been through a tough time. School's hard enough without having to work out who you really are. Hugo has always been another piece of this identity puzzle. I want my son to feel complete and will do anything to help him build his self-assurance and sense of who he is.'

'Oh. Poor lad.' Emily looked down at their hands, still intertwined. She let go and walked away, stopped after a few paces and took off her hood, turned around. 'I'm probably going to regret this, but okay. I understand more now. I'll help.'

Morgan felt as happy as the time she'd got an unexpected bonus at work and could pay for an ecstatic little Olly to go camping with Cubs. 'You really mean it?'

'It's not as if there's anything else going on in my life. As long as we're clear, this is about your Olly, not us revisiting the past.'

'You think we will?' asked Morgan and she leant forwards. 'Find Hugo, that is?'

'Of course. The Secret Gift Society never once failed, but it'll mean getting the others on board. The Case of the Missing Father could be a tricky one.'

8

PAIGE, EMILY, TIFF

Paige went to her desk, in her study, a room she'd hoped might one day be a nursery. She tied her Ted Baker wool wrap coat tightly, and sat in front of her laptop and the email she'd received a few days ago. Since meeting her old friends, she'd hardly slept, had lost weight, and taken up smoking again. Today's get-together couldn't possibly make things worse – could it? Morgan and Emily had found her on the internet and asked to meet up. Her business, North West Bodytalk, had a website with a contact page and her address. Perhaps they'd put her name along with Castlefield into the search engine, as Paige had mentioned to Morgan that's where she lived. In fact, Morgan and Emily had suggested meeting up nearby, at the end of Deansgate in New Chapter Café.

So Emily had clearly changed her mind and was now helping with the... what had they called it? The Case of the Missing Father.

Ridiculous.

Paige got up, walked through the living room and into the kitchen. On Sundays, she usually tidied up and did her admin whilst Felix had a lie-in. She downed a glass of filtered water. She should have been brave enough to tell Morgan, when they first met, why she'd never agree to spending hours investigating Hugo's whereabouts. The only thing that held her back was this sense that Morgan had an important secret agenda. But then why should Paige care? They were no longer friends. They no longer had sleepovers where they shared such secrets under the covers. Morgan, who'd once been like the sister she'd never had, who was going to do all those typical girlfriend things as they got older – share a flat, be godmother to Paige's kid, be best man at her wedding (girl power, natch).

Paige consulted her watch, turned up her coat collar and scribbled a note to her husband saying she wouldn't be gone long. She went into the bedroom and left it on a pillow, kissing him gently on the forehead before leaving. Outside, the Manchester air, crisp and unforgiving, cleared her head. Today, the time had come. She needed to drop her bombshell from the past, whatever the consequences. It was best for everyone.

* * *

The train hurtled past Stockport, the Plaza theatre, the old Debenhams. Tiff was on the road to fame, Paige had her own business and Morgan a child she adored. Emily had a looming divorce and P45 – she wasn't going back to the hospital, not that the emergency care matron knew that yet, she'd only insist Emily finish the counselling before making such a major decision. Emily had attended her first session on Friday. The woman with poodle curls and furry jumper sat opposite and dug her claws into Emily's childhood.

Like Olly, Emily only had one parent now, and even though she was thirty-five, it still felt like a blemish on her life. The train pulled into Piccadilly Station and she walked down towards Market Street, stopping to give a homeless man a fifty-pence coin. A retro street performer danced to 'Wannabe' by the Spice Girls, one-time heroes of the four girls, each determined to forge their own way in life, equal to men in the best ways. How her friends would have disapproved of Emily doing a striptease to that song for her husband, when they first got together. Lewis had loved their hits and she'd put on his Union Jack boxer shorts for full effect. Her throat hurt. Lewis. She missed him. But not his adamant belief that her future still lay in nursing, whatever the cost. He'd become active in the ambulance union now too, and part of her loved him for it. However, it wasn't in her any more, to give away so much of herself to a National Health Service in such a mess.

New Chapter Café came into view and an unfamiliar buzz flickered in her stomach. She'd come up with an idea of how to find Hugo and was keen to share it. Morgan was waiting outside and for one moment, the predictability of her old friend arriving first eased the ache that had made itself comfortable inside Emily for so long.

* * *

The problem with having a photographic memory was that you could burn a phone number but still remember it. The numbers danced around in Tiff's head for several days, willing Tiff on to ring Morgan. Instead, she mentioned to Mum that she'd been in contact with the girls.

'Oh love.' Her mum had teared up. She'd been so fond of her daughter's friends. For all her nagging ways, suggesting teen Tiff eat healthier, to start priming herself for a Hollywood career, Tiff always appreciated how welcoming her mum had been, letting her friends stay late at weekends. Now and then, Tiff's parents even joined in board games. 'You were such good friends,' she'd said. 'It cut straight through me, Tiffy, when you had that little argument.'

Little argument? But then Tiff had never explained to her mother exactly what had happened at the school dance. After Hugo's derision, for the first time, Tiff focused on becoming a success for herself, not just for her parents. She should have thanked him, really, because this made all the difference. How satisfying it would be to rub his nose in everything she was achieving. To show him that he was wrong – that the chubby little nerd was actually worth something. Maybe meeting him now would finally extinguish that need to seek validation from every colleague, date, fan, human. Tiff picked up her phone and typed in the numbers the flames had burned.

9

MORGAN

Morgan and Emily walked into New Chapter Café, which was decked out like an American diner with its glossy furnishings, chrome bookshelves, and black and white floor tiles. The walls bore literary drawings, like the large ones of Ebenezer Scrooge and Hogwarts. No sooner had they sat down than Paige glided in, bang on time. Lastly, Tiff arrived, all primary colours and pungent scent. Morgan and Emily sat opposite the other two, their lack of conversation replaced by the hiss of the coffee machine, knives cutting through slabs of brownie and the Sunday morning crowd enjoying their weekend.

'It's great to be together again,' said Morgan.

'Best to keep it real though,' said Emily, and she loosened a scarf covered in pulled threads. 'I'm only on board to help Olly. Then I'm going back to my life. The society disbanded a long time ago.'

'Agreed,' said Tiff. 'Once this case is solved, I'm off.'

Paige opened her mouth and then closed it firmly.

'Our usual drinks, my treat? I'll go up and order,' said Morgan cheerfully. 'Tea for Paige, Emily you always had orangeade, Tiff hot chocolate?'

'*Green* tea, for me, please,' said Paige, in a polite voice.

'Latte like in Marks, would be great,' said Emily.

'I'll have a cappuccino,' said Tiff, 'decaf, with oat milk, extra hot, no chocolate on top.'

Morgan glanced at Tiff, then Emily, Paige too, a small flame of humour flickering between the four of them, lighting up each face a little.

'Nothing wrong with knowing what you want,' said Tiff airily.

That's why the group used to work. No one would be singled out. Humour was always shared as a four, not enjoyed behind backs.

Morgan returned with a tray of drinks. 'Cheers, everyone.'

Tiff took her cappuccino and cleared her throat. 'Getting things out in the open is important. Before anything else, we should apologise for that prom night and the things we said. It's bad karma not to – my wellness advisor said so. Paige was right, the other week: we betrayed each other.'

'Let's not go there, Tiff,' said Paige and she frowned. 'I don't see how anything good can come of it. It's needless anyway, because...' She took a deep breath. 'You should all know that—'

'I'd have thought you'd be up for it, Paige,' interrupted Emily in a measured tone. 'I looked at your website, you studied psychology. I have a little, too. Isn't closure important? Our friendship fell apart so quickly that night.'

'Perhaps it was exam stress that made us foolish,' said Morgan quickly. 'Let's leave it at that.'

'Foolish?' said Tiff and threw down her napkin. 'You got pregnant! We'd spent five years hating that tosser, ignoring his nasty comments about us being geeks and losers, putting up with the sarcastic barks when we walked past, implying we were dogs, and as for the pinged bra straps... but then secretly, in the last term, one by one, behind each other's backs, we let him flatter us into' – she took a moment – 'falling in love.'

Emily cringed. 'Talk about screwed up. I feel sorry for whomever he's with now.'

'A classic move, revealing what he'd done, at the dance,' said Tiff. 'What a way to get back at the society for solving a case against him. I'll never forget his tone when he expressed amazement that any of us believed he found us attractive. How he said The Secret Gift Society was run by a bunch of childish romantics whose special bond, he'd proved, meant absolutely nothing.' Tiff bit her lip. 'Sometimes, over the years, I've wondered if he was right. A secret society? What were we thinking?'

'That's enough,' said Morgan. 'Please stop, Tiff. Don't do this. Don't ruin happy memories. Yes, it probably was a bit childish but—'

'You think?' said Paige. 'Swearing an oath, underground, in virtual darkness?'

The four of them exchanged wry smiles.

'We had good intentions, that's what matters. We helped other pupils,' said Emily.

The four women paused, nodded, and then knocked back mouthfuls of their drinks, as if they were gin.

'We were young,' said Paige, eventually. 'Naïve.'

Emily's face hardened again. 'You weren't quite as naïve as us, Paige, you'd at least dated several guys, unlike us three. *You* should have known better.'

'*I* should have known, if anyone,' interrupted Morgan. 'Boys used to make me cringe. I'd never dreamt of receiving declarations of love or red roses, like you lot used to, but somehow, with Hugo...'

'One hundred per cent,' said Tiff. 'If anyone was going to see through Hugo's game, it should have been you, Morgan. But Christ, instead you ended up sleeping with him.' She put her hands up. 'As for me, it was the first time a boy appeared to look past my podginess and I was bowled over, I lapped it up.' She shuddered. 'God, I was so grateful.' Her voice wavered. 'I told Hugo I loved him.' She didn't blink for a few moments as if watching a reel of a horror movie from 2004.

'I looked up to you three,' said Emily in a quiet voice. 'My closest friends who knew best about everything, who were always there when life got shitty. I was having a bad enough time as it was, because of my mum. I still think about how Hugo must have found the fact he was the first boy I'd ever kissed funny.'

'I'm sure we didn't mean everything we'd said to each other that night,' said Paige, her tone reminding Morgan of how she so often used to bring the girls together. However, today that conciliatory tone irritated Morgan, who couldn't keep the words in.

'You said I was gay! I didn't care what you thought about my sexuality, what hurt was the fact that I thought we knew each other, inside out.'

'Did we? You called me a princess, Morgan,' said Paige, colouring up.

'Better that than a slut,' said Emily and shot a grimace Tiff's way. 'I couldn't have had less experience with boys.'

Tiff got to her feet. 'You were right, Paige. I should have kept shtum. In fact, I should have kept away today, because you three have no idea how I suffered after that night. *Gay?* Paige didn't mean it as an insult, it was simply a misguided observation, not a critical comment about, say, your behaviour or appearance. As for *princess*, well, let's face it Paige, with your designer clothes and dad's Aston Martin, it was near to the truth. And *slut* was a common enough insult thrown by people at school to each other, no one really meant it, and you obviously weren't, Emily. But *Jabba*...? That name's repulsive image drew all the loudest laughs.' Her eyes shone and she went to go.

'Please don't leave,' said Morgan and looked around the table. 'Please. I need... I couldn't bear it if...' She gulped and knocked into the table as she got up and charged towards the toilets.

Tiff raised her eyebrows and sat down again. 'Oh. She's truly upset. Guess I would be, if I was the one to reach out after all these years and it didn't go to plan.'

Paige followed Morgan past the cake counter and into the small corridor. She was crouched at the bottom of a wall, a tissue in between her fingers, her handbag next to her, open, with an official-looking letter sticking out and a tube of Rolos, favourites ever since she'd been old enough to have pocket money. Paige took Morgan's hands and pulled her up.

'Look, Morgan, there's something I should tell you...'

Morgan's breath hitched. 'I don't need to listen to anything, unless it's you and the others agreeing to spend this time together, looking for Olly's dad, the four of acting as a team, like we used to.'

Paige tilted her head. 'There's more to this than finding Hugo, isn't there? Why are you so upset? You must have realised there was a chance we'd not hit it off again. What's going on, Morgan, apart from all this stuff with Olly?'

Morgan rolled her lips together. Paige waited, in silence, whilst Morgan's mind raced back to what had been the beginning of the end for the friends. She could exactly recall Hugo's face when he found out he'd lost his captaincy of the football team. It was the end of January, six months before the prom. The four friends were walking home, past the frosty, lit-up football pitch. Hugo was shouting at the coach, who pointed to the changing rooms and ordered him inside, to get dressed and go home. On the way, Hugo passed the girls.

'You frigid little bitches have caused this,' he spat, icy-white air shooting out from his lips like icicles. 'The headmaster's had a word with Coach. Coach wasn't happy with him interfering with the way he runs things, but said he couldn't help agreeing...' Hugo's eyes flashed with anger. 'Apparently, my behaviour doesn't fit with the *ethos of the team*.'

'That's what happens when you two-time the head's daughter,' said Paige smoothly.

'Amelia brought her suspicions to us, we were duty-bound to help,' Morgan had added.

'She was really upset,' said Emily, standing a little behind the others' backs.

'The truth always comes out eventually, however much you carry on denying it,' said Tiff, bravado at the fore.

'My dad's going to go apeshit. You've made the biggest mistake of your lives,' he'd hissed and jabbed his finger in the air.

Morgan shook herself and stood straighter. Wiped her eyes. Blew her nose. 'Sorry, Paige. I don't know what came over me. I should never have put that message in the newsletter. I'll find a way to track Hugo down on my own. Right... better go and wash my face. Take care. If they're still there, thank the others for me and say goodbye on my behalf.'

Morgan splashed cold water onto her skin. The headmaster's daughter was one of the few pupils who'd shot the girls sympathetic glances at the prom. Months earlier, she'd taken them to one side, explained how it was odd how Hugo was more interested in talking to her dad than to her, whenever he went around for tea, as if his mind was on something – or someone – else. Therefore, the girls had used their four gifts and the evidence they found left them in no doubt that he was cheating with a pupil in Year Ten named Sophie. She sat next to Morgan in maths.

Morgan wiped away the water and memories with a paper towel. The one thing she liked so much about maths was that if an equation went wrong, you could always trace it back to the first mistake – and then put it right. Life wasn't like that. What was the first mistake The Secret Gift Society made? Was it each falling for Hugo? Was it taking on Amelia's case and standing up against their nemesis? Was it forming the society in the first place?

Morgan left the toilets. Where was her handbag? Crap, she must have left it on the floor. She hurried back into the café. Emily and Tiff sat waiting, Morgan's handbag on the table. Paige must have picked it up and put it there. The café door opened and Paige walked in, cheeks drained of colour. She held onto the back of the chair for a second and then sat down.

'I just needed some fresh air.'

Had Paige been crying?

Paige gripped the chair back tighter. 'I've got something to say…'

10

MORGAN

'This isn't easy for me,' said Paige. 'I came here today to put an end to this reunion.' She exhaled, air noisily escaping her clenched jaw. 'But whatever's happened in the past, Morgan has guts for getting in touch, for asking us to work together even though the sense of betrayal is still so raw. This tells me she's pretty desperate. Aside from that, Olly's blameless in all of this. Us four started it when we took on his dad. Emily's right, we should do this for him. It's our responsibility. One last ever case, if you like.' Her tone sounded affectionate for a moment. 'Then we formerly, and properly, this time, disband the society. Right, Emily and Tiff?' She gave them both pointed looks, then sat down and took out her compact, looking thoroughly miserable as she dabbed the skin around her eyes.

Tiff drummed her fingers on the table. 'I'd say revenge is also good motivation. That's why I'm prepared to do this.' Tiff rubbed her hands together. 'I'll show Hugo that I had the last laugh. I bet he's stuck doing some crummy desk job.'

Morgan kept quiet, wondering why Paige couldn't stop looking at her.

'Although I've thought about how Olly must feel,' Tiff added, in a gentler tone. 'It must be so odd, never having met one parent. I look in the mirror and know where every feature came from. My mouth from Mum, my striking nose, thanks for nothing Dad... whereas Olly must look and feel like half is unexplained.'

Morgan had never thought of it like that. She imagined not knowing where her small feet came from, surprised at the sense of emptiness that would create.

'Remember how, at the beginning of every school year, with new teachers, the class would be made to introduce themselves one by one?' asked Tiff. 'We'd say a couple of lines about ourselves. How about we do that for us now? Just the basics. I'll go first.'

It was good to see Tiff so much more confident in herself. Back in the day, there was an awkwardness about her, and an apologetic air that didn't go with how she gave bullies the finger. She used to be larger than life, laughing, making dramatic gestures. Occasionally. Morgan used to wonder if it was because, inside, Tiff felt much smaller.

'I spent most of my twenties working in bars and taking any acting job – I got bit parts in pantos, did voice-overs, had walk-on roles in soaps. Finally, a top agent signed me up and now I'm finally doing bigger stuff. I couldn't believe it when I won an award for a West End play I was in, and then was cast as the top suspect in a cosy crime series, which was pretty big on Netflix. I've even been asked for selfies by people who've watched it, which is strange but amazing. I've got a month off before I start filming my next job, a thriller set on the Isle of Wight. And this time, I'm the lead.'

'Don't expect me to be the first to follow that glittering CV,' said Emily, in a tense tone.

'If it helps, I've never had a long-term relationship. Not that it's a big deal,' Tiff added with a fake Hollywood smile.

Emily shot her a curious look. 'Okay, well, I've done that at least. I've been married, but we're currently separated. I was a nurse. In A&E. Lewis is a paramedic.'

'A nurse? Wowsers. Go you, Emily,' said Tiff.

Morgan loved how that could have been teenage Tiff talking.

'I'm not surprised that you went into the caring profession,' said Paige, 'after the way you looked after your mother.'

'Well, I'm not a nurse any more...' she said, looking as if she'd just been asked to empty ten bedpans. 'Actually, working in the emergency depart-ment became pretty shit.'

The other three looked at each other. Words weren't necessary. No doubt Paige and Tiff read the news like Morgan, and remembered the lock-down clapping for NHS workers, a gesture that led to no changes to their gruelling work circumstances.

'What will you do next?' asked Paige.

'I'll sort something out. *No big deal.*' She shot the words towards Tiff as if fighting a duel.

'As you and Emily know, Morgan, I'm a body language expert,' said Paige. 'I advise people over non-verbal communication, stuff like body movements. I teach businesses and individuals how to get ahead by presenting themselves in a certain way – and how to read the behaviour of their competitors and customers.'

'You went to university?' asked Morgan.

'I studied psychology – and then did a master's in kinesics.'

'You used to like analysing people,' said Tiff. 'We forced you to do us once.'

'God yes, I remember you said I was a product of my parents in more ways than one,' said Morgan. 'Practical, you said I got on with life's mistakes, accepted there was no point fretting about things that couldn't be changed, like the time the hairdresser misunderstood and gave me a fringe. It was hideous, looking back! But you noticed I held my head high, clipped it back and wore headbands until it grew out, that I found it funny, when another girl might have thought the world had ended.'

'Whereas you saw that I was an open book, until I wasn't, when my mum fell ill, you said I changed, kept asking why I didn't invite you lot around very often.' Emily shook her head. 'I'd have thought the answer was obvious, as if I had the time to entertain you three in between washing Mum's hair and comforting my brother after a teacher had been mean.' Emily's shoulders hunched up.

'And I was a sensitive soul, you reckoned,' said Tiff, 'well suited to the creative industry. You said my emotions spoke through my hands.' She shrugged. 'Guess you were right. My drama school teachers had to knock

that out of me when I delivered lines.' Tiff held her hands together, now.
'Tell us about your love life, Paige.'

'Felix and I have been married five years,' she replied.

'Kids?' asked Emily.

Paige shook her head and muttered, *No big deal.*

'Well, as you know, I got pregnant,' said Morgan briskly. Paige's mouth
had turned down at one corner, it always used to do that when she was
feeling sad. 'I work in a supermarket, live in a council house around the
corner from Mum and Dad's, and I'm currently single.'

Actor, nurse, business owner... cashier. Morgan didn't want to feel like a
failure. Many of her colleagues loved their jobs and climbed the ladder,
becoming supervisors. Retail work had its plusses but wasn't what Morgan
had ever wanted. She took out a notebook and pen and moved the chat on
to talking about Hugo. She explained that she'd already searched online,
and also contacted the school secretary who was in charge of the alumni
newsletter, how she'd agreed to contact Hugo if he was listed and ask if it
was okay if Morgan got in touch. Morgan hadn't heard back. 'If you three
can help me piece together who Hugo's old friends were, I might approach
them if they are on social media.'

'No need. I've got a plan,' said Emily.

'You have?' Morgan leant forwards.

'I skimmed the last newsletter and was about to delete. Then I saw your
message. Did anyone else read the whole letter?'

They shook their heads.

'Remember Miss Moo Moo?'

Of course, their nickname for the French teacher, Mlle Vachon.

'She must be... what, pushing her mid-seventies now,' continued Emily,
'but is still as active as ever. She's set up a French club for adults. It's going
to be held in Dailsworth library every Saturday morning, starting in the
middle of March, the eighteenth.'

'She's still around here?' asked Morgan. 'I've never seen her.' But then
Dailsworth was a town, not village, with a population of a hundred and fifty
thousand.

'What's she got to do with Hugo?' asked Tiff.

'Once, when Hugo and I were... alone...' Emily pursed her lips. 'He mentioned how his mum and Miss Moo Moo were quite close, what with both of them being French. He kept it quiet. It wouldn't have been cool if people discovered he hung out with a teacher off school grounds.'

'She might know where Hugo and his family disappeared to,' said Paige.

Paige didn't sound enthusiastic, but she was helping out, Morgan couldn't ask for more than that.

'It's worth a shot,' said Emily. 'How quickly did he move away?'

'I did the pregnancy test two months after prom. Visited his house. It was empty,' replied Morgan. The black coffee stared up at her like it had that day back in 2004 when she'd gone to the girls' favourite café in Dailsworth and ordered a cup after seeing the pink line, all alone, as she would be from that point on. Oh, she'd have the support of Mum and Dad, when they'd calmed down, but it wasn't the same. The waitress had asked Morgan where her friends were and she'd burst into tears and run outside, not knowing yet, without it being born, that her love for that baby would carry her through the darkest moments; it would feel like the best moments of her life so far being rolled into one – winning the maths prize for three years running, solving cases like The Case of the Injured School Cat, sneaking out with the girls to go for a midnight swim in the school's outdoor pool, that buzz in the stomach at the first sight of snow, the purple gleam of the tin of Quality Street at Christmas.

'We could drop into the library at the end of this French club next Saturday,' said Tiff. 'I'm free.'

Emily drained her cup. 'Can we agree on a finite amount of time for this case? No offence, but I don't want it to drag on forever. Why don't we make a concerted effort, within a set timeframe?'

'I don't need to get to the Isle of Wight until Wednesday 12 April, after Easter Monday,' said Tiff.

'I work five days a week but I'm owed lots of holiday...' said Morgan. 'How about each of us try to find out what we can the next few weeks, hopefully that will throw up some leads, and then... maybe we could, say, spend a few days together, maybe even a week solidly working twenty-four-seven on this?' Morgan ran a hand across her forehead. 'I know it's such a lot to ask, but I feel like focus is the only answer.' She noticed Paige slowly nodding, which gave her the confidence to continue. 'How about the first week of April, from Saturday 1st to Saturday 8th? That way I can give my boss good notice that I want the time off. Unless any of you already have plans for Good Friday? It ties in really well for me because Olly's away on a Physics field trip that last week before the Easter holidays. I haven't put him in the picture yet in case it's a lost cause and our investigations come to nothing but dead ends. You work too, Paige. Does that timing suit?'

Paige took out her phone and checked her calendar app. 'There are only a couple of appointments I might not be able to move.' She shrugged. 'The first to eighth works for me. Felix is away on business that week. I guess it's as good a time as any.'

'Okay, and next Saturday, I'll see if I can switch shifts, a colleague owes me,' said Morgan. 'That way, I can go to the library too and go into the supermarket later instead. If we can at least come up with a couple of leads by Easter, then when you all... go back to your lives... that might be the point I tell Olly what I am doing, and he and I take it from there. I'm more hopeful now. Thanks so much everyone.' Her voice caught. 'You can't imagine how much this means to me.'

'What if our four *gifts* don't work?' said Emily. 'Christ. Doesn't it sound cringey now, calling them that, as if our strengths were oh-so special. I guess that's teenagers for you. But yes, I hate to be the harbinger of doom, but I reckon my gift has gone for good.'

'Remember our oath?' said Tiff and she smiled. 'It's as if we thought we had superpowers.'

'True, but even though everyone laughed at the prom, no one could deny how we brought answers to the questions that tormented other pupils,' said Paige. 'Mind you...' Her eyes twinkled. 'Our oath seems a tiny bit over the top now: The Secret Gift Society swears through its blood...'

Morgan joined in. 'To only act for the good.'

Emily started speaking too. 'Its four powers to serve those in need of defence. All hail...'

Then each woman spoke their own gift, in the appropriate place.

'Logic,' said Morgan, a shiver running down her spine.

'Kindness,' said Emily, in an unsure tone.

'Empathy,' Tiff said and she yawned.

'A sixth sense,' said Paige, humour in her voice.

* * *

As she drifted off to sleep that night, more relaxed than she had been in a long time, the oath whispered in Morgan's ear, emphasising the four gifts. The women had chuckled together after they'd chanted it – yes, actually shared a joke – about how they used to call Paige's gift a sixth sense. Paige agreed it sounded supernatural, wishful thinking on the part of those teenagers. A better label for Paige's strength, they all decided, would have been *strong intuition*.

Was Emily right? Had their gifts disappeared? Not Morgan's. She'd always loved the logic of maths, always been called practical, and as a member of the society, used to be able to detach herself emotionally and work out a problem. None of that had changed – unless it came to Olly. As for Emily, the kindness was harder to spot now, what with the sarcastic comments and no filter. Yet she'd agreed to help Morgan and seemed genuinely concerned for her son. Back in the day, her sweet nature inspired a sense of trust that lent itself to extracting information from people to solve a conundrum. As for Tiff, a prerequisite of acting was empathy, to be able to put yourself into the shoes of characters. Morgan couldn't afford streamed television so hadn't caught the shows her old friend had been in, but Tiff had certainly put herself in Olly's position, considering what it meant to him to be missing one parent. There was no doubt, too, about Paige's intuition. She'd guessed there might be another reason for Morgan wanting to find Hugo. But Morgan wouldn't think about that now and hoped Paige didn't mention it again. Instead, she allowed the oath to lull her to sleep.

11

PAIGE, EMILY, TIFF

Paige buried her face in the pillow, coming up for air after suffocating in memories of dancing at the prom, exchanging furtive, flirty glances with Hugo when she thought no one was looking. He'd even brushed her fingers with his as he passed – minutes before his nasty, revelatory speech. Yet she'd seen such a different side to him during their private trysts. He'd made her a bookmark with a daisy chain drawn on it. The chats turned to secret trips into Manchester. The first time they'd kissed, Paige took the lead, running her hand through his hair, down his chest, further down still the next time they got close. He'd buy her favourite cigarettes, a mate's dad ran a corner shop and Hugo could get his hands on them cheap. They'd smoke them in the park. Read books together. Through her, he discovered the classics. Everyone used to say how mature Paige was, but with Hugo, for the first time, she could let down her hair. They went on a day trip to Blackpool. She'd never been on a rollercoaster before. He even gave her a charm bracelet. Said he loved her. With the direct eye contact, the dilating pupils, he'd seemed so honest.

Paige dragged herself into the sitting position. She never usually minded Monday mornings and would get up early and make coffee, often drinking it on the balcony, even in the winter with a rug on her lap, watching Manchester surface after a weekend of hangovers. But after another restless night, she was late today. Eight o'clock and she'd not even got showered or dressed. All night she'd tossed and turned due to her secret...

The bedroom door opened and Felix walked in, bringing her back to the present. He carried a tray and a small vase with a rose in it.

She shuffled up and leant back against the pillows. 'What have I done to deserve this?'

He set the tray down on the bedside table, already dressed in his jogger bottoms and muscle-fit T-shirt. He ran a hand over his buzz cut, a nervous habit. 'I'm worried about you, Paige. You've hardly slept the last couple of weeks and didn't say much when you came in yesterday. You just let me go on and on about my trip next weekend. Honestly, it's as if I'm going to somewhere amazing like Dubai for a week... oh. Wait.'

Paige did her best to smile. Felix hadn't been sleeping well either and snapped occasionally; a lot was riding on his work in the Middle East. He worked for Prestige Fitness, a global gym business, helping them set up gyms around the world. He played an integral part in training staff, from the trainers up to management. Last summer, he'd gone to Sydney for three weeks, and in the January, Switzerland. She'd taken a week's holiday and joined him. They'd fitted in skiing.

'I looked online, it's thirty degrees in Dubai at the moment,' she said. 'I'll sneak some extra sun cream in your suitcase.' She'd also hide one of her gloves in his case – a romantic joke to do with the way they met.

'Sure you won't come? Jiggle your appointments?'

'I'd rather us book off a week together when neither of us are working. Let's have a day out somewhere nice when you get back, though. It'll be the Easter weekend so we'll both have that Monday off. You know sun's not my style – one reason I love living in Manchester.'

He passed her a plate – eggs, sunny side up. 'What's going on, Paige? *Who* was it you met yesterday?'

His voice was gentle, the gaze caring. Another man might have suspected Paige was cheating, but Felix and Paige shared a deep trust of each other. After the teen years, honesty had been the priority in all of her relationships. And yet... she bit into the toast. She didn't want to dump everything on him, not now, not when he was getting ready for Dubai. Just one word and it might all come spilling out, the dams of the painful past open with nothing to plug them. Prestige Fitness had suffered huge losses since 2020 and were struggling in a way they never had before. Felix didn't talk about it much, a sign he was really worried. His real passion also lay not in the glitzy gyms, but the charity projects the company ran on the side, in which he was heavily involved, setting up community hubs where disadvantaged kids could develop an interest in fitness and good health, a place they were safe and could make friends. Dubai was a last-ditch project to see if Prestige Fitness could get back on track and his bosses had made it clear it was down to Felix to make Dubai work and lay the foundations to expand into other areas of the United Arab Emirates. An intense seven days, they could only afford to send him for one week. If Dubai wasn't a success, the community hubs back in the UK would be the first arm of the company to suffer. Paige couldn't offload her turmoil since meeting up with Morgan, Emily and Tiff. It would act as a distraction that might jeopardise everything Felix had worked so hard for.

'Just friends.' Were they now? 'As for the lack of sleep, I've been brainstorming. A company I want to impress.' One little lie, the first of their marriage. 'They'll pay well. The fee could go into our detached house fund.'

'How about I cook tonight?' he said. 'Pasta, red wine, we can get a little silly...' He winked.

'Whatever do you mean, Felix Barron?' The anxiety inside her stomach unfurled into something much more pleasant.

Felix went to leave and hesitated at the bedroom door. 'No amount of money is worth you taking up smoking again, Paige.' He gave a sheepish smile. 'I smelt it on your clothes the other day. It's up to you, but I reckon you don't need cigarettes. You're one of the strongest people I know.'

Paige loved Felix to the max. He knew her so well. She reached for the handbag by her side and ran a finger over the packet of cigarettes. But she wasn't as strong as he thought.

* * *

Afternoon already. Emily's phone bleeped and she reached for it. The four women had set up a WhatsApp group and there was a notification. She let the phone fall back down onto her bedside table, glad to be in bed, not at work. Monday was the busiest time in A&E due to a lack of services over the weekend; health problems spilled over. Some patients didn't even bother trying their overstretched GP these days.

She used to put other people first, genuinely care about their wellbeing, but losing Mum had started the rot, magnified by 2020 and the strain on the NHS. Angry and frustrated patients. The government blaming nurses. Pay that hardly covered weekly bills and food. Emily pulled the duvet over her face as tears flowed. They didn't count if the world couldn't see them. She missed Lewis curled up next to her, gently snoring, tickling her behind the neck when it was time to get up, threatening to kiss her with his morning breath. They'd had such happy years at work before everything fell apart, exchanging stories each evening, united in a particular interest of looking after social outcasts, the people no one else loved. Each understood the stress of the job and after her difficult teenage years, Lewis renewed her faith in her vocation to look after others – for a while, at least.

Four paws landed on the bed. Emily pulled down the duvet. A wet nose batted hers. Emily ran a hand down Smudge's back and the ensuing purring gave her a small, much-needed sense of achievement. Mouth dry from last night's glasses of wine, not the full bottle for a change, Emily sat up as she recalled agreeing yesterday to find Hugo Black, telling Smudge about it as she sat up in bed. Despite the pain that memories of those school days brought back, she could face tracking down that lowlife because nothing could be as bad as what her career had demanded in recent times, like ringing relatives to tell them their loved one was dying, but no, they couldn't visit, or holding doctors in her arms as, masked up and gloved, in protective clothing, they suffered from physical and mental exhaustion.

Emily shoved her phone into the pocket of her hooded blanket and padded into the kitchen. She filled the kettle, blocking out the prospect of her counselling session later. She pulled an iced bun wrapper off her bare foot and dropped it into an overflowing bin. A strong cup of tea accompanied her into the living room and she sat looking onto her back garden. A

flock of ducks passed overhead and took her back to the small park behind
her childhood home. One Saturday afternoon, she'd escaped to it. Dad had
got back from another trip and she badly needed a break from waiting on
Mum hand and foot. There was a pond and to her surprise, Hugo was
there, holding slices of bread, so unexpected. Young Emily had found it
sweet that he fed ducks and he'd offered her a slice – the start of his plan to
woo her. She visited again the following weekend, curious as to whether
he'd be there. Hugo had brought a small picnic. Their first kiss, under a
weeping willow where no one could see was gentle, chaste, Emily
panicking about where his hands might go, if she'd come across as stupid
and naïve, Hugo taking it slow, seeming to sense this. The softness of his
lips that had released unfriendly words over the years, words that became
cruel after he lost the football captaincy, took her breath away. Deep in her
pelvis, a tickling sensation grew that she'd never experienced before. She
didn't want it to stop. Emily blurted out that she loved him. Taken aback,
he'd held her tightly.

A blue tit flew over to Emily's feeder. She'd have to fill it up. Emily
pulled out her phone and tapped into the WhatsApp group. Her eyes
widened. As requested, Morgan had sent over a photo of Olly.

* * *

Holy shit. Olly really was the spit of Hugo. Tiff studied her phone screen,
sitting in the lounge with Mum and Dad, who were re-watching a TV series
where she'd played a minor part. As the screen flickered, so did memories
of her relationship with Hugo. The smiles he started to give her, leaving her
wary. The day he'd snapped his chocolate bar in half and offered her some.
She'd ignored him at first, waiting for the insult that didn't come. No boy
had ever paid her any attention before, what with her lack of fashionable
cheekbones or thigh gap, or at least that's what she put it down to, especially a boy with such charisma, and how she'd longed for that validation.
Finally, she had romance in her life with someone who bought her milk-
shakes without judging. She was sixteen, in love, and rapidly stopped
asking the hows and whys. Up until then, only in her dreams had a boy run

his hands over her curvy stomach and hips. The first time, she'd flinched, self-conscious, afraid, until he'd whispered in her ear that she felt sexy.

Shame had trickled over her during the years since, quashed by the fact her friends had behaved equally badly.

'Popcorn, love? It's low fat,' said her mum and shook the bowl in her direction.

Here Tiff was, years later, still worried about what she looked like. Being slim, being seen as stereotypically attractive, had helped her, in part, get the attention she'd always craved, from directors and fellow actors, from fans. However, it was never enough, as if she were a movie that sold out in the cinemas, but was still hated by critics.

'No thanks, Mum,' she said and got up. 'I'll have something slightly healthier,' she said, a little sarcastically, but her mother missed it. Healthy was not denying herself what she truly wanted. Tiff got up and fetched one of the chocolate bars Dad kept hidden at the back of the tinned food cupboard. She sat up at the kitchen table with a pen and paper, making a list of Hugo's friends, in case the visit to Miss Moo Moo came to nothing. She broke off a piece of the bar, put it in her mouth and closed her eyes for a second as the creaminess hit her pleasure points. Then she clicked into the Dailsworth High Facebook group. Of course, Jasmine White was listed. She'd been friends with Hugo, but Tiff was going to keep her out of it because of the information she had on Tiff that Morgan, Paige and Emily must never find out about.

12

MORGAN

Dailsworth library was at the far end of the high street, further on from Tesco, squashed between two bigger buildings as if it were an afterthought. By the time Tiff arrived, the other three were waiting, making pleasantries about the warmer weather, as Saturday shoppers passed. Paige wore a classic black trouser suit, with a camel coat and court shoes, exactly how teenage Morgan would have pictured her friend as an adult – although she thought she might have quit smoking by now. At high school, Paige used to insist it was just a passing phase and that she'd have more exciting things to spend her money on when she was an adult. Emily was in muddy trainers, threadbare jeans and an anorak that had seen better days, as if she'd spent so many years caring for others, she'd forgotten how to care for herself. In knee-high leather boots, tight leggings and a suede jacket cinched in with a belt, Tiff looked so different not in the baggy clothes she'd worn in the 2000s.

A group of people filed out of the library. Morgan led the others in. In the old days, Paige would have been up front but today, she hung back after stubbing out her cigarette. From the outside, the building looked nondescript, a concrete box, but the insides couldn't have provided a bigger contrast. Aside from the many shelves of books, colourful paintings by children decked the walls, as part of a book cover competition. Comfortably upholstered, red chairs were dotted around the large room and in the children's area. A large tree was painted on the wall. Instead of leaves, pens and pencils hung from its boughs. Morgan felt lightheaded. Was this really happening? The four of them together again?

The expression on Mlle Vachon's face replicated Morgan's feelings. She put down a book and clapped her hands as the women approached.

'*Mes pucettes!*'

Morgan never did understand why 'little flea' was a term of affection. 'You remember us?'

'Of course. I never forget favourite pupils, and, well...'

'The prom...' said Morgan.

Mlle Vachon nodded. 'I'm so glad you've made it up and are friends again.'

Emily pulled a face as if she'd just worked a twelve-hour shift without being able to pee.

'I've often thought about you over the years.' Mlle Vachon wrapped Morgan in her thin arms that were still so strong. She always had been petite. A Parisian woman without the designer outfits, Mlle Vachon preferred slacks and jumpers and that hadn't changed. The pixie cut was still dyed brown, the glasses still gold framed and on a chain.

Mlle Vachon hugged each of them in turn and then stood back. 'Morgan... Banks, Paige Forbes, that's it, Emily Jones and Tiff... Anderson.'

'Tiff Tudor, now,' said Tiff proudly. 'It's my stage name.'

Tudor? That's why Morgan had never been able to find her on social media.

'You achieved your dream? Well done! And you other girls?'

'Unemployed,' said Emily.

'Self-employed,' said Paige.

'Under-employed,' answered Morgan.

The four girls looked at each other and out of nowhere, started laughing. Morgan could have cried. God, she'd missed this. They all regularly used to fall apart over something only slightly funny. Like when they'd walk to school together, singing at the tops of their voices, and a man in a corner house would always shout, 'Shut up,' out of his bedroom window.

'I have a son,' said Morgan. 'He's called Olly.'

An affectionate look crossed Mlle Vachon's face. 'A son? What a good name. I used to be very much in love with an English film star called Oliver Reed, from a distance, of course.'

They talked about the French club and how Mlle Vachon was finding retirement: busy, by the sounds of it, with theatre club, reading circle and, sore hip permitting, walks in the Peak District.

'You never wanted to move back to Paris?' asked Paige.

'*Non*. I have many friends here. I am godmother to two children. My heart has grown fond of Manchester. It has a buzz of a vibrant, diverse city, yet doesn't expect you to dress up just to go shopping. England is my home, in my bones. Of course I still visit France. My brother is retired now too. Later this year, we are holidaying together in Spain. I always wanted a family,' she added quietly. 'But it wasn't to be, my career became my baby.'

'As it turned out, you had more children than was humanly possible,' said Emily in a soft tone. 'My best teacher, by far. Once, in class, I got period cramps so bad, I couldn't stand up. You twigged and told me to stay until the end. Said you'd be back in five minutes.'

'I brought you a cup of tea and my packet of chocolate digestives!' Her eyes shone. 'You haven't forgotten?'

'No. My mother was always too... wrapped up in her own life to do things like that.'

Mlle Vachon reached out and patted Emily's arm. 'But enough about me. What can I help you all with? Verb conjugation, adjective agreements, or something less interesting?' She gave them a beady stare.

Their French teacher always did used to be one of the brightest. She pointed to the chairs and Paige turned a couple around so that the five of them could sit in a circle. Mlle Vachon rubbed her hip and Emily pulled a chair nearer, standing by until Mlle Vachon was safely settled.

'My son. Olly. I need to find his dad,' said Morgan. 'Things were... complicated at the beginning. I had him the year after we left school.'

The pencilled eyebrows knotted together. '*Ma pucette*, that must have been so difficult. But you always were a determined girl. I've not had a pupil since who was so set on learning the gender of every new word.'

'He dad was... is.... Hugo Black.'

Mlle Vachon looked as if someone had told her France had banned eating cheese. 'Hugo?' she exclaimed and shook her head. 'But how? I mean, the prom...' She placed her hand on her chest.

Emily pulled a tube of mints out of her bag and Mlle Vachon took one gratefully.

Morgan sighed. 'Yes, you know what happened at the dance, but I was already pregnant by then, I just didn't know it. By the time I found out and was ready to look him up, his family home was empty and he'd disappeared without a trace. I couldn't face asking his friends at the time, I never wanted to see anyone from high school again. But lately... Olly... my son needs to know.'

'You were friends with his mum, right?' asked Paige.

Still that lack of enthusiasm, as if Paige were simply going through the motions, yet any contribution filled Morgan with gratitude.

Mlle Vachon leant back in her chair. 'Ah, *oui*, Sylvie, such a beautiful soul. I've been lucky to have her in my life. Sadly for me, during your Year Eleven, Sylvie made plans to move back to France. Yet I understood. She'd grown up in a town on the outskirts of Fréjus and never got used to English weather. She and Hugo's dad, Garth... well, it's not my place to explain all the details, Sylvie was a very private person... In fact, perhaps I shouldn't say any more.'

'If I was her, I'd be so excited to meet my grandchild,' said Tiff, encouragingly.

'Oh yes, she would have been.'

'*Would* have?' asked Morgan.

Emily gestured for Mlle Vachon to take another mint.

'She and Hugo... left together. The marriage was broken.'

'Hugo moved to the south of France?' asked Tiff.

'*Oui*. They had happy times. Sylvie and I would call each other often. He became close to his grandparents.'

Hugo didn't live in England any more? Morgan didn't blink for a few seconds.

'But my darling Sylvie passed.' Her voice broke. 'Hugo was only twenty-five. A road traffic accident. A drunk tourist on a motorbike hit her. She never stood a chance.'

Oh. How sad. No one, not even Hugo, deserved that trauma. Poor Olly would never get to meet that gran. Poor Sylvie, a life cut short.

'Hugo wrote me a brief letter explaining,' continued Mlle Vachon. 'I sent back a sympathy card asking him to tell me when the funeral was, but I never heard back. I wrote several more times, rang as well, but he never picked up.' She turned her loose, gold watch around and around. 'It's hard, never having had the chance to say goodbye – especially as we hadn't spoken for a while. Sylvie's dad died and she was getting over that, trying to be there for her mum and Hugo as well. Everything went quiet. I didn't like to keep bothering her. Grief can take its time in loosening its hold.' She looked up. 'Apologies that I can't tell you more.'

'No, that's really useful,' said Morgan. 'I'm very sorry about Sylvie's accident.'

'I can text you the address they moved to if you want. Not sure what help that will be, though, a decade later. He might not still be there.' She took out her phone. 'If you give me your number, Morgan, I'll message you when I get home.'

'You won't confiscate her mobile, will you?' asked Emily.

'Enough of your cheek, Jones,' Mlle Vachon replied, looking more relaxed.

The conversation moved to lighter subjects once again, like Mlle Vachon's boyfriend, a retired travel agent. She asked about Paige's business, promised to look out for Tiff's Netflix series, and like in the old days, dug out anything pupils were holding back, prodding Emily to reveal she'd been a nurse until recently.

'Us staff used to sing your praises in private, Emily,' she said, with the familiar French lilt. 'Your grades only slipped a little, despite the care you were giving your mother. I was so sorry when she passed.'

The funeral had taken place two weeks before the prom. Morgan, Paige and Tiff told Emily they'd skip the dance and stay in with her, if she wasn't up to it. To their surprise, she wanted to attend the end of year celebration. The funeral had come out of nowhere. The girls hadn't seen much of each other for a few weeks, only going into school for exams, when Emily announced her mum had died. Her family had wanted the funeral to be a quiet, private affair. Morgan didn't even know where it took place. The next day, the girls took Emily to their favourite café but she didn't stay long, hardly spoke, made it clear she never wanted to discuss her mum's death or the burial. Morgan and the other two had found it odd, but then none of them had ever suffered such a loss, so who were they to judge.

'What about you, Morgan? Under-employed? Not a maths teacher, then?'

'I'm a cashier. Priorities changed when I had Olly.'

'As they should do. But he's eighteen now, isn't he, an adult? I didn't train to be a teacher until my thirties, you know.'

Mlle Vachon talked about how she'd worked for the family business for years, a restaurant in a suburb outside of Paris. Her parents had always expected her and her brother to take over. But a cousin died unexpectedly and it sharpened her sense that life shouldn't be wasted following the wishes of others. Morgan took in every word.

'It caused a ruckus. My parents didn't speak to me for a year, said it was too much for my brother alone. But then he started dating a chef and the two of them were keen to run the place when my mother and father retired. That's the thing with life, it has a way of working itself out. It's never too late, Morgan. Don't give up on yourself.'

Was that what she'd done?

All of them got to their feet, Emily helping Mlle Vachon.

'Girls, it has been wonderful to see you again,' she said as they walked towards the door. 'I hope I've been of some help. If I have, I'd appreciate a favour in return.' She beamed. 'It is my birthday on Easter Monday, 10 April. I am holding a little get-together at my house, 45 Greenacre Lane. It would be so lovely if you could pop in for cake. It's an informal affair. No need to answer now, you can just turn up. Or text me nearer the time. Morgan will have my number.'

Mlle Vachon had always been a guiding force, helping the girls navigate through fallouts. Like that Halloween in Year Seven when Morgan and Paige pretended they'd caught spiders and threw them at Emily and Tiff. The plastic toys looked so realistic. Mlle Vachon explained that one person's idea of funny can be scary for another.

'I'm so glad none of you forgot your Miss Moo Moo,' she said, and shot them a mischievous smile as they stepped onto the street.

Four faces flushed with the realisation that Mlle Vachon was still sharper than the lot of them.

13

MORGAN

Emily's smirk grew wider as Tiff took furtive glances around the room, clearly not keen to be recognised in a burger joint. Morgan's phone buzzed loudly, above the background music and chat of other customers.

'Mlle Vachon is efficient as ever.' Morgan shook her head, smiling. 'It's what... barely an hour since we saw her and she's sent over Hugo and Sylvie's address, as well as details about her birthday party. Midday onwards. No presents.' Morgan showed the others the address and message. 'She's signed off with a cow emoji.'

'Right. The Riviera it is,' said Tiff and she sipped her sparkling water. 'Presumably we'll fly out there the beginning of the week we agreed to really focus, so two weeks today, 1 April?'

'*Travel to France?*' said Morgan. Tiff couldn't be serious. The women looked at each other. 'I'd planned to simply write to this address. See if Hugo – or anyone else replied.'

'No point. He clearly didn't want to keep in contact with anyone here, and we don't have long to move this case forwards, international post isn't the fastest.' Tiff lowered her voice. 'Maybe he had something to hide. Maybe he had something to do with his mother's death and did a runner.'

'For Christ's sake, Tiff,' said Paige, cheeks colouring up. 'Hugo may have been a bully but he was never a murderer. If we stand any chance of helping Morgan, we need to act like grown-ups, not school kids. We aren't starring in one of your whodunit series.'

'Calm down, I was only joking.'

'Yeah, let's head to France,' said Emily. 'Why don't we go first class or even better, hire a private jet? It's not as any of us are jobless, facing divorce and looking to save every penny.' She sunk her teeth into her Big Mac with all the trimmings.

'I appreciate that you're willing, Tiff, but Emily's right. I for one can't justify money on an airfare or hotel when I'm saving as hard as I can to help Olly out at uni.' Morgan winced and rubbed her back.

'You okay?' asked Paige quickly.

'Just a twinge. Sitting in a cashier's chair dawn till dusk does it no good.' She put on a bright smile. 'I'll write to this address. You never know... and I'm also going to pluck up the courage to act on the leads we've found between us already about Hugo's friends.' She grimaced. 'Hopefully, they won't still call me Morgan Wanks.'

Paige hesitated, then went to talk, but changed her mind. Finally she spoke. 'Look... Felix and I have loads of air miles – they keep accumulating. He travels far and wide for work, and we go on holiday. I'm sure we've built up enough for four economy return tickets.' Briefly, she explained about his global job with Prestige Fitness.

Tiff went into Google on her phone, tapped away and nodded to herself. She looked up at the others. 'I have a French actor friend, Belle. We worked together on a project for Apple TV and she was the lead. Belle has a small villa on the outskirts of Fréjus, near her parents. It's slightly cheaper there than living in Cannes, which is where her mother used to work. Belle would volunteer at the film festival, every year, before her acting career took off. She's offered it to me free more than once, doesn't like it standing empty during the less popular months. I was just checking – it's not far from this address Mlle Vachon has given us. I'll ring her now, see if it's available.' Without waiting for them to talk it through, Tiff got up and went outside.

'Sorry. Nothing to contribute,' said Emily, in a flat tone. 'Perhaps I should stay in England. Money's the answer to most things.'

'That's where you are wrong,' said Morgan. 'You can't fight your own nature, Emily. Your kindness, it's still in there, however much you deny it, and—'

'Please stop,' said Emily, red in the face. 'You don't know me, not now.'

'But you're still so... so unaware. That's why you were cracking at helping the society solve cases. People never guessed you were pulling information out of them because you often didn't realise that's what you were doing.'

'What are you talking about?' she muttered.

'You softened Mlle Vachon today, made her happier to help us, what with those kind comments about her being your best teacher and in some ways being a mother to more children than anyone. How you fussed over her when she sat down, with the chair and tube of mints... It helped tease out the more personal details she wasn't sure about giving in the first instance.'

'Morgan is right,' said Paige. 'You gave a perfect lesson in how to put someone at their ease.'

Emily blushed and sat up straighter.

Tiff returned. 'The villa's available. It's got a view of the sea. Only two bedrooms but we can share, right? I've gone ahead and told her we'll take it.'

'I'm guessing you and Paige have up-to-date passports?' asked Morgan. 'I got one last year. Took Olly on a trip to northern France.' She was determined 2022 would be the year he got to fly on a plane, the year that he, for once, could go back to school talking about a trip *he'd* had abroad. They flew from Manchester to Brittany, stayed in a mobile home for four nights. Every morning, Olly got up early to go to the on-site shop and fetch a fresh baguette and croissants. Their budget allowed for eating out once and they found a cheap restaurant in the local town. Olly loved a bean stew called a cassoulet. He took photo after photo and couldn't wait to show his friends. He also made an album for Morgan when they got back. The French break made up for his disappointment over the school physics field trip to CERN, the largest particle physics lab in the world. Olly couldn't have been more excited to be going to Geneva. It was heavily subsidised but Morgan had fitted in extra hours to pay their contribution, a few here, a few there, so that Olly wouldn't notice and worry. However, the trip had to be cancelled at the last minute – the plane suffered engine trouble. So he and Morgan went to France instead, and, as it turned out, this year, Year Thirteen pupils who still wanted to go to CERN – like Olly – were being allowed to tag along with Year Twelve, as long as it didn't affect their studies. 'What about you, Emily?'

'Lewis and I were due to celebrate our ten-year anniversary this year with a couple of nights in Amsterdam. Both of us had always fancied going there with the canals and tulips, the pancakes. Looking back, we already knew we were dreaming when we applied for our passports. Both of ours had gone out of date the last year. We could hardly afford them, let alone the trip.' She studied the other three. 'But us four going away together... really?'

'I'll book open-ended tickets,' interrupted Paige. 'We might come straight back if we find nothing there.'

Emily threw down her burger. 'You're all totally mad. We're practically strangers. We can't willy nilly jet off abroad for a few days, to live together.'

'Willy nilly? Your mum used to say that,' said Paige. 'She was always up for a laugh, even when she was ill.'

'She was very young at heart too, wasn't she?' said Tiff. 'She'd joke about sex and drink in a way my mother never did, even during those last months. I've never forgotten in Year Seven how she explained to us what French kissing was.'

Morgan smiled. 'She was always so full of life.'

'Sure was,' said Emily, in an emotionless voice. 'Right to the very end.'

'You were so young, Emily,' said Paige. 'I can't imagine life without my mother, even now.'

Emily broke eye contact and stared out of the window. 'Oddly, it was a massive relief when she went.'

Morgan forced herself not to react, not to look at Paige and Tiff. She could understand such sentiment in terms of the hours of care Emily had put in, but it was the sincerity that caught her attention, almost as if Emily's mum's death hadn't bothered her on any level.

'You were an angel,' said Tiff, 'you sacrificed so much, gave her baths, shaved her legs, made sure your brother didn't tire her out. See, we know stuff about each other, intimate stuff... We aren't strangers at all.' Tiff waved her hand in the air. 'What have you got to lose apart from one week in dreary old Blighty?'

'My sanity?' Emily's eyes crinkled at the corners. She met the gaze of the others again. Their eyebrows raised as 'Hey Ya!' by OutKast came on.

'The one song that actually all of us liked,' said Paige.

'Because despite its cheerful beat, the lyrics are actually sad and about how couples sometimes stay together even though they are unhappy,' said Morgan. 'I think we connected that to the idea of how appearances can be deceptive and people shouldn't be judged by how they look.'

'I just remember the lyrics being kind of fun,' said Tiff and they listened. She shook her bottom, in her seat, when the words about shaking it came on, like they always used to. Smiles appearing, the others followed suit.

Paige cleared her throat and consulted her watch. 'Right. I've got to get going. I'll message you for details I need to book the tickets. Departure two weeks today, yes? We're... we're sure we want to do this? Morgan? It's your decision.' Paige bit her thumbnail. 'I'll go with whatever is best for you.'

Excitement hadn't infused Morgan like this since last year's trip with Olly. But it had nothing to do with going away to pastures new, and more to do with treading old ones that used to feel like home. 'Yes. Let's go shake it in France.'

14

PAIGE, EMILY, TIFF

Paige wrote a short, last-minute email to the others, confirming they should meet her inside Terminal 1, tomorrow, at midday. Their flight would leave at two thirty. They were flying directly to Nice and would then get a train from there to Fréjus. She pressed send and put down her phone. Felix sat opposite at their dining room table, by the window. He hadn't even been aware of her typing. The distant lights of a helicopter flew past. He followed them with his eyes, the plate of beef goulash in front of him no longer steaming. It had been like this, the last year, before each trip. Paige had urged him to look for another job but his was more like a vocation when it came to helping disadvantaged youngsters. His flight left at 7 a.m.

'How was tonight?' she asked. Felix had never looked more handsome, post-shower skin glowing. He brought the best out in her; she now offered free advice to struggling businesses. Paige had set up a page on her website where small enterprises could apply for her to visit and speak to the staff, to assess how they could improve their image and communication with clients.

'Jamal was on fine form. He's just turned sixteen. I've mentioned him before...'

Paige nodded.

'The lad's getting way too cocky for his own good and I told him as much.' A flicker of a smile. 'He can do fifty push-ups now, faster than me.' Felix tore off a chunk of bread roll. 'When he first turned up, a year ago, Jamal hardly spoke, wouldn't look anyone in the eye, had no direction. It took a while, but he's made good mates and when he leaves school next year, he wants to become a personal trainer.'

'That's brilliant, Felix. Has he got it in him?'

'Jamal's a bright lad. The other day, he said it made a big difference having someone believe in him.'

'You,' she said.

'His parents both have... issues. He doesn't blame either of them, both come from a difficult background, but coming to the hub is the first time he's ever felt that someone saw his potential. It sounds like his teachers wrote him off as lazy or stupid but I think he's just never had the support at home. A large part of his school's catchment is from a much wealthier area. When he started there in Year Seven, he says it was hard for him to even explain that he had no internet, no real work space, he slept on the sofa...' Felix ate the bread. 'Jamal slipped big news to me tonight. He's built up the courage to ask out a girl he's fancied for ages.' Felix explained how the lad had asked his advice about where to take her for a first date. Felix stopped talking for a moment. The Gorton hub where he'd been tonight was going to be the first one to close if Dubai didn't come off, then the one in East London, after that Sunderland. He sighed and put down his bread. 'Sorry, wrapped up in myself. What are your plans for this week without your husband around to blather on about his job?'

Carefully, she wiped her mouth with the linen napkin. Paige would tell him everything as soon as he got back from Dubai, but that didn't lessen her guilt.

'I'm actually spending time with M...' *Morgan.* She so wanted to tell him the truth. 'With... *myself,* on trips to the shops where I'll enjoy leisurely coffees, reading, when I'm not working – and imagine, the duvet, just for me. Bliss.'

Felix reached for her hand, brought it to his lips and kissed the palm. 'Everything's all right, isn't it?'

Paige mentally checked her body language. Shit. She was actually rubbing her nose, a sure giveaway of a liar. Her shoulders were hunched, she'd dropped her gaze, and her voice had become breathless...

She lay both her hands flat on the table. 'Never better,' she said in a steady tone and, with full eye contact, gave him a big smile.

Felix cocked his head and scanned her face before picking up his fork to eat the now-cold goulash.

* * *

France. With Morgan, Paige and Tiff. How was this happening? Emily pulled down an old suitcase from the loft and dragged it into the bedroom. Her chest twinged but not from the exertion. There was something from their schooldays that Emily had hidden from the others, not to do with Hugo. Something so big, it had overwhelmed her in 2004. She should have told them then, but it had been too hard and the prospect of telling them the truth felt no easier nineteen years later.

The doorbell rang, shaking her out of the past.

'Who the hell's calling by at this time on a Friday night?' she said to Smudge, who was asleep on a pillow. Ten o'clock. Normally, she'd be asleep on the sofa by now but she'd not needed wine to escape her life this evening. Tomorrow, she'd be escaping for real.

She sloped downstairs, opened the front door.

'Lewis?'

'I was passing, after my shift.'

'Just happened to be in the area, right?' she said and folded her arms. She wouldn't let herself be moved by the shadows under his eyes, deeper than ever, the raggedy nails he never used to bite; wouldn't let herself invite him in, put her arms around his. Caring got you hurt, her mother had taught her that. 'What do you want?'

He edged forwards.

She sighed. 'You can't stay long. I'm busy. Off to France tomorrow.'

'Yeah, right, and I'm having afternoon tea at Buckingham Palace,' he replied as he followed her into the kitchen and slumped at the breakfast bar.

Emily held the kettle mid-air. 'Do you want a coffee or not?'

He threw his keys down, next to her passport. Lewis raised his eyebrows. 'You're not joking about this trip? But why? How?'

'I'm fine thanks, Lewis, nice of you to ask.'

Lewis took off his hi-vis jacket. The bottle-green paramedic's uniform always had suited him. He leant his elbows on the bar.

'I can see how you're doing,' he said and he looked around the lounge, with the takeout boxes on the floor and days' worth of newspapers scattered across the furniture, next to empty mugs and plates. 'How's the counselling going?'

She sat down next to him and slid over a coffee. 'How's work?'

'Tonight, I got called a black bastard by a man who objected to my siren, even if it had meant getting his neighbour's heart beating again. Elsewhere, a patient blamed me for her husband's death a few months back, because he had a stroke on one of the strike days.'

'This is why you should jack it in. I've never been happier since leaving nursing.'

'Looks like it,' he said and waved his arm around. 'So, France... a new man?'

Emily looked shocked and then started to laugh, tears running down her cheeks. 'Oh Lewis, I did need that.' She wiped her nose. 'But no, I don't want to be with anyone at the moment. Just as well. With no job or prospects, I'm hardly dating material.'

Lewis sipped his drink.

'If you must know, I'm going with my old school friends, Morgan, Paige and Tiff. Morgan got in touch. She had a son shortly after we fell out and, well... her son's father is that Hugo Black I've told you about, last seen at the prom, ruining my life.'

He sat upright. 'Bloody hell, Ems. So you might come face to face with him again?'

'Yup. Let's hope he's aged as well as me.' She gave a wry smile. It was good to chat to someone familiar with the story. Emily had spoken to Lewis, over the years, about the best friends she'd ever had, and how Hugo had duped her and them.

'I'm glad the four of you have found each other again. This could be just what you need.'

'Oh, I won't stay in touch, not after this week. I'm happy to help this Olly lad, he's an innocent party in this, but those women let me down when I needed them most... I'm keeping it real.'

'Don't forget, those women were just girls when your friendship broke up. The teenage years... they're damn tough. You never know, things might be different now.'

Emily shook her head. Although Lewis was right. Like all teenagers, they had been young and foolish back then. Not that that was an excuse for the way they'd deceived each other over Hugo... nor an excuse for the big thing Emily had kept from them. She felt guilty about it, even now.

Smudge strutted into the kitchen. He meowed at Lewis, who got off the stool and picked him up, stroking his silky ears.

'Do you need me to feed Smudge whilst you're away?'

'Sheila next door is dropping by. You know how her grandkids love playing with him.'

Lewis put Smudge down, straightened up, rubbed the back of his head. 'You could have great friends back in your life, Ems. You could stay with a career that's been your calling. Everything is there for the taking.'

'Not this again. For God's sake, Lewis, leave it.'

He pushed his stool under the breakfast bar and went to the front door, dragging his feet as if he'd tried to resuscitate someone but failed.

Emily followed Lewis into the hallway as he put his jacket back on, a voice in her head imploring with him: *Don't leave yet. Have another drink. I miss the way you hum when you clean your teeth, never worked out how you managed it. And the way you whistle, out of tune, in the shower. I even miss picking up your wet towel.*

'It kills me to see you throwing away a life you were born for.'

And just like that, the voice stopped. She pursed her lips. 'It's different for you, Lewis. Your brother is a physio, your mum's a nurse too, your dad a porter, your granddad used to be a doctor and his father was a surgeon during the war. Medicine, the NHS, caring for others, it's ingrained in your DNA. It's different for me. My mother cared more about her appearance than any other human being, buying expensive pills to make her skin tighter, her hair thicker. She never even bought me and my brother cheap multi-vitamins and... and now, during these last difficult years...' Her breath hitched.

'Go on,' he said and nodded encouragingly, 'I want to understand.'

She folded her arms.

A hard look came over his face. 'There's another reason you want to leave your job, but you've dug your heels in this last year, Ems, refusing to open up even though we're married. Recently, I've sensed there's something in the background and hoped, one day, you'd let me in so that we could talk it over...' He shook his head. 'Honesty – if we haven't got that, we haven't got anything.' His voice wavered. 'I can't carry on like this.' He took out his car keys. 'The reason I've come by...' He took a deep breath and his face crumpled, blink and you'd miss it. 'I've contacted a solicitor.'

Emily leant one hand against the wall. He'd got *legal advice*? A hundred bottles of wine couldn't ease how deeply that cut. She'd tried to talk to him about how leaving her job was to do with her mum but couldn't bring herself to, the hurt went right into her core.

'I'm initiating divorce proceedings. We can put the house up for sale. Both make a fresh start. I can't live in that crappy little flat any longer, clinging to the possibility of you confiding in me. If you really want to find a different job, I'd support you, even though I think it's a huge mistake, but I need to know why you resent me so much, for simply wanting you to fly in a career you're brilliant at. I don't understand why that's wrong. I'm worried these jaded feelings of yours are just a temporary blip and that you're giving up everything you've worked so hard for and might regret it. Tell me, Emily. You can trust me. Whatever it is.'

Emily wrung her hands. She wanted to. She couldn't.

Lewis sighed and opened the front door. 'If you can hold a grudge against your very best friends for nearly twenty years, then what chance do I stand?'

* * *

As Marlon rolled off, Tiff faced the spotless bedside cabinet. She'd checked into the airport hotel late afternoon yesterday, having told her parents it was a really early flight the next morning. A hand squeezed her shoulder.

She turned around and admired the tanned skin, the pecs, those long legs. Marlon yawned, flashing his super white teeth.

'Hello gorgeous. How's Tiffany this morning?'

'Ready for breakfast,' she said and smiled.

'Wish I could stay but the gym's calling.' He got up and walked butt naked to the bathroom and left the door open. Marlon ran a cup of water and drank it back.

If they could see her now, the school bullies would choke on their nasty words about Tiff and the others being losers. A magazine on top of her suitcase caught her attention; it had an interview with her in it. This should be enough, incoming fame, men lusting after her. So why did Tiff still feel she had something to prove? What would stop the goal posts moving? She'd told Mum and Dad the trip to France was to see a friend, the villa's owner. Tiff couldn't have coped with the questions, the expectations, if she'd told the truth. Mum still talked about the four friends as if they were teenagers and might have invited them over for tea and a game of Twister. Her stomach clenched at the prospect of the week ahead, as if she were about to go on stage but didn't have any lines. Paige had always been the sophisticated one, grown up, in charge. Morgan talked sense, keeping them on track. Emily was soft-hearted, a calming presence, whereas Tiff was just seen as a joke, dramatic and impulsive. Well, things had changed and the others had better get used to it, otherwise she'd jump on an early plane back to England and cut all contact.

'Fancy accompanying me to dinner next Saturday, Marlon? I'll be back by then.' she called.

'Sorry, Tiffany. No can do. I'm meeting someone else.'

'No problem,' she replied in a carefree tone.

If they could see her now, they would, those school bullies *would* choke. Tiff wasn't a loser at all.

15

MORGAN

'Pyjamas?' asked Morgan. They sat on the sofa in the small lounge. She'd just switched off a Friday night chat show. They'd had takeout pizza as a treat.

Olly gave her a thumbs up. It was almost midnight. Vikram's dad was picking him up at ten o'clock the next morning to take the two pupils to the airport for their flight to Geneva. Morgan would get the train there, for midday. She'd not told Olly about her trip. The truth would get his hopes up – and lies about some fictional holiday would be even more dishonest. Morgan told herself there was no way they'd bump into each other at Terminal 1, even if they were both flying with BA.

Morgan hadn't foreseen life becoming so complicated as Olly got older. She'd kidded herself a childhood without his father would lead to acceptance. Her parents always said it was a mistake not telling him, that the truth would eventually come out, but they'd respected her decision. Yet all these years, Morgan hadn't respected Olly's needs, she could see that now.

'Wallet, charger and phone?'

Olly rolled his eyes.

'Deodorant?'

'Mum. That's enough. I'm eighteen and perfectly able to pack.' He drained his mug of hot chocolate.

'Then you'll have packed yourself a little first aid box too? Plasters, Paracetamol, that anti-itch cream in case you get bitten?'

'I guess it wouldn't harm to take painkillers in case I have a hangover.'

'There's a packet in my toiletry cupboard,' she said, not taking the bait. 'Get them tonight then you're all set for tomorrow morning.'

Olly sighed and went upstairs. Morgan smiled, imagining him sliding down the banisters on the way back, like he used to whenever he was younger and excited, when they enjoyed a far simpler life, happier times.

She took the pizza boxes into the kitchen, switched on the fluorescent light and went to dry crockery on the draining board, leaving herself as little to do as possible in the morning.

Crap. Olly was in her bedroom.

She dropped the tea towel and ran to the bottom of the stairs. 'Wait a minute, love, I'll—'

He appeared at the top of the stairs. She squinted through the dark hallway, lit only by the moon coming through a window behind Olly. Next to him was a pull case.

'What's going on? I found this behind your door.'

'Nothing,' she said brightly, 'I'm visiting... Blackpool for a couple of days. To get some sea air.'

Slowly he walked down the stairs. 'On your own? Why haven't you mentioned this before? You hate Blackpool. Too run down. Too many arcades.' He followed her into the kitchen.

She picked up the tea towel, went to the sink and turned her back as she ran the taps. 'I'm not completely over the hill. I'm allowed to be spontaneous now and again, aren't I, and change my mind?'

Morgan spun around at a smacking noise. He'd thrown her passport onto the kitchen table. 'This was on top of it. Why are you lying? But then you're the expert at keeping things from me, aren't you? Even though I'm now eighteen?'

'Love...' She moved towards him but Olly backed off.

'What else haven't you told me? Have you got a guy on the go? I wouldn't care, I'm not a child.'

'It's nothing like that...'

'What is it then?' His voice cracked and he slumped at the table. 'Is it me? Are you going away for a while?' He lifted up his head, looking at her through his fringe. 'Is it my fault?'

Morgan crouched by his side. 'Now you listen. You listen good. There is *nothing* you could ever do that would ever make me leave. I love you more than anything else in this world. What's more, I've never lied to you before. Wouldn't want to. Never could.'

A sob came from his chest and he covered his eyes, tears streaming down his face. His shoulders shook. Olly crying? In front of her? In the last year or two, he'd come down in the morning with red eyes, now and then. She'd ask if everything was all right, he'd insist he was fine. Then he came out, and she assumed that's what the upset had been about. He'd not cried in front of her since he twisted his ankle when he was fifteen. Her heart felt as if it were tearing apart, not in half but into a thousand pieces that only her son's happiness could put back together.

'It's all shit,' he said. 'Coming to terms with who I am, exam stress, not knowing my dad, and getting ready to go to university. Maybe he went and he could tell me what it's like, give me tips on how to cope, reassure me I'll be able to do the work, that I'll make friends?'

Morgan felt as if she'd been working methodically through a page of long division and the answer was wholly unexpected. Olly anxious about going to college? This time last year, he'd spoken about it with such enthusiasm. She'd opened a separate account and moved a little money in once a month to set him up with kitchen equipment and books, and cover other living costs when the time came, that wouldn't be covered by the student loan or grant. She slipped an arm around his shoulders and leant in, eyes wet. For once, he didn't pull away, his fight gone. When the tension in his body eased, she fetched them each a glass of water.

'Okay. The truth. I know I've told you about The Secret Gift Society in the past...'

Olly wiped his eyes with the back of his hand and sat up. 'That club you and three friends at high school formed? Remember how you made up stories about it when I was little, solving mysteries like the four of you used to? I used to think how cool it sounded.'

A nostalgic feeling ran through her. 'Yes. I remember. So... I put a coded message in the last Dailsworth High alumni newsletter, and reached out to the girls – well, women now. We've been in touch and the four of us are going to France.'

Olly's jaw dropped and he uttered an expletive. 'But didn't things end, like, *really* badly? Why would you bother now?'

'We're re-forming the society for one last case.' Her throat felt dry. 'They're going to help me look for your dad. We knew him at school.' Morgan took a deep breath. 'He's called Hugo. Hugo Black.'

Olly put down his glass. Didn't speak for a moment. 'Hugo. Hugo,' he said, as if trying the word out to see if it was a good fit. 'You're really looking for him?'

She nodded.

'I... I can't believe it. But that club was a kids' thing, right? It's not like you're actual detectives.'

Morgan told him about their visit to Mlle Vachon.

'My dad's half French?' He shook his head and repeated the name Hugo several more times, as if learning a multiplication table, as if scared he'd forget it, as if worried Morgan would somehow take it back if it wasn't engraved in his head.

'Your grandparents split up, but I've no idea why. It seems that Sylvie, your grandmother, took Hugo to the south of France, where she grew up, not long after the prom, and they lived close to her parents. But I'm so sorry to tell you, love, that... she passed away when your dad... when *your dad* was twenty-five. She apparently got hit by a motorbike. I've not learnt anything about your granddad, Garth, yet though. Sylvie's dad died shortly before she did, I don't know anything about her mum, Hugo's grandmother.'

Olly got up and paced the kitchen. 'Hugo. Sylvie. Garth. I can't take it in. Have you got a photo?'

Morgan went upstairs, pulled down the loft ladder and climbed up. The storage boxes were labelled alphabetically. Morgan had kept her old school exercise books, she wasn't quite sure why. She tore the masking tape off one of the boxes and rummaged towards the bottom, carefully sliding out a long, rectangular photo: the yearly snapshot of all the pupils. With her arm, she wiped off the dust before climbing back down. She placed it on the kitchen table. It was the last one ever taken, in Year Eleven. Sitting together, she and Olly scoured the rows. He pointed her out, hair short and spiky. Her eyes narrowed. Three rows up, the air of arrogance jumped off the print. She pointed to Hugo.

Olly got up. Took the photo into the hallway and stood in front of the mirror, by the front door. He looked in it. Studied the photo again. Olly came back, and sat down.

'I've got his nose, the same shaped ears. It's... weird seeing someone else who looks like me.'

'Weird in a good way?'

'It's like... I'm part of something bigger. How long did you and him...?'

'It's hard to explain.'

Olly pushed away the photo. 'I'm listening.'

Morgan studied his face, the shadow forming where he'd need to shave tomorrow morning, the hickey on his neck. He was older now than she'd been when she slept with Hugo, older than her three friends when they'd also been duped by him.

She pressed her palms against each other. 'Your father was a good-looking lad. Very charismatic, popular with pupils and teachers, he was good at sport, but you should know, love... he wasn't perfect and there's a reason I didn't want to tell you about him. You see, The Secret Gift Society revealed he was cheating on the head's daughter and...'

Olly's expression didn't change as she explained how he lost the football captaincy, and then how he got his revenge and fooled the four girls, how they'd betrayed each other. When she'd finished, Morgan downed her glass of water. Olly got up and sat in the chair next to her. A single tear ran down his cheek.

'Sorry,' she whispered. 'It must be hard to find out all that about your dad.'

'That's not it. This is the first time you've treated me like an adult. Finally trusted me to cope. Let me in.'

She covered his hand with hers. 'I'm sorry I didn't do it earlier. I do trust you, love. I'm so proud of the young man you've become but... it's always been the two of us. Protecting you has always been at the forefront of my mind, even when you didn't need it so much any more. It's been hard to let go, and I'm wary of introducing you to a man who hurt me... hurt my friends. Of course, we don't know what your dad's like now. We were all silly kids back then...'

'What are the other girls' names?'

'Paige, she's a body language consultant now. Emily, she... used to be a nurse, and Tiff is an actor, she's actually changed her name to Tiff Tudor. I still can't get used to that, but—'

'Holy fuck!'

'Olly!'

'Sorry, Mum.' His face flushed. 'It's just half the guys in my year fancy her. She was in a huge Netflix series last year... So do the four of you get on?'

'This isn't going to be some big, lasting reunion, the others have made that clear. But I'm grateful for their help. They've volunteered one week of their time.' She told him about the free flights and villa. 'If, by the end of that, we still haven't found Hugo...' She looked Olly straight in the eyes. 'We'll carry on. You and me. Track your father down together. Right?'

Olly gave her the kind of smile he used to when he was a little boy, full of respect, full of belief, full of... love.

He ran a hand through his floppy, chestnut fringe, like his dad used to. 'Did you ever... I mean you could have chosen not to...' He exhaled. 'You were brave to have me, Mum. What made you go ahead with the pregnancy?'

'I only considered other options for a matter of seconds. A knee-jerk reaction when that test turned out positive.'

'What changed your mind?'

'It was like... someone giving you an equation to work out, say... what is pi squared? If I didn't find the answer, it would always niggle me. As soon as I found out you were in my tummy, I wanted to know what you'd look like, would we be friends, would you be interested in the arts, or science, would you like Marmite... but more than that, I already felt attached, felt protective.'

'It's 9.86, by the way,' he mumbled.

Morgan sat more upright, as if the dark cloud pressing down on her had been blown away, by being transparent, by speaking with Olly as... an equal. Her son was about to make his own way in the world. Protecting a child was a natural, necessary instinct, but not a young adult, not if they were to become strong and independent.

'Thanks Mum. For looking for my dad.' His voice became clipped. 'I can't say I'm not still angry about how long it's taken, though. You might have found him years ago if you'd contacted your friends sooner. And now...' He threw his arms in the air. 'It's crap that I'll never meet my French grandmother.'

'I... I know.'

Olly drank his water, and put down the glass. It landed on the table a little too loudly. 'Everything you've told me has filled a gap, but opened up another one as well.' He ran his sleeve across his mouth. Took a moment. 'At least, now, things are more out in the open.'

'Yes, and in the spirit of that, there's one other thing I want to tell you. It's another reason I wanted to get back in touch with my friends. I haven't told it to them yet.' Her throat closed up as if she were about to gag, but Olly deserved to be the first to find out. She should have told him weeks ago.

Olly sat and took in every word. His eyes glistened. When she finished, he wrapped both his arms around Morgan tightly and she allowed herself to lean into him.

'Thanks for telling me,' he said later, as they climbed the stairs, after an hour of talking. They faced each other on the landing.

'I love you, son.'

'Love you too, Mum.'

16

MORGAN

Standing by the end of the queue for the BA desk, Morgan looked at her phone. Midday. Paige appeared in the distance, with an understated, black pull-case. Morgan's was white, an impractical colour that showed scratches, but it had been half-price in the January sales before her trip to Brittany with Olly.

'Paige.'

'Morgan.'

Paige gave her a cursory hug. Morgan wouldn't have been more surprised if the customer from yesterday who'd sworn at her for being slow on the till had taken her in his arms. She went to reciprocate but Paige stood back. They waited in silence, so unlike the old days. Eventually, small talk broke through: yes, the airport was busy, no, neither of them had been to Fréjus before.

Tiff appeared with a Louis Vuitton case and sunglasses pushed up into her hair, high heels, tight jeans: the worst outfit for relaxing on an aeroplane, in Morgan's opinion. She'd gone for flats, leggings, and a sports bra underneath a baggy sweatshirt. Paige wore wide-leg, soft trousers, with trainers and a blazer, different to the Burberry check one she'd worn when they met on the school grounds.

'This is really happening, us travelling together as if it's almost twenty years ago and we're going on a school trip,' said Tiff. 'It isn't an April Fool's joke.'

Paige gave a polite smile. Morgan's was warmer.

'I've checked with Belle and the keys are with a neighbour. She's had cleaning staff in and the fridge will be stocked with essentials. Did your air miles really cover the cost of flights, Paige?'

'More than.'

'Where is this villa, exactly?' asked Morgan.

'On the outskirts of Fréjus. It's a port town, in the south east. It's got Roman ruins, a Gothic cathedral, and beautiful sandy beaches. I actually went on holiday near there once, with Mum and Dad, when my first ever decent pay cheque came in. I treated them.'

Someone walking unsteadily in their direction caught their attention and the three women went over. Emily wore a winter coat, far too warm for France in April. Her small pull case had a broken wheel, and she looked as if she'd worked a week of night shifts. A slight smell of alcohol floated into the air.

'Let's get rid of our bags and go get a drink,' said Emily.

The queue moved quickly and once checked in, they headed over to a restaurant which was airy and light with basic tables. Its menu offered a favourite dish for each of them. Mac and cheese for Morgan, grilled halloumi and smashed avocado for Paige, a classic beefburger for Emily and a Caesar salad for Tiff. Three of them had hot drinks. One a vodka. Emily pulled off her coat and put it on the back of her chair. It fell off, but she didn't notice. They talked politely about holidays they'd taken over the years. When Olly was small, he and Morgan, along with her parents, would usually go to a holiday park in Wales. Swimming pool, soft play area, cheap bar food, job done. Aside from Felix's worldwide travels, when they sometimes attached a week's holiday onto one of his trips, Paige and her husband had honeymooned in Venice and went skiing as often as they could. Emily and Lewis always enjoyed two weeks in Greece. It was easy to book, they liked the same hotel, had made friends with the staff who cooked them English food. Like Felix, Tiff travelled with work: Croatia, Chicago, Canada. In between jobs, she visited her parents.

'No one else drinking? Aren't I supposed to be the quiet one?' said

Emily and raised her glass. She took a large bite of the burger and ordered another vodka.

'Take it easy, Emily,' said Morgan. 'You don't want to be ill on board. Those aeroplane toilets are tiny.'

'Of course. Morgan the sensible. Jeez, don't you ever let your hair down, even now?'

'There's no need to be rude,' said Paige and she put down her fork.

'Guys, guys, this week's never going to work if we argue before we even get on the plane,' said Tiff.

'Because this week's going to be perfect, right?' said Emily. 'Look at the four of us! We have so little in common now. We were always different, but I guess back then, I thought we had common values. But after what happened with Hugo, I asked myself if we'd ever really had a proper friendship.'

'Of course we did,' said Morgan.

'I remember you always saying how four was a special number,' Paige said to Morgan. 'That there were four winds, four seasons, four moon phases, four elements.'

'And four secrets,' muttered Tiff.

'Tiff's right. Or maybe there were more... Fess up, guys, who's still hiding something?' Emily stabbed a pot of ketchup with a French fry.

Tiff sat very still. Paige became engrossed in cutting up her halloumi.

'What's going on, Emily?' asked Morgan gently. 'What's this about?' She pointed to the glass. 'Can we help?'

Emily pushed away her plate. 'I found out last night Lewis is divorcing me and I reckon everything that happened with my mum is to blame.'

'Oh, I'm so sorry,' said Morgan.

'Me too,' said Paige.

'But your mum isn't here any more,' said Tiff. 'She never even met your husband, did she? He wasn't at school, right?'

'You know how Hugo won me over?' said Emily, with bloodshot eyes, ignoring Tiff. 'He said his father was ill too and that he didn't get on with him. Said sometimes he wished his dad were dead, that even though his father was a prick, Hugo felt he had to be nice all the time. He made me promise not to tell anyone. It would ruin his perfect image, the boy who had everything: brains, a nice family, looks. Around that time, I was feeling most like the odd one out, because none of you had the challenges I faced. It was as if Hugo was the only person in the world who got it. And so I opened up to him, told him how difficult my mum could be.'

'What a snake,' muttered Tiff, looking as if she'd read a bad review of one of her plays. 'I bet his dad wasn't sick at all. Hugo took advantage.'

'Idiot me fell for it,' said Emily. 'I mentioned Hugo's dad to mine once. Dad said he was always out in the pub when he was there, laughing and chatting with mates. He reckoned Hugo's dad was raking it in as a plumber. He looked tired a lot of the time, but what self-employed person doesn't? Any supposed illness hadn't held him back from enjoying a social life, from holding down a demanding job.'

'I went to my gran's funeral a few months ago,' said Tiff. 'I... always wished I'd gone to your mum's, to be there for you, to pay her my respects.'

'Respects? To my mother? That's a joke. She was a selfish bitch.'

The other three exchanged looks.

'Seeee, you never knew me *that* well,' said Emily, speaking as if explaining a complicated dosage to an elderly patient.

Emily's mum was never perfect. Back in Year Seven, Emily would often come into school with rumpled clothes, nothing but crisps and chocolate in her lunch box, unlike the healthy meal Morgan's mum or dad would always put together, and her permission slips for trips were never handed in on time. In Year Eight, a lot of that stopped. Emily learnt to take responsibility for herself. More than once, she'd said her mum had a life of her own, and had told Emily to follow her example and marry someone who wasn't around twenty-four-seven. A lorry driver husband suited her. Even when he was back, she still went out clubbing with colleagues from the betting shop. But Emily missed her dad and when she went to tea with Morgan, said how nice it was to see her whole family eating at the table together.

'I've observed a lot of deaths,' said Emily. 'The hardest to watch were those where the relationship between the patient and next of kin was conflicted. The last time it happened, there was a middle-aged son. He was gay and his mother had never understood his *choices*, as she put it. He did the minimum in her final days. Strict visiting hours only, sitting by the bed but not holding her hand. Then she went. Suddenly. A panicked voice rose out from that end of the ward – his. As white as the tiles on the ward's floor, he stood shaking as I confirmed the worst. You'd expect to see a sense of release, but it hit him hard. I'll never forget that howl – grief for the mum who'd loved him so much as a little boy, grief for what could have been in later life.' She shook her head. 'But however many times I've witnessed it during my career, I've never understood it with reference to my mother.'

Oh, Emily. Morgan wanted to hold her tight.

'A few months before the prom, my world fell apart,' continued Emily, in a taut voice. 'Perhaps Hugo sensed the trauma.'

'The funeral must have been devastating,' said Morgan and she nodded.

Red blotches appeared on Emily's cheeks and she fiddled with the cuff of her jumper's sleeve, looking away. 'No,' she said, eventually, 'it was about something else, just before that. I wanted to talk to you three, share what had happened. I cried myself to sleep every night, but we had exams and, of course, were all secretly hooking up with Hugo. I couldn't tell you about the biggest thing that had ever happened in my life.' She lifted her chin. 'If you three didn't guess I'd suffered a tragedy, when that sleazeball Hugo did, then what did that say about our friendship?'

A server came over to clear their plates. A tannoy announced their flight was boarding. Emily pushed herself up.

'Was it something to do with your mum dying?' asked Tiff.

'You could say that,' replied Emily in a flat voice. 'You see, the funeral never really took place.'

17

MORGAN

On the aeroplane, they fell into their old familiar pairs: Morgan next to Paige, Emily and Tiff together. Minutes before boarding, Tiff went to one side and took a call from her agent before hurrying aboard the plane with the others. She looked ruffled, happy, all kinds of impulsive. Paige gazed out of the window, and after the buzz of taking off, Morgan pretended to read. Emily's mother didn't have a funeral? She must have had a direct cremation then. Morgan's dad had bumped into Emily's father one day, asked how everything was going. He'd started to cry. Over a pint, it spilled out: the guilt at not being there for his wife, not going to appointments at The Christie cancer hospital, guilt at Emily having to carry the burden, at their young son struggling without either parent. But he needed his driving job; money had always been tight, what with his wife's social life. He'd spoken of the hours he spent trailing internet sites, looking for a miracle cure.

Despite her appearance, Emily's mum's spirit didn't wane, she was still full of jokes, of celebrity gossip, of the latest fashions. She would have definitely wanted a fancy send-off.

Halfway through the flight, a child suffered a panic attack, due to turbulence. Tiff waved to the air steward. 'My friend is a nurse, perhaps she can help.' She pushed Emily's shoulder, waking her up.

When they finally landed in Nice, despite her disgruntled expression,

Emily had insisted on staying with the child until the paramedics boarded. Finally, at the rail station, the women got on the train to Fréjus. Morgan lapped up the sights: the fields of green, Baroque-style churches, winding roads, the palm trees, the ocean in the distance, cyclists with the breeze blowing their hair. Halfway into their journey they passed through Cannes. Tiff leant nearer to the window, as if expecting to see the film festival's red carpet. Emily slept again and Paige stared straight ahead, deep in thought. Ninety minutes later, conversation was still at a minimum when they disembarked and got into a taxi. Tiff gave the driver her friend's address. Sure enough, it wasn't far, just on the outskirts of the town, following a drive passing medieval-looking buildings, terracotta stone cafés with tables outside and a shopping mall. Morgan wound down the window and inhaled. Even the air smelt different: of the vanilla plants winding up tree trunks along the boulevards, and the sweet aroma of pastries wafting out of a nearby boulangerie.

The villa itself was at the top of a hill and apparently a fifteen-minute stroll from the beach. Morgan clambered out of the car and stretched, basking in the Riviera, confronted by a pool that looked as if it had come straight out of glitzy movie. With all her heart, she wished that Olly were here. Wherever they'd gone on holiday throughout his youth, be the swimming option chlorinated or salty, be the beaches sandy or pebble-covered, Olly would be the first into the water and would always come up laughing. She wouldn't put it past him to try to swim in Lake Geneva.

For the first time it hit her, what Hugo had missed. An evening came back to her from a couple of years previously. She and Olly had debated physics until late into the night, one of their favourite activities until he became more distant. How water might feel wet, but that was only our perception of it. If you submerged your hand in a bowl of water, and kept it there, the sensation was different to that wetness. This led to a longer discussion about how we never really touch anything, because a human body's electrons repel those of other objects. This theory blew Olly's mind but Morgan explained; she read physics books for enjoyment, her parents had never been able to understand. She told him when he lay in bed at night, so comfy, when he felt that dip in the middle of the mattress, actually his body wasn't touching the bed at all. These chats were some of Morgan's fondest memories, the two of them swept up in a mutual passion. It was after that particular evening Olly thought seriously about studying physics at university.

Hugo had never even seen his son's first smile as a baby, the genuine one, not due to wind. He'd not been clutched by Olly's little hand on the walk to primary school, not watched his serious, oh-so-determined boy deliver his shepherd lines in the nativity show, with a tea towel on his head. Hugo had never wielded that parental power of a hug solving every problem, nor fought him for the last slice of pizza. Most of all, he'd missed the satisfaction of helping his bawling, purple-faced baby grow into a caring, hardworking, intelligent young man who knew his own mind, knew right from wrong. A son to be proud of.

Morgan took in the villa's whitewashed walls, the cream shutters, the terracotta roof tiles. Birds of prey flew overhead. Emily might know what they were called. The view, across from the pool, mesmerised Morgan. Down to the right was the sandiest beach that curved and disappeared into the distance. To the left, far away, stood the dusty mountain range between Fréjus and Cannes, covered in green vegetation. Back in Manchester, if she squinted through the back window of an upstairs bedroom, she could just spot the tops of the Peak District.

Tonight, they'd stay in and make omelettes. Morgan loved the artless decor, with understated white walls and chunky wooden furniture, and the watercolour of a field of lavender. The wash basin in her and Paige's room was old-school, with a large jug by the side. The tub in the bathroom was freestanding. The huge bed she and Paige would share was the biggest she'd ever seen.

Tiff poured four glasses of red wine and toasted Belle for her generosity in her absence and then sat down next to Emily, on the natural-linen-look sofa. Morgan and Paige made themselves comfortable on armchairs on the other side of the rustic, oak coffee table. They talked about Hugo and Sylvie, agreeing to visit the address Mlle Vachon had given them first thing tomorrow.

Tiff hadn't been able to stop fidgeting with her sparkly bangles. 'I'm sorry about things with your mum, Emily,' she blurted out. 'My parents have been... challenging, but I don't hate them. I used to think I did at school, and sometimes I wonder what career I'd have followed, given the chance to follow my own instincts... but they both had good intentions.'

Emily put down her untouched wine. 'Well, I've told you three how Hugo hooked me in, saying his dad was also ill. How did he succeed with you three?'

Paige remained silent. Tiff ran her finger around the rim of her glass.

'He said I was different from other girls, chatting for hours without a hint of flirting,' said Morgan quietly. 'He liked things simple – I sensed his life was very complicated. I used to worry there was something wrong with me, not raving about boys the way other girls did, more interested in maths than hot guys. I believed I'd never find a relationship, what with me finding clothes and make-up boring. I could never act ditzy around the opposite sex like Jasmine and her friends did. But then Hugo seemed to like me for just being me.'

'We did too,' Emily, in a measured tone. 'Or didn't that count?'

Paige glared at Emily.

'Of course it did. But no boy ever had. Hugo said he got sick of the attention he got and that I was a refreshing change.'

Tiff frowned. 'But that's why he used to hate us: because we didn't pander to him like everyone else.'

'I didn't take his shit at first,' said Morgan. 'I said it didn't make sense. But he said the attention had become like a drug, he didn't like it but couldn't get enough.' She shook his head. 'What a naïve fool I was. You only had to look at him at the prom after he'd given his little speech. When all the girls flocked around him saying sorry, they should have voted him prom king after all – he looked as if he'd landed the Sovereign Grant.' Morgan leant forwards, put her elbows on her knees and rested her chin in her hands. 'Then the sex stuff... I... I was scared I'd never lose my virginity – that no man would ever want to sleep with me and I'd end up as some lonely old bat with nothing in my life apart from books, biscuits and cats.'

Although now that didn't actually sound too bad.

'With Hugo, I was out of my depth and didn't want to stop falling.' The condom had come off. She hadn't been sure at what point. As soon as she got home, Morgan rang a helpline, to find out the odds of getting pregnant from sleeping with someone once. The woman listened to Morgan's situation, talked instead about STI tests, but Morgan persisted so she went through several leaflets and finally found the statistic. Morgan put the phone down, unworried by the one in twenty chance.

Maths had never let her down before that.

'You never showed any interest in a relationship,' said Paige. 'Why didn't you tell *us* the truth about how you really felt?'

'I guess if I kept it quiet then I could hang on to the possibility that I was wrong and one day, the right lad would come along. Boys were never my number one interest – teaching maths was my dream, not a big white wedding – but even so, I was still a young woman, and I still wanted to feel attractive.'

'I can relate to what you say about how Hugo got into your head,' said Tiff and she reached for the bowl of crisps they'd set out. 'He'd overheard me moaning to you lot about Mum. She'd read about a new celebrity diet, and her latest plan was for me to take elocution lessons. He apologised for the football pitch incident, said that he deserved to lose the captaincy, but had been dreading telling his dad who had such high expectations. He said his dad put on constant pressure and wanted Hugo to either be an international football player or a whizz on the stock markets. Hugo said he admired me rejecting the pressure from my mum to fit some ideal she had about how actors should be. He said I looked and sounded great and nothing was more appealing than someone happy in their own skin.'

'But you *were* happy with yourself, Tiff,' said Paige, frowning, and she put down her wine. 'So why was it so special, Hugo saying all that stuff?'

'You used to give the finger to Jasmine and her friends when they oinked,' said Morgan. Although, just occasionally, Morgan had wondered if it was an act.

Emily's brow knotted. 'You were just Tiff, to me. I was always too busy laughing at your stupid jokes to think about your size. In fact, I was jealous of your bust. I was in an A cup until my late teens. I never really got why Jasmine made a thing of your curves.'

'Really?' Tiff replied, coolly. 'Where did that Jabba comment come from, then?'

'From Mum, as it happens.' Emily rubbed her brow, suddenly looking tired. 'I'd been combing her hair, put on her favourite lippy, made her breakfast. She'd *pinched an inch*, as she said, around my waist. Called me Little Miss Jabba and said I'd never get a boyfriend if I ate so much cake. It was the first thing that came to mind, that night at the prom, because her comment had hurt me so much.'

'That's shit about your mum.' Tiff's jaw set into a hard line. 'But no excuse for passing the insult on. How could none of you have worked out my insecurities? Remember how we obsessed over *Love Actually* when it came out, the first term of Year Eleven?'

'Bill Nighy was brilliant,' said Morgan. 'You loved Hugh Grant, Paige. We used to argue about which of them was the best character.'

'Martine McCutcheon was so relatable,' said Emily.

The three of them looked at Tiff.

'I wanted to be Keira Knightly.'

'You said that was because you had a crush on Andrew Lincoln,' said Paige. 'That you wanted him to stand outside your front door reading those cards.'

'That was partly it, but mostly... she was pretty, so thin.' Crisp fragments tumbled out of her mouth as she spoke. 'Hugo's attention was too much to resist, for' – Tiff's voice wavered – 'a sexless chubber like me.'

'You were never that,' said Emily and looked quite fierce for a moment.

Tiff carried on as if she hadn't heard. 'How Hugo must have laughed because I told him to ignore me, as usual, in school. I didn't want my best friends finding out.'

'I told him that as well,' said Emily.

'Yup, ditto,' said Morgan.

'Me too,' said Paige.

'We made it so easy for him,' said Tiff and put the empty bowl back on the coffee table.

The four women looked at each other.

'He might still laugh at us, even now,' said Morgan.

'It doesn't feel real, that we might see him tomorrow,' said Tiff.

Paige swirled the wine in her glass. The sun was beginning to set. 'A few weeks after the football incident, he appeared by my side as I walked home one Friday night. He commented on my new school bag, which was designer, made by my mum's company. He said everyone thought they knew him because of the way he looked, because of his confidence, but they were wrong. It put pressure on him to act like the stud and left him worried no one would like him if he lost his coveted position as Mr Popular. Losing the football captaincy had devastated him. He suggested maybe I could relate, because of my background. He was right. People judged me too, by my parents' money, my accent, my clothes. It was refreshing to find someone else in the same position. He trusted me with his truth. I felt unique.' She turned to Morgan. 'He never called me a princess.'

Morgan blushed. 'Yeah, well, you fell for his lies too. I remember seeing Hugo out and about with his dad. He always had an arm around Hugo's shoulder, Hugo laughing at his jokes.' Morgan got up and went over to the French windows. The last rays of sun lit up ripples of water. She turned around. 'Hugo said at the prom it didn't take much to hook four silly girls whose heads were so easily turned by a few snogs – girls who couldn't be trusted because they gave up a supposedly strong friendship and principles for flattery and stupid presents.'

'He gave me chocolates. Of course he did,' said Tiff.

'A charm bracelet,' said Paige.

'Flowers,' said Emily. 'Mum was jealous. She didn't like the idea of her daughter getting male attention.'

'He bought me a small solar-powered calculator.' Morgan raised her hands in the air. 'But now it's obvious we betrayed each other for the deepest of reasons. Hugo gave us so much more than presents, like relatability, a feeling we weren't alone. He cut through the surface, tapped into things no one else saw: Emily's hate for her mum, Tiff's non-acceptance of herself, the pressure on Paige over her image, how I *did* want to be fancied.' Morgan collapsed into her armchair. 'We've punished each other, all these years, for simply being vulnerable teenagers.'

When it was dark outside, they got up and worked as team, like they used to, preparing dinner. Morgan lay the table, forks on the left, knives on the right. Before she knew it, Tiff had swapped them around: an old quirk of hers. Paige beat eggs, tentatively thrown to her by Morgan, one by one. Paige couldn't help but smile at their teen routine that often ended up with yolk on the floor and an angry dad or mum. Emily put out drinks and folded the napkins so that they stood up like fans. Paige's parents always used to ask her to do it if she was over and they were having a dinner party. And not unlike the old days, when Tiff sliced a baguette, she cut her finger and shook it dramatically in the air, shooting Emily a pointed look. Emily rolled her eyes and disappeared. Minutes later, she came back with a plaster and antibiotic wipes.

They ate, washed up, pulled on their coats, went outside and sat by the pool. Paige took out a packet of cigarettes, offered them around and then smoked alone. Morgan tracked the pool's ripples of water. What wasted years. If the truth had been revealed back then, surely they could have repaired the damage? Surrounding trees rustled as the mistral wind whispered against the leaves, perhaps telling secrets and spreading rumours. Perhaps spreading news of their arrival in France, to Hugo?

Would he scarper? Relish a confrontation? Issue an instant apology? Had he become a man worthy of her son? *Their* son. Morgan shivered.

A round to oval green leaf, with raggedy edges, blew across the ground by their feet as rain started to spit. It was the same shape as the leaves on a hazel tree, like the one by the disused basement at Dailsworth High. The hazel tree was steeped in myths. It represented wisdom, inspiration. The girls used to think it no coincidence that that was their meeting place. On more whimsical days, they'd say its magic had brought them together. Morgan went to pick it up but Emily beat her to it, peered at the leaf in her hand and gently ran her thumb across it.

18

PAIGE, EMILY, TIFF

Paige sat in front of the dressing table mirror and yawned. They'd closed the shutters. The rain fell harder. Now that the four of them were opening up, it was time to tell Morgan what she'd been hiding.

She put down the hairbrush and turned around to Morgan, who was on the bed, scrolling on her phone. 'There's something about me that might be a shock.'

Morgan looked up. 'Shoot. If we can get through talking about our past and Year Eleven, we can get through anything.' Her voice wavered. 'Things have been... tough for me, in recent months. Every hour us four spend together... it's more than I could have ever hoped for. It's... healing.'

'Right. Okay. Here goes... um... these days, I... I...' *Healing.* Morgan had said that. Could Paige really blow everything apart again? 'These days I... shop at Primark,' she blurted out.

Morgan burst out laughing. 'Is that it? Oh, very funny. I can't imagine that. Sorry, but your April Fool's joke didn't work. Whereas I'm still a big fan. That store has been a lifesaver with the cost of living crisis.'

Yet the first thing that had come into Paige's head happened to be true. The pound shop was a favourite too, as she saved for her and Felix's detached home. Also, because, at the back of her mind, she wanted to build up a money pot so that if his job ever became too much, he could hand his notice in and they'd have enough to cover bills. Not that he would. Felix had always been stubborn – or 'determined', as he preferred to call it. He'd pursued her steadfastly in the early days, asking her out until she said yes.

'What do you think is going on with Emily?' asked Paige. 'Perhaps the doctors got it wrong about her mum. But then the idea of her mother still being alive seems far-fetched, and why would her surviving such a terrible illness cause a big rift between them?'

'I don't know. Perhaps money was tight and they couldn't afford a big send-off. Maybe her dad was made redundant, on top of everything else.' Morgan lay back on the covers. 'I need to digest everything that's come out – how blasé teenage Tiff really had body image issues, and you, Paige, the most self-assured, collected person in the school, suffered from a pressure invisible to me, caused by your parents' status, their wealth...' She took off her watch. 'Do you think we'd still be friends, if everything with Hugo hadn't happened?'

'I reckon we would have gone to uni together.'

'That would have been fun. I've taken my maths A-level now, done evening courses, you know. Olly's passion is physics. I've always been interested in it, but nothing like he is. I'm excited to see where he goes from here.'

'You could still go to university,' said Paige.

'If I win the lottery. I've Olly's education to contribute to, for three years at least, before I can even think about going taking a degree myself. Student loans don't cover everything.'

'You could both work part-time. It's important to make plans for the future, isn't it? Just for you? Not to lose yourself. I see that so many times in my line of work. As people age, they lose self-belief. Their body language becomes closed, their heads drop, shoulders droop, they acquire an apologetic air, they don't meet the gaze of people they pass in the street as if, somehow, they aren't worthy of an interaction. Don't do that, Morgan. Olly moving out could be the start of a new chapter – for both of you.'

'Not in a world where every penny counts and you'll skip eating so that you can treat your kid, or you'll hide money problems from your own parents because they'd do the same.'

Paige couldn't find the words to reply.

Morgan got up. 'Do you want me to get changed in the bathroom?'

'No, it's fine.'

Facing Paige, she took off her top to put on her pyjamas. Her arms weren't as stick-thin now, but she was as pale as ever, with that small, brown birthmark on the right of her stomach in the shape of a hedgehog.

'Has there been anyone special over the years?' asked Paige. Had Morgan always had to manage alone? Paige had her own money, her own independence, but couldn't imagine living without her husband. When it came to Paige, his ability to read people far outstripped hers and more than once, he'd come home with a bunch of flowers, having detected a low mood simply from the way she'd poured a cup of coffee.

Morgan told her about Den as she folded her clothes, then asked about Felix.

'Our eyes met at a gin stall at the Christmas markets. It was snowing and we ended up buying a hot chocolate and standing talking.' Paige went into the bathroom but left the door open. 'Every anniversary we have gin in hot chocolate to mark the occasion. It's a combination that goes surprisingly well.' She brushed her teeth and got into bed. 'Do you mind if I turn the lights out? Felix and I had a late one last night.' She and Morgan used to have the best sleepovers. They didn't paint nails or watch romcoms. Instead, they'd often just gaze at the stars. Paige had a really cool loft room with a window in the roof. They learnt to recognise Jupiter and Venus and would spot aeroplanes and satellites. In the darkness, they'd imagine aliens staring in, concluding humans were odd creatures. Would they work out that eyebrows were to stop sweat running into eyes, or that hair was to keep the head warm and cushion the skull?

Takeout pizza in boxes was another treat. Paige's parents weren't fans of eating off cardboard but would let them have it when Morgan slept over. As midnight approached, they'd process their school week. The smarmy English teacher who sucked up to Paige, having met her parents and found out her dad was on some board at Rolls Royce. When Jasmine had bumped into her in the canteen, knocking over her orange juice. It went through her skirt and knickers, sweet and sticky, followed by bitchy comments that Mummy's designer label could easily provide her with new clothes.

Whereas Morgan would talk about those girls taunting her for having supermarket own brand items in her lunchbox. Or she'd mention one of the popular boys who'd always ruffle her short hair and push past, sniggering, 'Watch out, sonny.' They'd chat about the fun times too, like the history teacher and language assistant who were dating and sent silly notes to each other via the pupils who had their lessons back-to-back.

'I set the alarm for seven tomorrow morning and told Emily and Tiff to do the same,' said Morgan as the shutters rattled. The wind had got up. 'Hugo's old address is about a ten-minute drive away. He or whoever owns it now might go to work, so if we get there before eight, we stand a good chance of catching someone in.'

'Go to work on a Sunday?'

'Possible if they work in retail or hospitality.' She hesitated. 'Night, then.' Morgan tugged on Paige's hair and quickly turned away.

A wave of emotion swept over Paige. It used to be their sleepover goodnight ritual. It was now her turn to tug on one of Morgan's short locks, before going to sleep. But Paige was wary, so wary of losing her friend for a second time. She couldn't let herself get attached, couldn't go through that again. Instead of reaching out, Paige turned on her side, slid her hands in between her knees and closed her eyes.

* * *

Seeing the girls again. The flight. The villa. Too much wine with dinner leading to sad thoughts about Lewis, about her career. The wind that now howled intermittently. The rain that meant she couldn't get to sleep. Eyes wide open, Emily turned her head, stomach churning, feet restless, mouth dry.

'Tiff?' Tiff was still on her phone, muttering about making a booking. 'Isn't Paige quieter than she used to be? She's hardly said a word.'

'We've all changed.'

'Tell me about your love life.'

Tiff put down her phone and turned her head to meet Emily's gaze. 'I'd much rather you tell me about Lewis. How did you first meet?'

'It was ten years ago. Emergency departments have always been under pressure but there was a lighter atmosphere back then. I'd seen Lewis often enough before, wheeling in patients. We'd chat. Share a laugh. I mentioned once how much I liked Snickers bars, some days that was all I had for lunch. It was his favourite too and a few days later, he brought a multi-pack in. Didn't even expect to share. I knew, then, that he was a keeper.'

'Cute.'

'A couple of weeks after that, his mates wheeled in a trolley. Lewis was under the blanket and when they pulled it off, he sat up and asked me out on a date. He was holding a bunch of red roses.' Pretending to be dead was the most romantic thing anyone had ever done for her.

'How long have you been married?'

'Almost eight years. We both loved our jobs – making a difference in people's lives, meeting patients from a variety of backgrounds, watching them heal, witnessing miracles.'

'Then why leave the profession? Won't you miss it?'

'Nope.'

'I went through a bad stage with my career. Rejections at auditions. Directors taking me aside for "the fat talk", saying I needed to drop seven pounds. My agent's told me often enough I'd get more parts if I lost weight.'

'Sounds to me like you need a new agent.'

'The point is, it's my vocation. I can't imagine doing anything else. Surely nursing is like that?'

How many times had Emily been told that in recent months? Firstly by the emergency care manager. Then Lewis. His family. Her dad. Next door. The woman from the post office. None of them would last one shift and would have got out well before things became so desperate. At least Smudge understood and knew to keep quiet.

'You probably just need a break like I did,' continued Tiff. 'Two weeks in a spa in Cleethorpes sorted me out.'

Two weeks living in the Dalai Lama's palace wouldn't clear Emily's head. With a concerted effort, she'd stay calm with Lewis, in front of her parents, even her fucking therapist. But it wasn't in her to hold back any more. What was it with people, thinking that being a nurse meant you should put up with all sorts of other crap, on top of dealing with bedpans, catheters and commodes? Barely hearing the rain that slashed against the shutters, she jumped out of bed.

'So my needs still come last?'

'No, Emily, I didn't mean—'

'I've held the hands of dying patients desperate to see relatives who weren't allowed anywhere near them. I've worked shifts back-to-back in a mask, mummified in PPE. That's on top of the usual challenges of sore feet, a bad back, extended shift hours. Then I've gone home and struggled to pay bills and had no money to relax and unwind, to enjoy myself.' She paced the room. 'How are you so unable to put yourself in my position? Oh, but wait – that would require empathy. But you've lost it like I've lost my kindness, because adulthood has stolen our four gifts away.' Emily strode into the lounge, shouting at the top of her voice, 'The Secret Gift Society is an effing joke, set up by a bunch of silly girls who'd read too many Enid Blyton books.'

Morgan and Paige appeared.

'What's going on?' asked Paige.

Tiff looked at the other two and shrugged.

'I've lost my kindness,' continued Emily. 'Tiff has lost her empathy. Paige's intuition screwed up a long time ago – she never saw through Hugo's twisted plan – and Morgan's sense of logic must have worn away over time, because only a lunatic would reunite us after what happened.' Emily yanked open the French windows, went outside and stood by the pool, in the rain, arms outstretched, head tilted up at the sky, cotton nightie drenched, hair sopping. 'Maybe this will help me feel alive, getting back to the basics of nature, forgetting how complicated modern lives are. Come on, clouds, do your worst,' she hollered.

Morgan, Paige and Tiff stood frozen by the French windows.

Tiff looked at the others, then back at Emily. 'Oh, for fuck's sake,' she muttered and then went outside too. She stood by Emily and slowly stretched out her arms, head tilted up, silk pyjamas soaked within minutes. Morgan came next. Then Paige. More of the round to oval green leaves, like hazel tree ones, tumbled down from branches. As the mistral blew them, they danced around the girls, who stood shivering by the pool, water trickling down their cheeks. The others' pained expressions looked just like

Emily's as she remembered what an utterly close friendship the four of them had ruined, back in 2004.

* * *

And I was always labelled the dramatic one. Tiff replayed last night in her mind. She brushed damp hair out of her face and shook her head. She reached to her bedside table and picked up her phone for the umpteenth time. Lying under the covers, she read another text from her agent. A great audition had come up for a romcom on Amazon Prime, about a love triangle. Tiff was in the running to play one of the three leads. The actor they'd set up for the role had bailed just before contracts were signed. Tiff hadn't been the casting director's first choice but this was a unique opportunity. The audition was last-minute and the day after tomorrow. She'd need to get to London as soon as possible so that her agent could fill her in properly.

Tiff had booked a flight for a few hours' time. The others would understand. This was her future. Three heads would be as good as four. As Emily said, Tiff had lost her empathy, so what was the big deal? She'd strived not to analyse Emily's behaviour last night, trivialising it as her friend making a fuss. However, the truth was, standing there in the rain, she knew exactly how Emily had hoped to feel, in that basic way children and teenagers did before the responsibilities of adulthood put barriers up, keeping out raw nature, raw emotions. When was the last time Tiff had run as fast as she could through a field, collapsing with laughter onto fresh grass? Or lain on the ground to inspect an insect, almost crying at its beauty? Beaches had become all about the swimsuit and tan, not about singing along with the breeze, lying in the tide as the ocean covered you with a salty water sheet and then pulled it back. As for hikes, they were more about the calorie burning instead of enjoying a sense of oneness with wildlife. Tiff had forgotten how it felt to have everything frivolous stripped back to what was important.

She looked at her phone again. Her agent had emailed her the audition scene, a monologue. The director wanted *feistiness* – a word her agent usually hated, saying it was sexist and subtly undermined women who were simply assertive.

Emily snored by her side. Her friend hadn't dropped off until a couple of hours ago. They'd come in from the rain and gone to bed without saying anything. Then hadn't been the time for Tiff to announce her premature departure. Tiff hadn't slept. Nothing new, the night before a big day on set, she'd be unable to switch off the lines going around her head. Concealer had become her best friend, along with eye drops, facials and the occasional sleeping pill. She'd even taken a line of cocaine once, at a party. Someone said that it gave you such a rush, but the subsequent crash meant that tiredness set in, and, Tiff hoped, deep sleep. That rush certainly did take her breath away, filled her with power and confidence, and she'd had sex with her director – but she still couldn't sleep afterwards.

Emily's eyelids fluttered. Tiff jumped up and went for a shower, not sure how to admit she was bailing. By the time she'd got dressed and fixed her hair, it was seven fifteen and the others were in the living room, drinking coffee, not talking. It reminded her of the first day of rehearsals, meeting actors with a reputation. You believed you knew them because of their past work, but actually didn't know them at all.

Slut. A hateful word. Wholesome, young Emily hadn't deserved it, she wasn't even sleeping with Hugo, never had with anyone. Tiff, Morgan and Paige were more streetwise, but Hugo being able to take advantage of Emily was less surprising. Tiff gazed at Morgan, in jeans and a T-shirt, no make-up, no false face. Then Paige in her crease-free, cotton trousers and blouse tucked in, still effortlessly stylish. The four of them used to joke that they had each other's backs – and their fronts. Like the time in Year Seven when the Home Economics teacher asked the class to come up with a healthy baking recipe. Pupils created bakes swapping in low fat butter and wholemeal flour. Tiff chose to make a cheesecake topped with lots of fruit, excited at how colourful it would look. However, their exacting teacher tore her apart in front of the other pupils, in a sneering, clinical voice. Said Tiff was tipping towards tubby and no wonder, if she thought simply adding healthy ingredients would cancel out a dish's high saturated fat content. Tiff laughed it off in front of the class, but Morgan, Paige and Emily found her sobbing in the toilets afterwards. She said it was the teacher's rude tone that upset her. They persuaded Tiff to make a complaint to her personal tutor, Mlle Vachon.

Having poured herself a coffee, Tiff sat down next to Emily on the sofa, sun rays shining through the windows, the clouds of yesterday gone. Morgan and Paige nodded from the armchairs. They'd all had toasted baguette and jam for breakfast.

Tiff took a deep breath. She couldn't put it off any longer. In the next half an hour, she'd need to leave for the airport. 'I have something to say...'

Emily face crumpled. 'Me too. I'm sorry.' The words burst out. 'Sorry for letting you three down in Year Eleven... You were the sisters I never had.'

Despite the sense that someone had jumped a scene, jumped to a climax and left Tiff to ad lib, the right words came so easily. 'I'm so sorry too,' she mumbled. 'I shouldn't have called you a slut, Emily.'

'I shouldn't have called you Jabba.'

'I'm sorry too, everyone,' said Paige and she turned to Morgan. 'Especially you.'

'Same here,' said Morgan. 'You were never a princess. I just chose the word that would hurt most. You deserved better from me...' She looked around. 'Each of you did.'

Many times over the years, Tiff had wanted their support. Even now, when starting a new show, Tiff would picture her three friends in the wings of the stage at school, cheering her on. As for the fun they had... Paige arranged a trip into town the first weekend of Year Eleven and said it was time to get more fashionable bras. They got pocket money, and earned extra too: Morgan from her gardening work, Emily from a paper round and Tiff from babysitting a neighbour's children. Even Paige, who helped out in her mother's offices during the holidays – her parents, as ever, were firm about their daughter learning the value of what they called, 'a hard day's graft'. The girls had giggled as Paige refused to let them buy comfy sports bras, instead pulling out ones with lace trims or a deeper plunge. She said it wasn't for boys, it was for themselves. 'Treat yourself well and you'll walk taller,' she'd announced. Whilst eating her burger afterwards, Tiff couldn't stop scratching hers, and over dinner that night, her mum had insisted Tiff took off her shirt. Sulkily, she'd shown her the new bra. However, her mum liked it, agreed the four friends were growing up, but had hinted that she thought it looked a little tight.

Whereas Paige, Emily and Morgan had said how well it fitted her gorgeous curves.

The others got up to wash their dishes. Tiff remained on the sofa, swirling her drink around. This director wanted feistiness. He sounded like a dick. Tiff wasn't one to disappoint, so in that spirit, she took out her phone, went into the text conversation with her agent and typed:

Sorry. Please cancel the audition. Something more important has come up.

19

MORGAN

The taxi driver drove through the town that had a café next to a small building with a yellow and blue sign on the front and the words *La Poste* – obviously the post office.

'That's proof that maths is much more difficult to learn than languages,' said Morgan. 'With French, you can often guess the meanings. With maths, there's no way of guessing answers. You always have to work it out.'

Paige, Emily and Tiff exchanged smiles.

'I don't think Mlle Vachon would agree,' said Paige.

Paige had said Morgan could still study maths at uni, that she should make plans for the future, but doing that when she'd first found out she was expecting had taught Morgan a lesson about setting herself up for disappointment. Pregnant Morgan had sworn she'd still study, get a degree, give her and Olly the life she'd always dreamt of, with a detached house in a leafy suburb, one of those big SUVs to drive around in, and a bonus each year that would pay for a holiday abroad. She wrote a five-year plan. Applied to sixth form college. But then the baby arrived and reality set in – sleepless nights, money needed straightaway for nappies, clothes, so many other things. Her parents were supportive but made it clear she needed to take responsibility.

Morgan used to cry in bed at night until Olly provided her with a different aspiration: to be the best mother ever, to give him the chances she'd now lost.

A tight sensation rose in her chest.

Years ago, teenage Tiff had moaned that her parents hadn't achieved their dreams, so were trying to live through her instead. Was Morgan in danger of being like that? The toast from breakfast came up to the back of her throat.

The driver turned into a long, narrow road and passed cyclists coming in the opposite direction. At the end, he pulled up outside a grey, stone house. Like the other properties, it had eggshell-blue shutters. Next door, a wrinkled man in a beret stood on his lawn, despite the grass still being wet from the rain last night, digging vigorously into the border of soil. He glared at them. Morgan pulled her spring anorak tighter, despite the morning sunshine. She paid the taxi driver and then took a photo of the house. Number 14. It took her back to the girls' fourteenth birthdays, Morgan and Emily's were in September, the others' in October. They went to Afflecks, the quirky indoor market in Manchester city centre, and found a stall selling cheap silver jewellery. They each bought the same necklace bearing a small leaf pendant, representing the society's beloved hazel tree.

As soon as she got home after the prom, Morgan had thrown hers away.

Behind her, Paige stood in her blazer, Emily a thick jumper – her winter coat was too warm – and Tiff in a tailored, suede jacket. Morgan flexed her hands. Her heart pounded as she reached for the doorbell. She had a rucksack on her back, organised as ever, containing plasters, painkillers, a water bottle, an umbrella. Paige sported an understated beige handbag. Tiff's was Louis Vuitton to match her suitcase. Emily wore a black bum bag.

Morgan pressed the doorbell again. Then knocked. She went to the front window and peered in. The bookshelves and magazine rack were bare, a small table clear and the fire grate empty. She went to look down the side of the house. A tall gate prevented a look in the back garden. She made her way back to the others who were waiting at the end of the drive.

'The building is empty. Out of all the scenarios I'd imagined, that wasn't one. What next?'

The man gardening next door shot them a scowl.

'Despite his frowns, that man keeps going to get up but then crouches down again,' whispered Paige. 'Might be worth going over. He's definitely got something to say.'

'His expression isn't very friendly,' said Morgan.

'*Bonjour!*' called Tiff and waved to him. 'If I was him, I'd want an invitation to talk,' she muttered to the others.

The man stood up and came over.

'*Parlez-vous anglais?*' asked Morgan.

'Yes,' he said and folded his arms.

'You've made our day by wearing a beret,' said Emily.

'Yes, I have a string of onions somewhere too,' he said and rolled his eyes.

Emily's smile widened. 'Of course, us English drink only tea and eat scones, whilst talking about the weather and Royal family... Your English is very good, by the way.'

For a second, his tanned face looked less wrinkled. '*Merci*. I've worked in the tourist industry along this coast my whole life.' Begrudgingly, he held out his hand. 'Henri. Has the house finally been put on the market?' he said. 'Are you four moving in?'

'No. We're looking for the previous owner – or owners,' said Morgan.

He glanced at Number 14. 'Did you know Gervais? I'm sorry to inform you that he passed a few months ago. A heart attack.'

Gervais? Had Sylvie remarried? 'Oh, no, we didn't, sorry about that,' said Morgan. 'Actually... we're looking for information about a mother and son who used to live here, Sylvie and Hugo. They moved here in 2004. She died but he might still be here.'

He shrugged. 'Sorry. Before my time, Gervais lived alone. The Duponts on the other side didn't move in until the year after me, in 2018, so couldn't help you either. When I arrived, a man around your age owned the house, let his friends live there. They played music at full volume, dumped rubbish on the front lawn, revved engines and more than once, I smelt weed. I suspected the worst when your group turned up. I couldn't go through that again.'

'He wasn't called Hugo?' asked Morgan.

Henri shook his head. 'Whereas Gervais was a blessing. The quietest, most polite man on earth.' He leant on his spade. 'Delphine, opposite, she's lived here longer than anyone and...' He pointed. '*Voila*, there she is, filling her bird feeders. She doesn't speak English; if you like, I could interpret.'

They crossed the narrow road. Henri went up the drive and spoke to her. Carrying a bag of bird seed, she approached. Large sunspots lay on her hands and cheeks like small pools of coffee. Henri spoke to her and she replied in rapid French.

'She says Sylvie was a lovely lady. She rented the house, having grown up around the corner. Her parents passed not long before she did. The dad had a stroke. Sylvie used to say her mum died of a broken heart. Just two days before her accident, Sylvie and Hugo moved into her childhood home. It made sense as the mortgage was paid. This house, opposite, where they used to live, stood empty for a while but eventually, new tenants moved in.'

'That could explain why Mlle Vachon never got a reply to her sympathy card,' said Emily. 'Sylvie hadn't given her their new address yet, and they hadn't spoken for a while. Perhaps Hugo didn't go back to the old house to collect post, and if Mlle Vachon rang him on the landline, no one would have been in their old address to pick up.'

'Imagine losing the three people you cared about most, one after another like that,' said Tiff. 'If that was me, I wouldn't be on top of everything.'

Silence fell for a moment.

'What happened to Hugo?' asked Morgan, voice coming out raspy.

Delphine spoke some more. '*Bon*, okay,' Henri said and he turned back to Morgan and the others. 'Hugo called by to see Delphine a few months after Sylvie passed, said he couldn't live on the estate any longer, too many memories. She's very sorry but she's forgotten the rest of what he said. You see, the morning of the day Hugo visited, her husband had packed his bags – dropped it on her that he'd been having an affair and was leaving. That day and the following weeks are a bit of a blur.'

Morgan gave Delphine an understanding nod before staring back at the house. She half-expected Hugo to stride past, cocky as ever. Right this minute, he could be a few streets away, living his life, unaware he was a father. Unless he'd had kids with someone else by now. Olly could have siblings he knew nothing about.

'Henri, can you ask where he worked?'

Henri quizzed Delphine. Gave her a thumbs up. 'A surf shop. On a beach, she doesn't know which one. But the shop is called Sea Breeze, or was back then, the name of her favourite cocktail. She meant to drop in, to have a proper chat, but couldn't face socialising for months after her husband left, and after that, it felt too late.'

Delphine spoke some more.

'Hugo had been so excited when he got the job. Delphine had been out the front the day he learnt he'd been the lucky candidate. She'd ask him about it whenever their paths crossed, and he hoped to work his way up and be put in charge of a new branch one day; the manager often talked about expanding in the future. Hugo spoke as if he'd finally found his place in the world. He loved the beaches. The waves. The sun. Delphine says they were a lovely family and to give Hugo her best wishes if you find him.'

Morgan thanked the two of them profusely, and Tiff rang for a taxi whilst the others searched for the shop on their phones.

'It's still there,' said Emily. 'Sea Breeze Surf Shop.'

Morgan studied the website. '*Etabli* 1991. Assuming that means *established*. Okay, this is good and it sounds as if he was happy settling in France. There are now three branches of the shop, across the Riviera, two smaller, so we should start with the big one.'

'Wonder how many French hearts he's broken,' said Tiff.

'Maybe none,' said Emily. 'Perhaps the stereotype is true and French women are more sophisticated in the ways of love.'

Neither Morgan nor Paige, spoke. The taxi pulled up and they got in. Morgan showed the driver the location of the shop on her phone. In heavily accented English, he said that beach wasn't the most popular with tourists, but was excellent for surfing and it attracted a lot of dog walkers. She got in the front, the others in the back, attempting conversation.

'Lewis and I had dreamt about retiring next to the coast. He loves sunny days with deckchairs and ice-creams, whereas I enjoy a bit of bird spotting and collecting shells.' Emily gave a small sigh and looked out of the car window. Tiff patted her arm before taking it back quickly.

Paige talked about the charity work Felix did through his job. 'Last year, as a treat, his team took the kids to Debdale Park in Gorton for windsurfing lessons. They were so excited, didn't even mind the torrential rain that came out of nowhere.'

'He sounds like a great guy,' said Morgan.

Paige gave a small nod.

'I have a neighbour, in London, obsessed with swimming. He'd love living somewhere like this,' said Tiff. 'Joe lives in a flat above a shop, next to my house.' Prodded by the others, she explained how Joe was in his late twenties and a drama teacher at an inner-city school. They'd started to run into each other when jogging. 'I know,' she said and pulled a face. '*Me*, running. Then once, he caught me unawares, said he was off to the pool for a thirty-minute lane swimming session, and did I fancy going with him. His running kit is always so sensible, with the black shorts and hi-vis jacket. I couldn't help laughing when he came out of the changing room in trunks covered in llamas.'

'And this Joe is just a friend, right?' said Morgan from the front, head turned around to look at the others, top lip twitching.

'He sounds fit, in more ways than one,' Emily chipped in.

'Llamas sound like fun,' said Paige and nudged Tiff's elbow.

Tiff sat up airily. 'Sorry to disappoint. We're simply friends, through and through.'

As they neared the beach, Morgan zoned out of the chat and went into her gallery on her phone, staring at the photo of Sylvie and Hugo's house. She'd promised to keep Olly updated, and would send it to him via Facebook Messenger when back at the villa.

They reached the beach at nine-thirty. The driver pulled into the car park. Morgan got out and inhaled the fresh air, dizzy as if it contained Class A drugs. Paige followed, lit a cigarette and took a long drag. Morgan hurried over to the shop, a wooden building with large windows, a palm leaf thatched roof and huge doors at the front.

Slowly Morgan went up to the doors. A sign on the front said the shop... was closed on Sundays from November to April.

Another setback. It was as if the universe was telling her to turn back.

She pressed her nose against the window and scanned rows of colourful surf boards and wetsuits, along with piles of shorts, tins of wax and board bags. She went to turn away when a row of framed photos caught her attention, behind the till. She narrowed her eyes. One was of a blonde-haired woman, on a beach, standing next to a surf board. A large medal hung around her neck. Next to her, with a wide smile on his face, was a well-built, tanned man with short hair. Not a paler, lanky boy, with a floppy fringe. But it was still Hugo.

Seagulls circling overhead, Morgan raced towards the beach. Memories flooded back of his lips on hers. She'd never daydreamed about him, or doodled his name in class, but Morgan had grown to care for Hugo. He'd been so thoughtful, it was unexpected. Would he be interested in a son? What would it do to Olly if he wasn't? Almost losing her balance, she pulled off her shoes and ran across patches of seaweed and into the sea, the cold water coming up to her ankles. The tide frothed as it circled around her feet, then it disappeared to sea again, leaving crushed shells in its wake. She squidged her toes in the sand, a comforting sensation.

Paige caught her up. 'Everything okay?'

Morgan could hardly breathe. Tiff and Emily arrived too. Tiff pulled off her shoes.

'We're really going to come face to face with Hugo. His photo is up on the wall; it's definitely the right place,' Morgan stuttered.

'I feel like a teenager again,' mumbled Tiff.

'Nervous. Excited. Angry,' said Emily.

Paige didn't say a thing.

Morgan shivered and Paige led her back to the dunes near the shop. The four of them sat huddled in front of one, protected from the coastal breeze, on a patch of dry sand, arms rubbing against each other – the closest they'd been for almost two decades. Morgan opened her rucksack to take a swig of water. She offered it around. The others hesitated and then drank out of it. As she put it back, Morgan spotted an item she'd forgotten to unpack at the villa. She pulled out the notebook. Tiff gasped. Emily's eyes widened. Paige started to laugh.

'Christ, what were we thinking?' Paige took it and read the front. 'Top secret. Closed cases. We were just a little self-important!'

'It was a serious business,' said Emily and she reached for it. She flicked through, the others leaning to look. 'The Case of the Stolen Packed Lunches. Milly... Smith, that was it. This case was at the end of Year Nine.

Do you remember? She kept finding her lunchbox, in her locker, with items missing – an empty crisp packet or a sandwich without filling?'

'Logically, it could have only been her best friend, Imani,' said Morgan. 'Their lockers were next to each other and I quizzed Milly. She hadn't thought to mention that they shared keys as she never suspected her best friend, they'd been in the same classes since nursery. Milly said they stuffed smelly PE kits into one, and would keep their books and lunchboxes in the other. They got replica keys made in town. Imani was the obvious culprit, hiding in plain sight, or so I believed. So you had a chat with her,' Morgan said to Emily.

'We had geography together,' said Emily. 'Both of us found it so boring. I complimented her new hairstyle: braided cornrows. When Imani smiled, I noticed how tired she looked. Whilst waiting for the teacher, I mentioned how my sleep was crap. Mum was always coming in late, singing at the top of her voice. Imani said she was awake half the night. I asked if everything was all right. Then the teacher came in and she clammed up.'

'But you kindly searched her out after school, didn't you?' said Tiff.

'I saved her half of my chocolate bar from lunch. Anyone else would have if they'd seen how much she needed cheering up. Slowly, it came out: how she'd been diagnosed with Crohn's. It was really painful and she had to be careful what she ate. It couldn't have been her randomly eating Milly's lunch. She even refused my chocolate.'

'I'd always empathised with Milly,' said Tiff. 'She was a bit overweight, like me. I found her crying in the corridor once. A boy from the year above had called her thunder thighs. It made me think that perhaps she was on a diet, and made up the stealing story to hide the fact she did care and was attempting to lose weight. I totally got that. Then we saw her mum at parents evening and I empathised even more.'

'She was stick thin and so glamorous with her costume jewellery,' said Paige. 'Aggressively opinionated too, the way she spoke to the teachers. She kept embarrassing Milly, saying what a sensitive child she was. My gut told me she had something to do with it. I reckoned she wasn't filling the sandwiches, emptying crisp packets, because she wanted Milly to slim down, but didn't want to make her upset.'

'Milly's face, when we told her.' Morgan lifted up a handful of sand and let it trickle out of her fingers. 'It all fell into place.'

'Shocking behaviour from a mother,' said Paige.

'Not even mine would have gone that far,' said Tiff.

'Mine would have,' said Emily. She picked up a bit of driftwood and drew circles in the sand.

They flicked through the notebook some more, memories flooding back of their friendship. A French bulldog trotted past. Emily called it over and stroked its head. The striking owner said, *'Bonjour'* and bowed his head, rugged, laidback and effortlessly handsome. When he'd gone by, the four of them glanced at each other and grinned.

'What were we like back in high school, playing detective,' said Paige and she shook her head. 'If I'm honest, I saw myself as Scully out of *The X-Files*: cool and assertive, following leads...'

'I fangirled over Jessica Fletcher out of *Murder She Wrote*,' said Emily, 'Mum called it a boring, old-fashioned television show but Dad and I used to hunt it down on digital channels.'

'Sherlock Holmes for me.' Morgan bowed. 'His brain works like no one else's.'

Tiff gave a sheepish smile. 'Daphne out of *Scooby-Doo*. Her clothes were so glamorous.'

The four of them laughed with equal pitch and equal warmth. Paige was the first to stop. She gulped and turned away for a moment. Morgan understood. After so long apart, the harmony felt overwhelming.

'Remember tic tac toe?' asked Emily. They'd played noughts and crosses in Mlle Vachon's lesson many times. Tic tac toe was the name of that game in French. A catchy phrase, the girls started to use if one of them dropped a secret – it meant the others had to follow and share one of theirs too. 'We shared everything, or so we thought,' said Emily. 'Crushes. Fears. The best thing was that no one ever laughed. We supported each other. Until the prom.'

'I... I've missed that,' said Morgan quietly. Without waiting for an answer, she stood up. 'I need a bracing walk.' She held out her hand. Paige hesitated and then took it, as Morgan pulled her to her feet. Then Paige pulled up Tiff. She pulled up Emily. They brushed themselves down.

Morgan put her trainers back on and they walked along the sand, Tiff's ankle giving way, now and again, in her heels. Talk soon turned to their families.

'My mum works at a different branch of the supermarket now,' said Morgan. 'She got a promotion and is now supervisor. Dad is still a warehouse manager.'

'I always admired your parents sticking together from such a young age,' said Emily. She glanced down at her left hand, at the wedding band she hadn't removed yet.

'They've been a great help with Olly over the years. I know they're going to love meeting Vikram, his boyfriend – not that I'm allowed to call him that.'

'You haven't turned into an embarrassing mum, have you Morgan?' asked Tiff and she grinned.

Morgan grinned back. 'Goes with the territory.' She turned to Paige. 'Although both your parents were always pretty cool.'

'They've retired now and are not in the slightest bit cool, spending most of their time baking in the sun at their Thai holiday home. Felix won't be cool either in Dubai at the moment. Not that he'll have any time to sunbathe. The future success of the company he works for is depending on him doing a good job.' She turned to Tiff. 'What about your parents, how are they doing?'

Tiff groaned. 'They are about to celebrate their fortieth wedding anniversary and have already hinted about me taking a plus one.'

'How about taking that Joe?' said Emily, a mischievous look on her face.

Morgan and Paige nodded.

'I don't think they'd like llama shorts,' Tiff replied. 'How's your dad, Emily?'

Emily waited for Tiff to say more about Joe and raised an eyebrow, but a stern look crossed Tiff's face and she folded her arms.

'Okay, okay… well, Dad works in B&Q, loves it. My brother's an aspiring musician and lives with his bandmates in Stockport.'

Eventually, they walked back to the car park. Tiff held Emily's arm to keep her balance until they reached the tarmac. Morgan rang for a taxi, Paige holding onto her elbow whilst she took off one shoe to shake out the sand. The two women smiled at each other as Paige wobbled and had to grip on tighter. Since 2004, The Secret Gift Society had been like a maths puzzle with no solution, however many times Morgan had gone back to work out how it could have imploded so badly. But the last few days were filling in gaps and offering hope that, once and for all, the puzzle could be worked out and leave the four of them with satisfactory answers.

Morgan sat in the taxi with Emily and Tiff, feeling almost as happy as she did when she caught Olly whistling or dancing to music.

'Paige? Coming?' she called.

Paige was staring out to sea. She flinched, turned around and got into the car.

20

PAIGE

Tic tac toe, tic tac toe, she couldn't hold it in any more. The longer Paige withheld the truth, the deeper her deception cut, the more the others were going to blow when they found out.

It was so much harder than she'd recalled, to put on a false face, to stay in the background, to watch that she didn't get caught out.

The time had come to tell the others that Hugo didn't go by his old name any more.

She knew that for sure. What's more, she knew exactly where he was now. Because...

Tic. Tac. Toe.

Felix was Hugo.

21

MORGAN

The waiter delivered croissants and coffees in elegant white cups, each with a gold teaspoon and a tiny amaretto biscuit on the saucer.

'I can't eat,' Morgan announced, the buttery smell of the pastries almost making her retch. 'I could be moments away from meeting Hugo if he still works at Sea Breeze. What if he doesn't believe Olly is his?' Her hands shook as she went into her phone's gallery and pulled up a photo of her son. She'd show him that one. There'd be no denying it.

'We're here for you. We'll make him listen,' said Emily.

'From his point of view, you've come all the way to France to find him,' said Tiff. 'He's not going to imagine you're joking.'

The other three tucked in. Paige had spotted the café down a side road, yesterday, just before the taxi driver had turned into the beach car park. Somehow, they'd got out early this morning, after a late night talking about Dailsworth High. How the new head, Jasmine, back in the day, had made other pupils' lives a misery, too. She'd spread rumours that Imani and Milly were dating. One girl with a facial birthmark avoided her at all costs because Jasmine used to ask if her mum had drunk too much Vimto when she was pregnant. They'd chatted about their collective crush on PE teacher Mr Dane, how annoyed they'd been at themselves, it was such a cliché. They talked fondly of the librarian, Mrs Keen. One day, she'd told the girls never to change, to never lose sight of who they really were, never to bend themselves to fit some ideal. At that point, Tiff had gone very quiet, leading to the conversation petering out. The four of them went on their phones. Morgan had sent Olly the photo of Sylvie and Hugo's house earlier and he'd responded with a thumbs up and tonnes of questions. She texted everything Delphine had said. He replied with 'THANKS' in capital letters, and a shot of Lake Geneva.

They'd decided to beat the Monday morning traffic and have proper, strong coffee before the surf shop opened. With its dim lighting, dark wooden tables and floor, the olive walls, and the tall ceiling and gilt bar, the café was more suited to a Parisian setting.

Paige signalled to the waiter for a glass of water. When it arrived, she slid it over to Morgan. 'Drink this, you've no colour in your cheeks.' Paige folded her napkin in half, kept going until it was too thick to fold any more. She ran her finger along the edge and then lifted her chin. 'Reminds me of when I had my appendix out in my late teens. I looked deathly white despite my tinted foundation. Oh, and that swine flu outbreak in... 2009? I ran such a fever, I hallucinated.' She put down the napkin. 'How have you lot been health-wise?'

Why was Paige going on about illness? If she was trying to distract her, it wouldn't work. Not here. Not today. Morgan flicked through more photos of Olly.

'Can't complain,' said Emily. 'The usual nursing ailments – aching joints, stress. Nothing compared to what patients go in to A&E with.'

'I had a cervical cancer scare a few years ago, but a biopsy came up negative,' said Tiff. 'Oh and... my heart rate rocketed once after taking diet pills. Couldn't get to A&E quick enough,' she blurted.

'Well done for having the sense to get it checked out,' said Emily.

'Those things should be better regulated,' said Morgan.

'Must have been scary,' said Paige.

Tiff swallowed. 'I've never told a soul before. Anyone but you guys would call me an idiot and say I got what I deserved. It's like we've flashed back to the 2000s for a second.'

Morgan glowed inside.

'How about you, Morgan?' asked Paige.

'What? Oh...' She sipped her coffee. 'I developed a frozen shoulder once, that was extremely painful. The man I was seeing, Den, got me through it, doing a lot of the housework, giving me massages after a day on the till. Apart from that, I can only remember the times Olly has been poorly. He caught chicken pox at nursery and broke his arm at primary school, falling off a climbing frame. That's another reason he wants to find his father. Little things over the years, like his bad hay fever and double-jointed thumb... he's wanted to know if he's inherited certain conditions.'

Tiff's agent rang. She cut off the call and put away her phone.

'Could that have been a certain Joe?' asked Emily and playfully pushed Tiff's shoulder. 'You ignored a couple of calls last night.'

'That was my agent,' she said, ears turning red. 'Honestly, Joe is a friend, that's all. He's a drama teacher so we've got lots in common. He came over for takeout the other week as his oven wasn't working.' Dimples appeared. 'He almost left when he saw the tin of pineapple. Joe is a bit of a traditionalist when it comes to pizza.'

'That always was your favourite,' said Paige. 'Are you sure his oven was broken?'

'Yes, there's no case to solve here,' she said sharply and bit into a croissant.

Paige and Emily exchanged glances.

'Look, sorry,' said Tiff. 'I do actually sometimes feel a spark between me and Joe but I don't want to get involved.'

'Why not?' asked Morgan. For the first time, she stopped looking at her phone. 'You date other guys. See him casually, have a bit of fun.'

'I'd be worried it wouldn't stop there.'

'Isn't that a risk with all the men you see?' said Emily.

'No. The two I'm seeing at the moment, Carter and Marlon, both travel with work. I date who is nearest when I'm free. They understand the arrangement, that I want to keep things simple.'

'Do they know about each other?' asked Paige. 'Dating more than one guy sounds anything but straightforward.'

'No, but they wouldn't care.'

'How can you be so sure?' asked Morgan.

Tiff exhaled. 'You're all as bad as my parents, especially Mum. It's not enough that I've got the career she always wanted for me. Now she drops hints about a wedding and grandchildren.'

'Perhaps she just wants you to be happy, like she is with your dad?' said Paige. 'To have a companion, someone to lean on.'

'I totally understand where Tiff's coming from,' said Morgan. 'My mum still hasn't recovered from the fact I turned down Den's proposal.'

'A wedding is *never* going to happen,' said Tiff.

'Why?' pushed Emily.

She sighed. 'Jeez, one reason I love my job is that it's so much easier talking if the words are already learnt. Okay. You asked for it... after what happened with Hugo, after what happened with *you four*... the trust went and has never found its way back. That summer, I couldn't eat, I was so unhappy, felt so worthless, I lost two stone. In fact, Mum worried I was anorexic.' She gave a wry smile. 'I thought she'd be happy. The casting director at my drama club certainly was. Then I got into drama school on the back of talent, but also a low BMI and cheekbones.'

'I'm sorry,' said Emily.

Morgan and Paige nodded.

'Have you got any photos of Carter and Marlon?' asked Morgan, a glint of mischief in her eye. 'Those names sound... glamorous.'

Perspiration appeared on Tiff's forehead as if she'd been cast in an action movie and asked to do her own stunts. 'They may be fake names. Who cares?'

Confusion spread across the others' faces.

'I've not told anyone this before, either.' Tiff clenched her hands together. 'They're escorts. I pay them. I always use the same high-end agency. The fees are a bit pricey but I've never had a bad experience, have always felt safe and Carter and Marlon are both absolute gents. Gorgeous too. Charming. Sexy. This way, I call the shots and I can easily end it if I feelings develop.' Heat flooded into her cheeks once more. 'It's nothing sleazy. They just meet me for dinner or accompany me to events. Some-times... things go further, but that's by mutual agreement and money's never involved if that happens.'

Wow, thought Morgan. How exciting. Glamorous. Heartbreaking.

'I get it,' mumbled Emily.

'You do?' asked Tiff.

'Lewis found a way through the defences I put up when everyone else had failed. After the prom, after what happened with my mum... I had no intention of ever trusting a person again. I took a risk with Lewis and it paid off – until it didn't. But I don't regret anything, Tiff. Sometimes you have to take a chance. We've had happy years together.'

'You definitely won't get back together with Lewis?' asked Paige.

'He wants a divorce. Things haven't been right for ages.'

'What do *you* want?' said Morgan.

'That's a question I haven't asked myself for so long.'

'What about your mum?' asked Tiff. 'Come on, Emily. No more secrets. Why wasn't there a funeral?'

'Tic tac toe,' said Morgan and she smiled. 'Hugo's Olly's dad. Tiff dates escorts. Paige? Emily?'

Emily looked as if she'd just lost a patient.

'Shit, I'm only joking,' said Morgan, and reached across to pat Emily's hand.

'Tic tac toe was a strict rule, wasn't it,' murmured Paige, voice sounding uncharacteristically shaky, the colour drained out of her face. 'We never let each other off, because talking about secrets always made things better. But I'm not so sure, now I'm an adult.'

'What have you got to hide?' asked Tiff in a teasing voice.

Paige studied the others one by one, as if trying to judge their reaction to something she hadn't said yet.

'I still believe sharing secrets makes things better, easier,' said Morgan. 'I should have been upfront with Den from the start that I never wanted another child. It would have saved a lot of hurt.'

'Okay...' Paige wrapped her arms around herself. 'I've been meaning to tell you all from the moment we met up again. It's been so hard keeping this to myself, but please, hear me out...'

'We're here for you, whatever it is,' said Emily.

'You were always there for us,' said Tiff. 'Straight-as-a-die Paige. Up until Hugo tapped into our weaknesses, you were the most honest, eye-wateringly sometimes – but that's why we trusted you.'

'We should have seen it was simply Hugo who'd fucked up our group,' said Emily, 'if he could persuade you, Paige, to get devious, when you were so robust, so dependable. Sorry, Morgan, he may be Olly's dad, but Hugo was one slimy bastard.'

Paige crossed her legs. 'Perhaps he's changed.'

Going by Emily's face, Paige may as well have told her hospital waiting lists had halved and nurses' wages doubled.

'It used to be me who saw the best in everyone, Paige,' said Emily. 'But the truth is, some people haven't got a grain of decency.' She took Paige's hands. 'You can tell us, whatever it is.'

Paige swallowed. 'Okay. Right. My husband... Felix... you see... he's really...' She took Morgan's water and knocked back a large mouthful. 'He's really...'

The others made reassuring noises. Paige drank in the smiles she'd longed to see so many times, over the years.

'He's really... supportive. Things have been difficult as I can't have kids.' The words tumbled out and she broke eye contact with the others. 'I... I didn't like to mention it before in case any of you were having problems too, it could have been triggering. I didn't mean to hide anything when you were talking about motherhood, Morgan.' Paige looked at them again and wiped her brow with the napkin. 'Felix and I... we've been trying for eighteen months. I wish we hadn't left it so late, but we wanted to wait until we'd bought our first place, established our careers.'

'It can take couples that long,' said Emily. 'Have you talked to your doctor?'

'I can't face it in case they do tests and confirm my worst fears.'

'What does Felix say?' asked Tiff.

'He wants kids but says it doesn't matter if we can't. I'm the one he wants to spend the rest of his life with.'

'He sounds pretty perfect,' said Emily.

'He is, to me,' said Paige in an almost inaudible voice. 'Sorry. I don't know where all this came from. I haven't told anyone else. Not even Mum and Dad.'

'A bit like me with the escort business,' said Tiff and she sighed. 'Although, to be fair, apart from fretting that dating escorts would never lead to a wedding, Mum would probably worry and not understand the agency is safe, or think that the men might sell their stories if I find more success.' Tiff shook her said. 'They say being a parent is hard – being a child ain't a piece of cake, either.'

The four of them smiled with understanding, like they used to in the old days when one of them was moaning about a parent. How Morgan's mum and dad would make her earn every penny of her weekly allowance by setting the table, keeping her room tidy, weeding the borders. Whereas Paige's insisted on teaching her about boring grown-up financial matters, such as tax returns, pension pots and mortgage agreements. Emily's mum's latest escapades were the subject of her complaints, before she got ill, anyway. Like the time she went out in a tutu skirt, and how she'd filch Emily's sanitary products as she always forgot to stock up.

A sensation swelled within Morgan, toasty and comforting, as Paige talked about the nursery plans she'd made and the others made sympathetic noises. Morgan had hoped so much that the spirit of their friendship was still there, the four of them cheering each other on, coaxing out problems, offering support.

'Tic, tac, toe, okay, my turn,' said Emily quietly, and she placed her palms together. However, her watch caught her eye. 'Wow. Look at the time.'

'I need to get to that shop,' said Morgan. 'I don't want to miss any chance of meeting him. Sorry to stall you, Emily... you'll tell us later, right?'

Emily had already drained her cup and stood up. Morgan got to her feet too and grabbed her coat. Emily hastily followed as if she'd been let off an extra shift. Paige said she'd be a minute and Tiff followed the other two outside.

22

PAIGE, EMILY, TIFF

Paige sat in front of her empty coffee cup.

'Madame?' The waiter gave a small bow and handed her a glass of water with a slice of lemon in it.

Her eyes stung as she drank. *Don't be kind to me. Don't.* Paige really had meant to tell the others about Felix but had failed again. When the women had met in New Chapter Café in Deansgate and Morgan had sat on the floor outside the toilets, Morgan had left her handbag and Paige had taken it back to the table. Her eyes had fallen on the official-looking letter sticking out, and one word on it had jumped out. She'd had to go outside to get some fresh air. Shocking as that word had been to read, it made sense of why Morgan had wanted, so badly, to meet up again and spend time rebuilding the friendships, if possible.

And now it felt even harder to reveal Felix's identity, now that the four of them were closing the space between them. So she'd blurted out another secret instead, about her worries that she'd never have a baby. Her mum had got pregnant days after coming off contraception. She always used this to make sure Paige understood that as long as they were taken properly, precautions were highly effective and gave women choices. Paige's gran got pregnant on her honeymoon. Paige never thought she'd have problems conceiving. At thirty-five, had she left it too late? Both she and Felix only wanted one child, so where was the harm in delaying? Hers was a happy childhood, close to Mum and Dad in a way she might not have been with a sibling. Felix's hadn't been so straightforward. His parents had struggled enough coping with one child so he balked at having more than that.

'Of course we haven't left it too late,' said Felix, the last time they'd discussed it. 'All in good time.'

'I'll be called a geriatric mother on my medical records.'

He'd raised an eyebrow and wiggled it. 'There's nothing elderly about your eggs or my sperm.'

Paige had done the research. She ate well. Didn't drink too much. Or smoke and suffer much stress – not until recently. Lots of women got pregnant in their thirties. Now Olly proved Felix's fertility was fine so maybe all this meant that there was actually an issue with Paige's 'wiring', as her gran used to call it. She loved Felix. He filled a gap she didn't know existed. With her doting parents, the lifestyle that left her wanting for nothing, life had felt complete. Felix tore up that story, as if it were a first draft that needed rewriting, the money, the image, fell away, and together, they'd rewritten it. Now, wanting a child had done the same again. This was another reason she'd put off seeing the doctor. She didn't want being childless to become this big thing between Felix and her.

'I'm sure it will be fine,' he'd said. 'But if having a baby is going to take more work, I'm here, by your side, all of the way. Diet, tablets, injections, whatever it takes, for either of us, however long, whatever the cost. We're in this together. If we don't get the outcome we want, there are options. We'll explore every avenue...'

Paige met Hugo – Felix – again, for the first time in 2016. At twenty-eight years old it had been twelve years since she'd last seen him, at the prom. She was coming out of Harvey Nicks. Ahead of her was a line of wooden festive market huts, the air smelt of hot chocolate and mulled wine, people bustling with bags full of artisan pickles and cheeses. It was a crisp Saturday afternoon, the week before Christmas. Paige had been working so hard, she'd not bought any presents yet. She walked forwards towards a gin tasting stall, taking off her gloves. She'd tried a couple of gin samples. It was her flatmate's favourite drink. She stood next to a tall man in front of her talking to the gin maker who handed him a plastic bag containing two bottles. The gin maker made a comment and the man laughed.

A punch to her stomach.

She'd only heard a laugh like that a few times, in private, like trickling water that started to run faster, gurgling in an infectious manner. The floppy hairstyle had gone, replaced with a buzz cut. Instead of school uniform, he wore a fur-lined cutler jacket, tight jeans and trainers. There was no mistaking the copper eyes, the wide lips that reminded Paige both of vindictive words and passionate kisses. However, his stance had changed. The slightly hunched shoulders no one else would probably have noticed had been replaced by a straight back. The hands that were often shoved in his blazer pocket, or that touched his nose or pulled on his ears whilst talking were by his sides, palms open. As the gin maker leant forwards, chatting about distillation processes and botanicals, he leant forwards too, head tilted, unlike the Hugo from 2004 who'd lean back when people talked to him and nod whilst looking in a different direction.

Giddy, Paige span around and headed right, towards the Tudor pub, the Old Wellington, not really focusing on where she was going. However, a hand gently caught her arm.

'Excuse me, you dropped one of your gloves.'

Crap, crap, crap. She came to a halt. Hugo appeared in front of her.

'Paige? Paige Forbes?' His mouth fell open.

'Hugo,' she'd said, politely and took the glove. 'Thank you.'

'Actually it's Felix now,' he said. 'Long story. Wow. How are you?'

'Fine. You?' she'd said stiffly.

He'd held her gaze for what felt like an hour. She held his back.

'I'm good thanks. Or was. Until seconds ago. Look... I have to tell you this: I've never shaken off the shame about our Year Eleven and the prom.' He exhaled. 'I'm more sorry than words could ever express for the way I treated you, Morgan, Tiff and Emily.'

Oh.

'If I could take back what I did, I would in a heartbeat. Are you still in touch with them?'

'What do you think?'

They stood in silence. Eventually, he pointed behind her. 'Can I buy you a hot chocolate? Explain?'

'What's the point, Hu... Felix? What's done is done.'

'Just half an hour? I'll even throw in marshmallows.' He'd gazed straight at her. 'There was a reason I behaved like I did. I couldn't share it at the time. Not that I'm making excuses...'

'Fifteen minutes.'

Wondering how Felix was getting on in Dubai, wishing she could talk to him about what was happening, Paige finished the water the waiter had brought over, left a tip and went out into the fragrant sea air, so different from the scent of Manchester's city centre that had notes of cannabis and petrol fumes. She lit a cigarette. The nicotine calmed her nerves as the other women edged nearer to finding the man they thought was still called Hugo. Paige didn't know how much the surf shop owner knew.

She took a long drag. Since meeting up with Morgan again, finding out her friend was a mother, since hearing about Olly... all of this had only magnified Paige's fears around her fertility. Olly had turned Morgan's life upside down. What if that happened to her marriage? What if Felix lost interest in having more babies? Even though it was only for a few weeks, what if he couldn't forgive her for keeping his son a secret?

The way Felix spoke about that kid Jamal, at the Gorton community project, Paige had no doubt that he'd make a great dad. God, she loved him so much, wanted to ring him right then. But Felix might even leave Dubai immediately, risking everything he and the company had worked for, risking their much-needed charity work. It was all such a mess. Telling him about Olly would be like revealing a positive pregnancy test. A tear ran down her cheek. Except she wasn't the mother, Morgan was. The child wasn't a baby, he was a young man who looked so very much like his father. Paige was happy for Olly that he'd meet his dad. And Paige was happy for Felix because Olly sounded like a good lad. She just wasn't sure if she was happy for Paige.

* * *

Emily looked behind her. Walking quickly, Paige caught them up. They crossed the car park and headed to the surf shop. *No regrets.* Emily was still digesting the comment she'd made earlier about Lewis. It had surprised her. The others had got her thinking about the divorce. As soon as Lewis had mentioned it, she'd assumed it was a done deal, not really asked herself if there was anything she could do about it. She loved Lewis for lots of reasons, one being the way he was with her father. From the very first day they'd met, Lewis had sensed a rawness, a deep sense of hurt in her dad, which had made it easier for Emily to tell Lewis the truth about her mum. The two men talked lorries and ambulances in a way Emily didn't – about important things, they'd say, like engine sizes, petrol consumption, those cheese-scented hanging air fresheners in the shape of bare feet. When she announced they'd got engaged, she wasn't sure who Dad was more pleased for, Emily or himself.

However, away from her home, from England, without him, Emily could see how much her relationship with Lewis had changed. The last few years had turned them into different people.

Or that's what it felt like. Tears threatened.

She'd clung onto their old house, not moved his things out of their bedroom, avoided the first lawn mow of the year because he enjoyed doing that, she still kept one of his favourite beers at the back of the fridge. After too many wines, she'd lie down on the sofa, face right next to Smudge, and whisper that the couple were just going through a rough patch. Smudge often replied by patting Emily on the nose, *tap, tap, tap*, as if to say, *There, there, sooner or later you'll face up to what's best for both of you.*

Too much damage had been done. They both needed that fresh start. The fallout from 2020 was still happening, she'd seen it in hospitals with waiting lists, depressed colleagues, patients with long-term after-effects. Her marriage was another casualty to add to the list, because recent stressful times had brought up old issues for Emily.

Wanting was the wrong word when it came to divorce, or hers at least. Perhaps *acceptance* was more appropriate, even when the best decision was often the hardest.

Emily continued walking. Her steps should have felt easier, now she'd come to a decision, thanks to the perspective being away from Manchester had given her. However, instead they felt heavier than ever as she a followed her old teenage friends into the surf shop.

* * *

Tiff squeezed Morgan's arm. If facing meeting Hugo was giving her stage fright, for Morgan, it must have felt like the night before debuting on Broadway. They headed towards the cash desk and walked around a couple of young men who were athletic-looking with thick heads of hair, laughing. One clapped the other on the back. Good physiques. Good fun. Their vibe reminded her of Carter and Marlon.

How had Tiff's love life become so shallow? She'd dived into the deep end with Hugo and almost drowned. She'd been caught out a couple of times since as well. Take the third escort she'd ever met, Devon, with his sexy afro fade, his ability to make her find humour in the most inopportune moments. Up until then, sex had been a serious business. Devon opened her eyes to the fun side. Like the time she'd got bad cramp and pushed him off a little too hard. He went flying onto the floor and stayed there laughing whilst she frantically apologised. Or when, in the throes of passion, they couldn't get a condom packet open, and neither of them could keep a straight face. He was never in a rush to leave, either, and sometimes they'd order room service. She ghosted him in the end on all social platforms. Hated herself for it. But he might have hurt her like Hugo and the girls had.

Her mind drifted to Morgan with that Den. Paige with Felix. Emily with Lewis.

Joe had messaged her on Facebook last night. Said he was coming up to Manchester for lunch, the Saturday of Easter weekend, to meet an old uni friend who was setting up his own drama school and wanted Joe to be involved. Would she like to meet up on the Saturday night for dinner? He'd booked a hotel, was staying over, and could do with someone to talk through his friend's proposition, as apparently Joe would need to give a swift answer. Tiff had read the message umpteen times.

Now she realised why.

Tiff missed him. Joe felt like a safe place. She'd only had that once before in her life, outside of family: with Morgan, Paige and Emily. New actor friends appeared more attractive, more accomplished, and Tiff could never shake off a sense of competitiveness. Whereas Joe kept it real. He worked in an inner-city London school. He saw children at the sharp edge of life in the 2020s, with their trousers too short and mouldy bread for lunch, with lack of internet access out of hours. Yet it didn't put him off. Quite the reverse: it fuelled him. More than once, she'd crossed his path as he carried a bag of food into work to hand out free to certain pupils. He volunteered at the breakfast club. She was... fond of him, because of this.

Tic tac toe. Aside from the escorts, there was something Tiff hadn't told the girls, something much closer to home. She wished Joe was here, to talk to, about her secret to do with the new headteacher, Jasmine. Tiff took out her phone and was about to look at his message again, when a man started talking.

23

MORGAN

'*Bonjour Mesdames.*'

'*Bonjour, parlez-vous anglais?*' asked Morgan.

The man in his fifties, with short, grey hair, tanned, lean, in a striped shirt and shorts, bowed his head. 'Of course. Millions of tourists visit the south of France every year. No English would make my life difficult. How can I help?'

'Is Hugo in today, please?' Morgan squeezed the words out. The man frowned. She pointed to the photo on the wall. Tiff and Emily were already there, staring, while Paige was pacing up and down. 'Hugo Black. He's older now. A former neighbour of his said he worked here. Or is he at one of your other shops?'

'Ah, yes! What a much-loved member of staff, so charming with the customers. Sales went up whenever he was in.'

Morgan wished Paige would stand still.

'I'm sorry but Hugo and I have lost touch,' he said.

'He doesn't work here any longer?' Was this the universe warning Morgan off once more? Emily and Tiff shot her sympathetic glances. 'When did he leave?'

'Let's see... 2014, the February, that's right, just after a terrible storm in

Brittany. The woman who replaced Hugo came from there, she'd only been in the job one week. We were all so shocked when we saw it on the news, but I remember how especially upset she was.'

'Right...' Morgan didn't know whether she felt disappointed or relieved. She wanted to see Hugo again. She didn't.

'Did he get another job in the area?' asked Morgan.

The man rubbed his forehead. 'You are good friends of his, *oui*?'

'Not exactly... we went to school with him, and... he's my son's father,' she replied. 'It's complicated.'

'Isn't love always?' he said and folded his arms. 'I don't know if I should share—'

'This is a wonderful shop,' exclaimed Emily. 'The breaking wave mural is fantastic and it's really customer friendly, the way you've set out all the products. The free coffee machine is genius too, gives it a really homely atmosphere. Hugo must have been reluctant to leave this oasis.'

'That's very kind,' said the man, chest puffed out as if he'd surfed the highest wave ever. 'It's my life's work. I put a lot of time into choosing the decor and floor design. Hugo helped me refresh it before he left.'

'Wouldn't it be great to know where Hugo is, and that he's okay?' said Tiff. 'You must have been curious over the years. I would have been.'

'It's true. I've Googled his name and looked on social media, but nothing has ever come up. He was never on Facebook or Instagram when he worked here. We talked about it once. Hugo enjoyed scrolling as much as anyone else, and was excellent at keeping the company's platforms up to date, but said he didn't feel comfortable posting private stuff. I didn't like to ask why. So anything could have happened to him since he left here. I have no idea.'

Morgan held onto the glass counter by the till. For the first time, she considered the possibility that Hugo might have died. Despite everything, she didn't wish him ill and Olly would never forgive her if it was too late to meet his father.

'I did wonder if he was in trouble,' said the man and he rubbed one arm. 'He left very quickly, you see. Came to me in a hurry, one morning. Said...' A conflicted expression crossed his face. The man stopped talking and looked at the photo frame.

'Please, go on,' said Morgan. 'We've come a long way to find him. It's important not only to me, but to Hugo too. He doesn't know he's a father.'

'*Bon*... okay... Hugo said... someone was after him and he had to move away from the area immediately. Hugo was upset – and angry, but wouldn't explain. I worried, if this person or people found him, it could turn nasty, if this was the reason he'd never posted anything about himself online. I gave him a month's pay upfront. At first he refused but I insisted.'

'Any idea where he went?' asked Tiff.

The man scratched the stubble on his chin. 'He gave me no details but might have taken up this job offer he got. A few weeks earlier, an English tourist came in who ran a sea sports school in England, at one of the top surfing destinations on the north Cornwall coast. He'd seen Hugo out on the waves. He owned a seaside activities business and wanted Hugo to work there. His was based in a prime location, not far from a big International Surfing Centre. He was keen to build his brand and turn it into a solid competitor. However, Hugo adored the Fréjus area, our Riviera lifestyle. This tourist made him take his number, nevertheless, told him to get in touch if he wanted more money and career prospects. I practically pushed the man out of the door at that point.' The shop owner smiled. 'On the way out, he listed the water sports they taught –kayaking, canoeing, paddleboarding, beach volleyball as well and they had an outdoor gym. Hugo was a bright young man. If he really needed to get away, it's possible he went there, to broaden his skill set. I could tell he was interested.'

'Where exactly was the man's business?' asked Morgan.

'The name of the beach sounded like our famous mistral wind...' said the man.

Tiff and Emily searched online, Paige looking over their shoulders.

'Fistral Beach, Newquay. It must be that,' said Emily and pointed to her phone's screen. She scrolled for several minutes. 'Yes, there's a big international surfing school there and... nearby, this must be it, a smaller school called Ocean Activity Centre. It offers all those water sports you mentioned. There's also a couple of smaller schools that just teach surfing.'

They thanked the man and booked a taxi. With the owner's permission, Morgan took a snap of the photo on the wall. Paige was quiet on the way back to the villa, in the taxi, and Morgan passed over her bottle of water.

Paige drank it back greedily, said she'd not slept well and that it was catching up with her, but that she'd be fine after something to eat and a rest. The other three made sandwiches, insisting Paige take it easy. They talked about how keen Delphine and the surf shop owner had been to pass on their best to Hugo. But then he always had been charismatic. After lunch, they sat around the pool. Morgan talked about her job and how challenging dealing with customers had become over the last couple of years.

'Customers can be annoying at the best of times,' continued Morgan. 'Guess how many times one rolls up with a full trolley and says, "I only came in for one item"? I'm expected to laugh *every* time.' The others chuckled as Morgan pulled a face.

'That's literally me,' said Paige. 'And if a product doesn't scan I always say, "It must be free then."'

'Yes!' said Morgan and she groaned, playfully punching Paige on the arm.

'Well, you wouldn't believe the complaints people turn up with in A&E, like kids sticking popcorn kernel in their ears... and worse,' said Emily.

'Love that!' said Tiff. 'I shared a bag of popcorn with Keanu Reeves once, you know. Total fluke. He thought I was a producer. I played along as long as I could.'

'Holy crap, Tiff! What was he like?' exclaimed Morgan.

'As good-looking as on the screen?' asked Paige.

'As kind as everyone says he is?' Emily leant forwards.

Tiff beamed. 'Yes, he was down-to-earth, humble, unostentatious – and an absolute God.'

'I might text Lewis and tell him,' said Emily and she took out her phone, 'he's a huge fan of the *Matrix* movies.'

'Joe is too,' said Tiff. 'He made me hot chocolate to wheedle out as much information as possible.'

'Text him,' said Paige with authority. 'You want to.'

Morgan exchanged glances with Emily and Tiff. Small smiles. This was the Paige she was familiar with and Morgan lapped up the sense of familiarity. Paige always had called her, Tiff and Emily out for not facing their truths.

'You reckon?' said Tiff.

The four of them pored over Tiff's phone as if they were back in 2004. Emily spotted the word Manchester in Joe's last message and Tiff explained he was coming up this weekend. The three others chorused that they should definitely meet up. Tiff went to type but changed her mind. In the end, Paige grabbed the phone and ran inside, locked herself in the toilet and stayed in for several minutes, despite Tiff hammering on the door, the others laughing. Finally, Paige strode out and casually passed the phone back.

'I've said you'd love to meet him in Manchester that Saturday, and put a kiss on the end.'

Tiff looked outraged. Emily wiped her eyes, Morgan held her ribs, Paige airily smiled. They collapsed onto the sofa and armchairs.

Paige researched flights. 'You can't book direct from Nice to Newquay. We'll have to fly to Gatwick. From there, it takes nine hours by train or five by car. So it's best to fly again. All in, with the change at Gatwick, if we have an early start, I can get us there tomorrow evening. Then that's the last air miles used up.'

'Are you sure you don't mind draining your supply?' asked Morgan.

'No problem. Felix's current trip to Dubai will already have started a new pot. But let's try ringing that Ocean Activity Centre first. No point going there if he's not there now.'

There was no reply. They rang the other surf shops in Fistral just in case Hugo had arrived in the area and found work elsewhere, but neither could help.

They couldn't waste Paige's air miles for nothing. 'Let's leave it and just go home,' said Morgan, putting on her brightest voice.

Paige studied her face. 'No. I love Cornwall and haven't had a break from work for a while. Let's do it. Like I said originally, Felix and I will never use up all our air miles.' She looked at Emily and Tiff, her eyebrow raised.

'It's not like I've got anything better to do,' said Emily.

'And we might find him...' said Tiff.

Paige gave the thumbs-up to Morgan who, looking relieved, swiped up and down on her phone, scrolling through hotels. 'There's a little B&B not too far from Fistral Beach. I could book two rooms, if that suits everyone?'

'Yes. It won't cost much split between four,' said Emily.

Morgan's cheeks reddened. 'I'll pay. I don't assume you all—'

'No you won't,' said Emily firmly. She looked at the other two, who agreed.

'I'm so grateful you three are on this journey with me,' said Morgan, looking as if a customer had spoken highly of her service to the manager. It happened more often than her colleagues approved of. 'Thank you.' Her voice wavered. 'I'm so very thankful.'

Emily's phone bleeped and she smiled.

'Good news?' asked Paige.

'Oh... just Lewis. He's sent me a *Matrix* GIF and a wow face. He also liked the photo of the beach I sent him. Said it reminded him of our honeymoon and first time in Greece. We chose a peaceful area, so far so good. But then most of the restaurants closed early, our bedroom aircon didn't work and our toilet got blocked.' She smiled. 'It's a while since we've laughed about something together.' Emily put away her phone. 'How about a meal out tonight? I couldn't provide flights or a villa but I can stretch to a dinner and bottle of wine. I might need to borrow some make-up and shampoo, though. I didn't pack much.'

'Remember how we used to love alcopops?' said Tiff. 'Your mum was always happy for us to raid her stock, Emily. She was so cool.'

'Yeah. Booze didn't affect her treatment, that's what she said.' Emily grimaced. 'She had quite old-school tastes in alcohol, looking back, cocktails out like Pina Coladas, Martinis or alcopops at home. She'd get them cheap from a bargain booze shop down the road and drink them in front of the telly at night with a bar of chocolate.'

'She used to drink Babycham as well, I remember,' said Morgan, 'my gran's favourite.'

'My mum always did like to get attention for being different,' said Emily and sank into deep thought for a few moments. 'You liked Reef, didn't you?'

'Yes,' Morgan replied. 'It was fizz free. Paige preferred Apple Sourz.'

'I did – it wasn't as sweet as the others. Emily, you liked Two Dogs.'

'Always a fan of lemonade, and the label was cute. Tiff, didn't you drink... Bacardi Breezers?'

'Sure did. They sounded so Hollywood.'

Emily disappeared into the kitchen and came back with a bottle of wine from the night before. She poured the last inch into a glass. Knocked it back.

'Right. Who's going to do something with my face?'

24

MORGAN

They found a pizzeria a short distance away, with an open kitchen, the chef spinning the dough in the air that was filled with the aroma of garlic, herbs, and tomatoes. The server wasn't in a waistcoat, nor did chandeliers beam out light, but disdain hung in the air from Tiff asking if she could have pineapple on her pizza.

'Wine, Morgan?' asked Paige and lifted the bottle.

She shook her head, preferring water.

'Everything okay?' asked Paige. 'Back in the day, you hardly ever turned down alcohol. Mind you, opportunities to drink it were far less common, when we were at school.' She gave an awkward smile.

'Just thirsty,' she said and smiled back. 'Tell us, Paige, about your work. You teach companies how to improve the way they deal with people?'

'Effectively, yes. Non-verbal communication is like our superpower; it enables us to influence others secretly. Also, if you learn how to read it, you can tap into people's thoughts and feelings just from their gestures. Say, for example, you work for a PR agency and are pitching to a potential client. You tell them you can double their profit in six months, but if you're nervous, your body language won't match your words, and the likelihood is the client will sign elsewhere and...'

Morgan listened to her friend, full of admiration for her drive, her work ethic, despite her well-off background. Morgan wasn't a daydreamer but occasionally imagined winning the lottery. She'd buy Mum and Dad a detached house, with decking and hot tub, like they'd always talked about, one for her and Olly too, with a telescope room in the loft for him. They'd travel to Iceland, Olly had always wanted to see the Northern Lights. She'd never craved fancy possessions, only things you couldn't see, like job satisfaction and Olly's happiness.

'I love this silk blouse you've lent me,' said Emily to Tiff. 'Even though it's a bit of a squeeze. Is the showbiz industry really still as harsh when it comes to appearance?'

Tiff sipped the Merlot. 'I was once told to lose a stone in two weeks. I tried practical things – went to the gym twice a day, only drank juice, manifested a size six. In the end, with no energy, stomach pains and light-headedness, I pushed back and lost the part.'

At least it didn't matter what Morgan looked like for her job. In fact, quite the opposite. These days, customers often didn't even meet her eye, packing the reduced and essential line goods she swiped through, paying the card reader, dragging their feet away as they studied the receipt.

'I reckon I've put on a stone the last couple of months,' said Emily. 'Too much sleep. Too much Netflix. Too much wine, according to Lewis. My therapist wants me to get out at least once a day, even if it's just for a walk around the block.'

'Therapist?' asked Paige.

'Yeah. Work has... screwed me up. Don't get me wrong, I loved my job for years. The emergency department is a unique environment. The pay-off is often fast, seeing patients arrive in distress, waving them off hours later, more cheerful and mended. You see the very best of human nature – brave patients, supportive friends and family who'll go above and beyond to get their loved one fixed, and colleagues giving more than 100 per cent. It's high-pace, high-stress. A big adrenaline rush of a career – combined with gentler moments, like holding a patient's hand, softening the shock of having their clothes cut off, of being examined despite the hurt. Looking after traumatised relatives.' She stopped for breath. 'But it's all gone to shit in recent years. The final straw was New Year's Eve. A man came in drunk, he stank of whiskey, couldn't walk straight. He didn't want treatment. He'd come in to throw abuse. He cornered me, by reception, said it was my fault his wife had died here, the week previously. The ambulance had been delayed, then she had to wait in a corridor for eight hours. She'd been coughing up blood, didn't get to intensive care until it was too late. She died from sepsis. He said we didn't care.' Her voice caught. 'Sorry to kill the atmosphere. I've not even spoken that much to my therapist.'

'So you've left for good?' asked Morgan gently.

'Yes, although my manager assumes I'm going back and Lewis says nursing is who I am.' She shrugged. 'I've always felt he knew me so well, but lately... We used to seem like such a good match. Looking back, he brought me out of myself. I was still a little shy in my twenties, but Lewis, he... he gave me confidence, laughed at my jokes, wore the jumpers I knitted even though the arms were always too long, even though his mates used to tease him about them in the pub.' Her face lit up for a second. 'I knitted him a pair of boxer pants for a joke, one Valentine's Day. Every Valentine's Day after that, he wore them to work, even though they shrank and developed holes.'

'What are his family like?' asked Paige. Emily had so many happy memories with her husband. Like she did with Felix. Paige couldn't bear the thought of losing him.

'His parents welcomed me with open arms. They've always reminded me of your mum and dad, who always took an interest in us and invited us to their fancy parties. I remember your mum chatting to me about nature, and she'd ask Tiff about her acting and your dad liked to throw maths puzzles at Morgan.'

Paige's parents had been great. Their lifestyle couldn't have been more different from hers, but Morgan could always relax and be herself in their presence. Whereas Tiff's irritated Morgan, because she could see how they put pressure on their daughter, probably without even realising it. As for Emily's, she hardly ever saw her dad, and Emily's mum... she was a good laugh but sometimes made jokes at the expense of Emily, and Morgan didn't like that either, didn't understand it.

Their pizzas arrived. The four of them cleared their plates. Afterwards, having studied the dessert menu, they shared ice cream.

'Is afternoon tea still a thing in your family, Morgan?' asked Paige. 'Your mum always made it on your birthday. We'd pile around after school and she'd have made a batch of scones, and as a treat got clotted cream.'

'Loved those,' said Tiff. 'She'd make tiny sandwiches cut into squares and triangles.'

'With white bread especially for me,' said Emily.

There was never much money when Morgan was growing up, but Mum and Dad always gave her a great birthday. 'Me and Olly carried on the tradition when he was little. An alternative one, Mum didn't approve. He'd want peanut butter or crisp sandwiches, and scones slathered with Nutella.'

Tiff drained her wine glass. 'I need to stretch my legs or I'll never sleep. It was only five minutes in the taxi, let's walk back. I've got Google Maps.' She was about to put on her coat when her phone pinged. She read the message. 'Joe,' she said. 'We're meeting on Saturday. He's suggested dinner at Mowgli's. Joe loves Indian food so clearly he's looked up Mancunian curry houses online. I'm assuming we'll be back by then. Tomorrow's only Tuesday.'

'Wit woo,' said Emily and took the phone. 'Ooh, a return kiss on the end.'

Paige wasn't messaging with Felix, but then he was away on an intense business trip. Den used to message Morgan with all the emojis, the hearts, flowers, kissing faces, a side he kept hidden at work, with his cutthroat sales pitches. But it wasn't Morgan, not really, and she'd just send funny GIFs back. Den never said anything but she hoped he was with someone now who appreciated the romantic frills.

Emily paid and they went outside. The wind that had blown since they arrived at the villa had dropped. They headed up the hill... arms linked. Step by step, they huddled closer, stopping to admire the intricate, wrought-iron gate leading to a cemetery; it had spikes on the top and a circular pane of flowers worked into its centre. The church stood behind, daunting in the moonlight, with its sharp spire, grotesque gargoyles looking down from under its eaves, and, as Emily pointed out, bats swooping above it.

'Let's go in,' whispered Tiff, as if the dead might be listening in. 'I love reading gravestones. They do say your only legacy is the way you make people feel, and that's reflected in what relatives have engraved.'

'But the writing will be in French,' said Morgan.

'We've got our GCSE to fall back on – and Google translate.'

The gate creaked as they went in and Morgan felt like a schoolgirl again, stealthily making her way to the unused basement to meet the girls, being careful not to let anyone follow her. She breathed in the smell of damp soil, the cemetery lit up by night lights on the church. The grass was overgrown and covered many of the graves, along with bunches of dead flowers. The occasional plot stood out for being weeded and adorned with ornaments or windmills. They passed worn gravestones, decades old, some of the letters unreadable now. Tiff stopped in front of a rather grand affair, a vault made out of pale-brown stone. She took out her phone and looked up some words.

'The stars shone more brightly because he was here. Jean Paul Blanchet, 1950 to 2019,' she said. They walked on and stopped in front of an arc top headstone, moss clinging to parts that had crumbled. 'Goodnight Sweetheart. Until we meet again. Annette Charvet, 1911 to 1975.' They turned to the right and the back of the church. Tiff stopped by a square top headstone, by a bench. '*Allé au bowling*, Claude Dupont, 1960-something to 2011... I love that. "Gone bowling".' Tiff bent down and pulled out a weed that was obscuring the date.

'1968. That's the year my mum was born,' said Emily, and she sat down on the bench. The others joined her. She linked her arm through Tiff's, on her left, Morgan's on her right. Paige gave her an encouraging nod as if she understood Emily was about to open up. 'We didn't arrange a funeral for Mum because, well... you see...' She took a deep breath. 'I'm so sorry I never told you. I can see now that... that it was a huge thing to keep secret. You see my mum... she was never even ill.'

'*What?*' said Tiff.

'Not ill?' said Paige, her jaw dropped.

'But the tubes... the weight loss...' Morgan stuttered. Was Emily tipsy?

'Yes... and on the other hand, there was the laughter as loud as ever, the booze she kept drinking, the way she always insisted she was fine to go to hospital on her own, the way she never lost interest in make-up and nail varnish, not even for one day.' Emily's breath hitched. 'All the signs of her deception were there.'

'Surely she wouldn't pull a prank like that. I mean, she was your *mother*,' said Paige.

Morgan shivered. Emily had to be lying. Or mistaken. Perhaps she was on drugs. If not... was it possible that Emily had deceived her friends, day in, day out, for *months and months*? But then Morgan looked back through a different lens. The laughter, the gossip, every time they went around, the glamorous look, the content expression across Emily's mum's face as she watched her favourite TV shows. Morgan had never once seen her wince with pain, wipe her eyes or steal away to her bedroom when the girls made a noise... If what Emily said was true, then it was her mum who'd really carried out this deception on such a huge scale.

'She was only my mother in name,' said Emily in an emotionless tone. 'Looking back, she used Dad for money, tolerated us kids as long as we didn't impinge on her social life. Mum took us for mugs: me, my dad, my younger brother. When she first fessed up, it made sense in a warped way. She'd never liked doing the cleaning or cooking. This way, she got me to do all the skivvying.'

To make up cancer to get out of housework? Morgan shook her head. That would be like finding out if aliens existed, only so that you could play *Alien vs Predator* more effectively. It made no sense, to do something that big, for such a trivial reason.

'But then she finally told us the real motive – in front of Dad. Didn't give him space to save face. I hated her for that.' Emily inhaled. 'She admitted to having an affair with a customer from the betting shop. The supposed trips to The Christie were to shag him. He worked shifts, she fitted in around his routine. So that's when she gave up her job, and she wanted to look her best, so she made me prepare salads and stir fries, all of a sudden, to lose pounds, not fight the "cancer". I even spent ages knitting her a scarf, for if her treatment changed and her hair ever fell out. I didn't tell her that was the reason, but she didn't like it anyway, said she wasn't over eighty yet. Apparently woolly scarves aren't sexy.'

With her hands, Tiff acted out her head exploding in disbelief. 'And I thought I was a good actress!'

'What self-belief to think she could carry it off,' said Paige and she took Emily's hand.

'It's like some misleading tabloid headline,' said Morgan, 'where the cancer turns out to be in a pet hamster. What a betrayal.'

'You're not far wrong,' continued Emily. 'I'm sure a story in the newspaper is what gave her the idea. She talked once about an article she'd read, a couple of years previously, about parents who faked their kids having cancer, to get money, to get attention. It was odd that she sounded impressed.' Emily's nose wrinkled as if she'd been asked to clean up after a patient with a bad stomach upset. '"I'm in love," she said, as if that excused everything. Mum said she couldn't help it, was only human. She told me I'd understand one day. I never have. My mother and lover boy then disappeared off to Spain. She's still running a bar in Marbella, I think.'

'I'm sorry, so sorry, at what you must have gone through,' said Tiff. 'But...' She pursed her lips.

'What? asked Emily. 'No more secrets, right? Tiff?'

'Okay... why didn't you tell us? This is *huge*. Why keep it to yourself?'

'Shame, I guess,' she muttered. 'It was easier. I wanted to forget about her when I was with you. And how would I have found the words, Tiff? It sounded so ridiculous. So horrific. I think I was in shock at the beginning, just getting through each day as best I could.

'But we were *best friends*. Buzz and Woody.' Tiff's voice shook. 'What other secrets were we all hiding – on top of our affairs with Hugo?'

Morgan held her palms vertical in the air. 'Let's not do this. We... we're just getting to know each other again, beginning to get some perspective on what happened with him. As adults. Women. Those young girls made mistakes, of course they did, and they should have been allowed to, it's part of the process of growing up.'

Tiff shook her head. 'Not ones like this, Morgan. It's massive. You talked about giving her clothes to a charity shop, Emily, about your dad having bereavement counselling. I'd get that for when the other pupils asked questions, and even the teachers. But us?'

'He did get that counselling,' she said shortly and took her hand away from Paige's. 'There are different types of grief, different ways of losing someone.'

'In adulthood, life becomes complex and makes you behave in ways you normally wouldn't...' said Paige, voice sounding strained. 'But in our teens, life was a lot simpler. You wanted to tell us the truth, right Emily?'

'No, I bloody well didn't! The whole situation made me look like an idiot. And *simple*, back then? Not for me it wasn't,' said Emily. 'Living with honest, straight-as-a-die Lewis has been far more straightforward than living with my mother ever was. Look, it wasn't about you three,' said Emily, in a tense voice. 'You look so hurt, Tiff, but I was in absolute bits. Rock bottom. No further to fall. So was my dad. My brother too. School and our society were an escape, the one place I could pretend none of the deception had happened.' Her voice cracked. 'If I could have told you, I would, but some things are so... so huge, so overwhelming. I had nightmares for weeks afterwards. With you guys, I just wanted to pretend none of it had happened, because there was no way of getting away from it at home, with Dad zombie-like and my little brother crying.'

'You still lied,' Tiff said. 'Like Hugo did. I'm sorry. I am sympathetic. In fact, there are no words to describe how much I'd like to go back in time, to be there for you. But it's a lot to take in.'

Emily gasped. 'You dare compare me to *him*? The only thing Hugo lost was the football captaincy and stupid prom crown.'

An odd expression crossed Paige's face.

Emily folded her arms. 'You're really going to make me do this, aren't you, Tiff? It may be nineteen years later but I've not forgotten. And I'm not that naïve teenager any more who used to find it difficult to stick up for herself. I won't be portrayed as the only one of us who kept a terrible secret.'

The indignation drained out of Tiff's face. She loosened the top of her jacket.

'What are you talking about?' asked Morgan.

'Emily?' said Paige.

Tiff stood up and wiped her hands on her trousers. 'Emily, don't, look, I...'

'Don't? After you berating me? When you were a blatant liar for no good reason?' Emily's eyes glistened. 'You've brought this on yourself, Tiff. Now it's your turn to explain yourself. Why were you secretly friends with that total bitch, our tormentor – Jasmine White?'

25

PAIGE, EMILY, TIFF

Tiff bolted and left the others standing by gravestones. Her heels tip-tapped into the distance, the creak of the gate sounded.

'See. I'm not the only one who held things back,' said Emily, red blotches across her face. 'Don't ask me anything about Jasmine. It's up to Tiff to explain.'

'Friends with *Jasmine?*' Paige could hardly get the words out. That would have been such an utter betrayal. That girl's insults were always aimed straight to the core, laughing at, belittling the four of them for simply being themselves.

Morgan's face had hardened. 'That bitch wasn't just cruel to us. She made life hell for some of the less resilient pupils. Remember Kath Mitchell? How we reckoned she changed schools because Jasmine made such fun of her lisp? She'd started missing lessons. How could our Tiff get close to a monster like that?'

The three of them made their way up the hill in silence, Morgan's hands deep in her trouser pockets. Paige hung behind and lit up again. She inhaled deeply. Emily must have got it wrong, although... Morgan loved trivial facts, and had discovered that the noise humans attributed to pigs in Japanese was *boo boo* and in French was *groin groin*. So, the four of them would shout those noises back every time Jasmine and her clique oinked at

Tiff. However, a few months before prom, they'd chatted about how they hadn't had to do that for a while. For some reason, the vile oinks had stopped.

Paige inhaled again. As for Emily's mum... She blew out smoke and stopped walking, as Emily's story sank in. Eyes blurry, Paige tossed the cigarette onto the ground. Emily, pure-hearted Emily, so soft and obliging back then, she often came to school with split nails and chapped hands; her parents didn't have a dishwasher, and she scrubbed floors, changed beds, cleaned windows. Emily had muttered once how her mum told her to do jobs she never used to bother with herself, as if getting sick had suddenly made her houseproud. Paige, Morgan and Tiff had always protected her, but never once considered they'd need to defend her against her own mother. As for Emily's poor dad... no wonder he'd needed counselling. After the funeral, the three of them had clubbed together and bought Emily a bunch of flowers. She'd thanked them and said she'd put them on her mother's grave. What had happened was life-changing for Emily on so many levels, yet she hadn't felt able to tell her three friends the truth.

Perhaps she had confided in Felix – or rather Hugo, as he was called back then. The young people at the community project confided in him about their problems, and he kept their confessions and worries confidential, only ever occasionally mentioning the surface stuff, like Jamal wanting to be a personal trainer. Paige lit another cigarette and took a long drag. Perhaps he had known.

When she and Felix had met for the first time as adults, that Saturday in 2016, he'd looked nervous as he ordered hot chocolates. The barest of pleasantries were exchanged, they talked about their jobs. Five minutes in, Paige looked at her watch, prompting Felix to talk about what mattered. At times, his face turned red, fists curled; at others, his eyes teared up. The longer he spoke, the smaller he looked, like an anxious teenager, like a genuine version of the Hugo back then, not the one he showed the world, full of smarm and charm.

Felix had ended by explaining his name change. Fifteen minutes stretched to two hours and lunch in the Old Wellington. He also talked about why he'd left France. Except the word he'd used was *fled*.

* * *

Morgan and Paige sat on the sofa, Emily on one of the armchairs after closing the shutters. She did her best to get comfortable, like a patient in A&E getting used to lying on a hard, medical bed. Tiff went over to the French windows and looked out at the pool. She slid down to the floor, facing the other three, let her jacket fall off her shoulders, kicked off her high ankle boots. Tiff bent her knees and lowered her head onto them.

Emily should have kept her mouth shut. There was nothing to gain from dropping Tiff in it. It wasn't as if Emily cared about her old friends. It wasn't as if she'd ever see them again. Emily listened to her inner voice raving, like a Friday-night drunk in the emergency department, in denial, saying they'd only had one pint.

'I'm sorry,' said Emily and looked at the others. 'Over the years, I've felt bad that I kept Mum's illness to myself. I know you'd have all been so supportive and done whatever you could to help. Like the time you bought me my favourite box of chocolates, Morgan, even though you were saving every penny of your pocket money for some book about Pythagoras. And you made me a lasagne, Paige, even though you despised cooking. Tiff, you'd come around with a DVD and snacks and help with housework so that I had a free moment to chill out.'

'Did your mum pretend to be ill with her friends as well?' asked Paige.

'Yep. Dad being away so much made it easier for her to lie to everyone, casually saying she'd been to appointments that he'd have wanted to hear about, in great detail, if he'd been around. She must have known, at the back of her mind, one day she'd be running off to Spain, so she didn't care.'

'How was she found out?' asked Tiff.

'Bit by bit, her story didn't add up. Her explanations of what happened at The Christie hospital, each visit, were always sketchy. I used to watch documentaries about cancer patients when she was upstairs in bed and my brother wasn't around. She never looked as ill as them. I assumed she'd need either chemo, radiotherapy, or surgery, but she said the tablets were enough. In the end, I rang the hospital, pretended we had an emergency at home, that I badly needed to speak to my mother and she wasn't answering her mobile phone. They'd never heard of her. I told Dad and he went mad at me, saying Mum would never lie about something like that. But they had a terrible argument the next day, after he'd slept on it.' Her voice broke. 'She never said goodbye. That was the worst thing, especially for my brother. One morning, she was there. The next, she wasn't.'

Tiff stood up, hesitated and then went over. She squeezed into Emily's armchair, next to her, like she used to when they were teenagers. She slipped her arm around Emily's shoulders. Emily leant in.

'You shouldn't have to apologise to us,' said Tiff. 'What a messed-up situation. I don't blame you for keeping it quiet. We were so busy anyway, what with it being Year Eleven, and if you'd tried to tell us, where on earth would you have started? I can see now how difficult it must have been.'

Emily caught her breath. A shudder turned into a sob. She buried her head onto Tiff's shoulder for a moment, shaking as the tears came. Tiff understood, she got it. 'It's such a mess, still,' she said in a muffled voice. 'Even now, I'm so angry.' She looked up. 'I've spent my life caring for others, as if to prove I'm not a mug, that other people genuinely need me. Mum left me feeling so... pathetic. But after the last few years, with all the abuse, with nurses being taken for granted, it's as if I've been taken for a mug again. Yet... guilt overwhelms me, sometimes, at not wanting to stay in the profession.'

Morgan passed her a tissue. 'Maybe you will go back to nursing. Maybe you won't. A vocation isn't a life sentence.'

Emily exhaled. That was the first time anyone had said that.

'I'm a cashier,' Morgan continued. 'It's not my dream job but shit happens and you have to get on with it. Mlle's Vachon's story about how she eventually followed her aspirations and embarked on a new career in her thirties has given me hope that maybe it really never is too late to switch direction.'

'Have you told anyone how you feel, Emily?' asked Paige. 'Lewis?'

'Lewis knows about Mum's deception but not that, in the last year or two, I've been feeling like that sappy, gullible teenager again whom I should have left behind. It's hard to explain because with him, I'm confident. I know Lewis can tell I'm holding something back but he sees this capable nurse on the outside. I... I'd feel like a failure in his eyes if I told him the truth and I couldn't bear it if he brushed it aside, because part of me would feel that yes, he's right, I should have got over Mum by now and it's pathetic that I haven't.'

'You were never sappy or gullible,' said Tiff firmly. 'You were compassionate, through and through. There's a big difference.'

'Maybe you *should* tell him,' said Paige.

To Emily's surprise, saying the truth out loud hadn't confused matters further; instead, the opposite had happened. Morgan was right. Emily was only thirty-five. Hardly anyone had a job for life these days. Why should nurses be any different? Plenty of colleagues of hers had left since 2020. Looking back, she could see it hadn't been an easy decision for them either. They'd clung on as long as they could, until their mental health or living bills gave them an ultimatum.

What else was she qualified to do, though? Emily wiped her eyes, sat up straighter and blew her nose. Private hospital receptionist? Medical sales rep? Cat whisperer?

The prospect of change blew a gap in the clouds that had settled over her head in recent months.

* * *

Tiff prised herself out of the armchair and made coffees. She brought the mugs over and put them on the table in the middle before sitting on the floor, cross-legged, as if time had spun back nineteen years.

'I'm sorry too,' she mumbled. 'It's... true. All of it. Jasmine and I became friends.'

'How could you?' said Paige and she folded her arms. 'We all stuck up for you over that "oink oink" business. Were you and Jasmine laughing at us behind our backs?'

'No! Of course not.' Tiff shook her head vehemently. They mustn't think that.

'It was bad enough that we all betrayed each other over Hugo, but Jasmine... she'd always had it in for us, year in year out, viciously,' said Morgan tightly.

Tiff interlocked her fingers and squeezed her hands tightly together. 'Jasmine approached me in Year Ten. She'd almost failed another assessment. A new boyfriend had distracted her. She asked me to coach her in English as I was such a fan of drama and reading. It was the only subject I always got As in. I told her to eff off but she offered to pay me, a good rate. You know how guilty I felt about my parents spending any spare money on *making me a star*.' A heavy sensation settled in Tiff's chest as she recalled those times, the fatigue when Mum announced she'd signed her up for yet another singing or dancing class. 'Jasmine would give me a piece of work, I'd mark it up, highlighting areas she could improve and mistakes, give it back.'

'I couldn't even bear to be in the same room as her,' said Morgan, an edge to her voice.

'Same for me, at the beginning. But we'd speak on the phone now and then. She came across as more human. Jasmine was given a load of fancy chocolate for her birthday, didn't want it so gave me some. My mum liked racy reads and Jasmine spotted one in my rucksack. I lent it to her and that became a habit.' Tiff bit her lip. 'She was callous, cold-blooded, no doubt about it, on the surface – but underneath, I saw a different side. A vulnerability. I caught her crying once. We were in her bedroom, I'd nipped to the loo. When I came back, she put her phone away. Her boyfriend had dumped her and she muttered something about always being treated badly. I gave her a hug, expecting to be pushed away, but she held on, wouldn't let go. My sleeve was damp afterwards from her tears. We never talked about it. I just got a vibe that something had happened to her once. I never found out what it was, but I think that's why she put on a form of armour in public.'

'*Jasmine* crying?' Emily tilted her head.

'I know. And then we talked about *Animal Farm* once; it was in our syllabus. How the animals overthrew the farmer and took over, to create a life more equal? But it simply meant a new hierarchy was created. Jasmine said school was like that. If she and her friends weren't the populars, others would be. She saw school as the survival of the fittest. It doesn't surprise me that she became a head teacher. Her favourite character in *Animal Farm* was dictator Napoleon.'

'Jasmine White. Hugo Black. Their names don't reflect the fact that most people are a shade of grey,' said Paige. 'No one's an absolute villain or hero.'

Tiff hadn't been able to resist the lure of being friends with someone like Jasmine. The oinking stopped and she began to see herself less like one of the downtrodden pigs in *Animal Farm*.

'It knew it was wrong,' said Tiff, 'but I told myself my friendship with her was justified because, in some small way, I was helping my parents financially. But' – Tiff bit her lip – 'at night, in bed, a voice would whisper in my ear that I was betraying the three amazing, funny, caring girls who made my school life more than bearable.'

No one spoke for a moment.

'How long did you know about Tiff and Jasmine, Emily?' asked Morgan, tone softer now.

'During our very last exam, English GCSE, halfway through, I caught Tiff giving Jasmine a thumbs up. Afterwards, I asked her what was going on, threatened to tell the invigilator that I caught the two of them cheating, sending each other hand signals. After everything to do with Mum, I wasn't so inclined to give people the benefit of the doubt. It was two days before the prom. I refused to speak to Tiff.'

Tiff had been so nervous, convinced her secret would come out at the dance. Morgan and Paige hadn't noticed the tension between her and Emily, they were still on a high about exams finishing.

Morgan rubbed her head. 'I predicted that us all getting together again would bring back difficult memories of Hugo, but I never expected other secrets to surface.'

'Me neither,' said Tiff and she looked around. 'Are there any others between us from back then?'

26

MORGAN

Emily paused and then slid down from the armchair, onto the floor, to sit next to Tiff. 'Don't laugh but whilst I liked our PE teacher, I also had a massive girl crush on Mrs Davies.'

'Our geography teacher, in Year Seven?' asked Morgan. She slid down to the floor too, and crossed her legs like Tiff. 'But she was so mean. She'd rap pupils on the hands with that roll of tracing paper. I wish I could go back and report her.'

'I totally get it, Emily,' said Tiff and unfolded her arms. 'She was so *on it* – never took any crap from anyone and she oozed confidence. No other member of staff could have carried off that tangerine jumpsuit. If we're talking crushes, I secretly fancied Tommy in our tutor set, until Year Ten, when he viewed girls as the trophies he and his rugby team collected.'

'Tommy was sweet before his hormones kicked in,' agreed Morgan. 'He was always the first to offer a pen or ruler if another pupil had lost theirs.'

Paige was staring at the watercolour of a field of lavender. Morgan caught her eye. Paige smiled and moved from the sofa to the floor.

'What about the secrets we kept together?' Paige said. 'Like on the trip to France in Year Ten. How the hostel had windows you could remove completely, in case of a fire.'

'Christ, I'd forgotten that!' said Tiff.

'Me too,' said Emily.

Morgan grinned. 'What we were like, taking them out that night, so we could slide down the drainpipe and go into that little town?'

'Then Mlle Vachon caught us on the way back,' said Paige. 'It's the only time I ever saw her looking angry. She split us up for the rest of the trip and told us we were only to speak in French when together.'

'As she anticipated, that stopped us making any other plans,' said Tiff. 'Fate must have been on my side when I scraped through my GCSE.'

The four talked about happier times at school, a large part of which was solving the cases. Morgan fetched the notebook and they turned its pages, marvelling at how they'd named bullies, called out cheating partners and brought thieves to justice.

'We were fearless back then,' said Tiff as she ran a hand over the notebook's cover.

Emily took it and flicked through again. 'The concept of right and wrong was very important to us.'

Morgan took the notebook from Tiff. 'We were good kids, with well-meaning intentions, a strong team.'

Paige hugged her knees. She didn't take the notebook when Morgan offered it to her. 'This is nice,' she said, simply.

Morgan wanted to hug her.

'Many times, over the years, I've wanted to call one of you for a chat,' whispered Emily, tears in her eyes. 'It wouldn't have solved my problems but would have made me feel better. Stronger. More ready for the fight.'

'When there's been good news too,' said Tiff and the others nodded. 'Mum and Dad took me out for dinner when I landed my first Netflix role, and I spent the evening imagining the celebrations us four would have had.'

Morgan would have been so excited, asking everything about how a show was made, the technical details from the set. Olly would have been interested in that too. She reckoned Paige would have asked about the behaviour of her acting colleagues, and if everyone was as shallow as made out in gossip magazines. Emily would have simply listened, letting Tiff talk to her heart's content about her achievement.

'I've missed you three just being there,' said Morgan. 'I haven't ever been married, I've not made close friends, I've got my parents but I have to protect them from things. And Olly... there are no barriers with him, or weren't when he was younger. I'm working on getting back to where we used to be. It's important because he and I always showed ourselves to each other in the raw, and... that's what us four used to do.'

'What about everything with Hugo?' asked Paige in an uncomfortable tone.

Slowly, Tiff reached out both of her hands, one to Emily, one to Paige. Emily reached for Morgan's. Morgan reached for Paige's. They sat in a circle with their fingers intertwined like they used to.

'We never should have let a boy get between us,' said Tiff. 'My gift, as we called it...' Tiff smiled at the others. Morgan understood. The idea of The Secret Gift Society sounded almost arrogant, all these years later. 'My gift for empathy,' Tiff continued, 'honed in on Hugo, instead of you three.'

'Same here with my kindness,' said Emily.

'My intuition failed big time,' said Paige.

'Logic should have told me that you lot would never give up our friendship just for hearts and flowers,' said Morgan. 'But now we understand why he succeeded in splitting us apart. What happened with him... it doesn't diminish the friendship we had.' She side-hugged Paige. The four of them got up, arms around each other. Morgan wiped her face with the back of her hand. 'Jesus, I never cry,' she said. Not often, anyway, only for big things like childbirth, when Olly's been ill, when the UK's lost the Eurovision song contest again.

'Are we going to Mlle Vachon's birthday party next Monday?' asked Tiff. 'It... would be good to see her again.'

'Yes, I mean... it would be rude not to go, right?' said Emily.

Morgan could have jumped in the pool to celebrate.

Paige's arms dropped and she stepped back from the circle. 'But... what about the things about our lives now, that we should tell each other?'

'We'll all have things to say about our grown-up lives that we aren't proud of,' said Tiff.

'It wouldn't be normal if we didn't,' said Emily.

'But let's just enjoy this moment,' said Morgan.

The rest of the night – or rather early morning – they chatted, laughed, drank too much coffee.

'We've got so much catching up to do,' said Morgan, back on the sofa. 'Favourite takeout? Mine's pizza – because it's Olly's.'

'Not Chinese,' said Paige, 'because Felix and I get competitive over who can use chopsticks best.' She gave a small smile.

'At the moment, any and all,' said Emily.

'Fish and chips, but I rarely allow myself that,' said Tiff. 'How about favourite movie ever? I'll start. *Shallow Hal*. I really like the message. Beauty is in the eye of the beholder – or it should be.'

'*Yes Man* with Jim Carrey,' said Emily. 'I love the idea of life not being planned out, just saying yes to everything and seeing where it takes you.'

'Perhaps that's what you need to do, Emily?' said Paige. 'Your life has been so structured, I imagine, following protocols, administering and monitoring to a schedule... perhaps, now, you simply need to go with the flow and not overthink what you do next – accept the first opportunity.'

Emily sat up straighter.

'*Interstellar*. Olly and I can stay up all night talking about it,' said Morgan. 'As he gets older, our passionate discussions about physics and maths are like when us four would lose our sense of time when discussing a new case.'

'For me...' said Paige, 'nothing has ever beaten *Finding Nemo*. I've watched it so many times over the years. It's a comfort thing. I like the idea of never giving up. You have to keep going, however tough things get.' She paused and then lifted her arms. The others knew exactly what she was going to do and in unison the four of them performed breaststroke in the air, smiles on their faces as wide as Dory's.

'All of us loved that movie,' said Tiff, everyone's arms now back by their sides. 'I really related to the sharks fighting their fish-eating addiction.'

'It reminded me of us,' said Morgan. 'Each of us different but working together as a team.'

'I related to Dory,' said Emily. 'Flawed but accepted for who she was.'

Not long after, the women admitted defeat and gave in to tiredness. Morgan clambered into bed after Paige. She turned off the lights, calmer, warmer inside than she had been for a very long time. She glanced left.

Reached out and tugged on Paige's hair, then turned over and closed her eyes.

The bed remained still until slowly Paige turned around. She reached out and tugged Morgan's hair back. Tears trickled onto Morgan's pillow for all the right reasons.

27
———
MORGAN

Tuesday dawned with palm trees against a blue sky, sunrays sliding through their parakeet green fronds, exactly how Morgan had imagined the south of France. On the way to the airport, she wound down the taxi's window and savoured the fragrance of vanilla one last time. They passed lines of slender, conical cypress trees. A teacher's wage could bring her here again. Could going to university be a reality? Emily was considering changing her career. In some ways, Tiff was just at the beginning of hers and Paige was now trying to become a mother. None of her friends' lives were static, they still had hopes, ambition. Why should Morgan's be any different?

Friends.

Despite the early April afternoon chill, as they got off their second flight of the day, at Newquay, Cornwall fulfilled her fantasies as well with a violet and peach sunset meeting the sea, on the horizon. Ocean Activities Centre opened at nine o'clock tomorrow. They'd agreed to get there early. All being well, they'd be in London by teatime. Tiff had said for them to stay the night at hers, then the four of them could go up to Manchester the next morning by train. Tiff still had a few days to spend with her parents before filming started on her next show in the Isle of Wight next Wednesday. Olly would be back from Switzerland on Saturday and had sent Morgan several photos of the Large Hadron Collider. He'd briefly explained what he'd learned about energy particles. She'd re-read his messages several times, pride growing in her chest at how his knowledge outstripped hers. Missing someone wasn't so bad if you knew they were having a good time. Thinking about her friends over the years, Morgan hoped tragedy hadn't struck their lives. She'd worried about car accidents, job losses, bereavements. As it turned out, they'd not had it easy. She was glad she hadn't known what they'd been going through during their estrangement.

Too tired to visit one of the local fish restaurants, they ate in the B&B. Paige spoke in monosyllables by the time their mains arrived. Morgan had hoped she'd be more like her old self after last night, the four of them having talked everything through. But still something worried her friend, she could see it. Paige used to get this look on her face ahead of exams, if the girls had a silly fallout, or if rumours said Warner Bros was cancelling *The West Wing*. She'd worn that look, on and off, ever since Saturday when they'd met at Gatwick airport. Paige left most of her chips and pushed her plate away, excusing herself and heading to the Ladies.

'Paige is on a downer,' said Emily.

'Perhaps it's to do with her husband,' said Morgan. 'She's not contacted him at all this week.'

'Maybe talking to us about her problems getting pregnant has made her dwell on them,' said Tiff.

'I've got a cousin who couldn't get pregnant. It destroyed her marriage, they were both desperate to have kids. It must be devastating.'

'We should try to cheer her up,' said Emily. 'Paige always liked Scrabble, didn't she? I spotted a box by the bar. I'll ask if we can borrow it.'

By the time Paige had got back, the women had already set it up and ordered two big ice cream sundaes with four spoons.

Paige beamed and selected her tiles, taking charge of the pen and scoring pad. As usual, she took the lead, Morgan coming a close second, Emily refereeing as Tiff made up ridiculous words.

'Let's add up the final scores,' said Morgan and she took the notepad and did the sums. She raised her eyebrows at Emily and Tiff. 'Wow. That's a first. We've caught Paige up and are all even.' She checked the numbers again.

'I was lucky getting that triple word with a letter z in it, otherwise I'd have been way behind,' said Tiff.

'Slow and steady kept me in the game,' said Emily.

'That's why our secret society worked,' said Paige. 'Each of our approaches was different, but equal in helping solve cases.'

'Like in Hugo's case and finding out he was cheating on Amelia,' said Morgan. 'His best friend on the football team skidded on ice one morning on the way to school. He fell over and grazed his hand. Even though he used to join in with Hugo's teasing, you stopped and kindly offered him a plaster, Emily.'

'He was taken aback. Thanked me,' said Emily. 'He explained he was always getting scrapes at football practise, was clumsy, and had a bad fall at the weekly practise, the previous Tuesday, after school. Hugo usually heaved him to his feet but had recently missed a couple of those sessions, including that one.'

'Very strange considering he was captain. There was no logic in it, so I followed Hugo one night,' said Morgan.

'You ended up at Sophie's house,' said Paige. 'So I observed the two of them at school together. Their body language was a dead giveaway. They stood so close together, I caught a couple of lingering looks, they gave each other such full eye contact but broke it as soon as Amelia entered the room.'

'The final piece of the puzzle was when I spoke to Sophie,' said Tiff. 'I was in the canteen reading one of my celebrity magazines. We did drama together. I liked Sophie and never understood what she saw in a loser like Hugo. We got talking about a story. A woman had an affair with a married footballer, the newspapers had made her out to be the villain. Sophie asked me if I agreed, kept pushing for my opinion, which is exactly what I'd have done in her position.'

Their chat moved back to the game as they packed it away.

'Remember how the highest score in Scrabble, from a single word, if the tiles are put in the right place, over triple scores, is...'

'One thousand, seven hundred and seventy-eight,' the others chorused and groaned.

'You used to tell us that *every* game,' protested Paige.

'Glad you haven't forgotten,' said Morgan airily. 'As you may also recall, the word is oxyphenbutazone.'

'How could we ever forget?' said Emily, exchanging humorous glances with Paige and Tiff.

Morgan grinned. That was another thing about real friends – you knew their teasing was just playful banter. As for that high score, they all agreed it was almost certainly unattainable, but, back in their schooldays, the slightest possibility kept them playing. And the possibility of them all being friends, once more, had kept Morgan going during recent weeks, following the bad news she'd received. People said never look back, always move forwards, but what about if you've lost something – or someone – important along the way? When Olly was a boy, he'd lost a cuddly bunny once. They'd looked for it every day, in the park. Finally, they found it, under a bush. One eye was missing, a bicycle had ridden over it, and a paw had been torn. None of that mattered to her son, who said it was what was inside that mattered.

Life had changed the four school friends, but their characters were still there, if hidden within a story each had chosen to tell. The story Emily told was that the world was an ungrateful place that took advantage of kindness, yet her good nature still shone through. Tiff's was that you had to be larger than life to be loved, yet her empathy still connected to the smaller things. Paige's story was completely authentic, she'd embraced her intuition and chosen a career that revolved around reading body language. Her intuition had brought the four of them on this journey as she'd acted on it and persuaded the others.

That was why she and Paige had been especially close. Both were straight-talking and scrupulously honest. Emily might tell white lies to avoid hurting someone, Tiff might lie outright to save face or cover up embarrassment, but Paige always told it how it was. Morgan trusted her completely. Even now. Paige had changed the least and Morgan was as happy as Olly had been with his bunny, to have her back.

28

MORGAN

Morgan put her hand across her brow and squinted in the sun, an information leaflet from the B&B in her hand. Fistral Beach stretched in between two headlands. She stared into the distance, at the northern one and the iconic Headland Hotel on top; it was over one hundred and twenty years old. Here on the southern one, Ocean Activities Centre was smaller than she'd expected and did teach many water sports but not surfing. However, at the northern headland was a large complex on the beach that, as well as restaurants and shops, housed the bigger International Surfing Centre that the man who'd tried to recruit Hugo, in France, had mentioned. Morgan drank in the camel-coloured sand and denim waves giving seagulls rides, the rugged cliffs covered in grasses and gorse, and the sulphury seaweed smell in the air. Morgan was no longer in the more sophisticated Riviera, but a place with a coarser beauty.

The four of them stood outside the grey, square building, with its blue canopy and mural of fish. Paige hung back as they went in.

'Good morning. I'm Sal. How can I help?' A woman with short, grey hair stood behind a counter in turquoise jogging trousers and a matching hoodie. On the counter sat a bottle of hand gel and a large basket filled with any serious surfer's essentials – sun cream, lip protection balm and Haribo fish. 'If you're interested in lessons, we currently have a special offer on paddleboarding, two sessions for the price of one. The weather's due to be outstanding this weekend, for early April, so we've a barbecue event with a beach volleyball tournament. Summer can never come too early at Ocean Activities Centre.' She briefed them about the staff's qualifications and how they'd just had new changing rooms fitted, with state-of-the art power showers.

The four of them clearly didn't look like water sports fans, Emily in furry ankle boots, jeans and jumper bearing a picture of a mug of coffee and pile of books. Tiff wore high heels and a sparkly blouse with a tight leather jacket, as if she were in New York and not Newquay. Paige hovered in linen trousers and an elegant jacket. Sofa-loving Morgan looked the sportiest in trainers, jeans and a sweat top. Olly would have laughed about that.

Olly. That's who this was for. Morgan's parents didn't know she'd come looking for Hugo. They'd didn't know he was the father. When she found out Hugo had left town, back in 2004, she was going to tell her mum and dad. But the night before she had it all planned, she'd overheard them talking in the lounge. Word had got around that Hugo and his family had disappeared. Dad talked about how he'd run into the father a couple of times in the pub, said the man was a complete tosser – Dad didn't swear often – and never bought a round. Apparently, he came onto the female bar staff, too, even though he was married. Dad said, from what he'd heard, the son was no better, a bit of a player, and how glad they were Morgan had the sense to stay away from lads like that, because one day he'd probably end up being as rotten a father as his own dad.

So Morgan refused to tell. Her parents had reduced her to tears, pressing her for a name, saying that a baby needed its dad, that she was a fool not to chase child support money. It had made Morgan ill and she was hardly sleeping. The doctor was concerned and this brought her mum and dad to their senses. Morgan guessed they'd try again after the birth, but by then she was a mother and the strength it gave her took Morgan's breath away. She didn't want Hugo anywhere near her baby and had become sure of that after bumping into people from school, over the summer. Gossip was rife as to why he'd moved away and without him around, pupils who'd been in awe instead opened up about how they actually hated him. Morgan told her parents that if they kept asking, she'd move out as soon as she could, and they wouldn't see their grandson again.

'Thanks but we aren't actually looking to do paddleboarding,' said Morgan. 'We're looking for someone. We haven't seen them in a very long time. Does a Hugo Black work here?'

The receptionist tilted her head. 'No, sorry.'

'Oh.' Morgan looked at the others. But then it probably had been a long shot. The only evidence was Hugo's French employer vaguely remembering a place that sounded like mistral.

'It must be hard to retain staff names. I expect you have temporary workers in the summer, and quite a turnover for a job like this,' said Tiff.

'Yes, it is actually, and what with the customers, it's bedlam here in the high season.'

'Hugo would have started in 2014,' said Emily. 'Were you here then, Sal? Something tells me you must have been. You seem to know everything about this place.'

She gave a broad smile. 'Thank you. I have been here more years than I care to remember but that name doesn't sound familiar...' She looked at the four of them. 'Hold on, he's busy but I'll ask Rob to come out. He owns the place.' She disappeared and came back a few minutes later, with a man in his forties in turquoise jogging pants like hers and a cap with a shark on it.

'How can I help?' he asked pleasantly, water bottle in his hand. He took a swig and put in on the counter.

'We're trying to trace a man called Hugo Black,' said Morgan. 'It's possible he might have started working here, in 2014.'

His brow furrowed.

'He's... my son's father.'

'Right, No, sorry. The name isn't familiar.'

Paige stood by the door, away from the others.

'Wait, this might help...' Morgan pulled out her phone and went into her photo gallery.

Rob's eyes narrowed as he focused, and his face broke into a smile. Sal looked over his shoulder at the snap.

'Ah, of course, he worked here, yes,' said Rob. 'Decent guy. Loved him. I spotted him working in a surf shop in Fréjus and offered him a job. To my surprise, he turned up a few weeks later, out of the blue and stressed. I didn't ask many questions.'

'Is he in today?' From head to toe, nerves sprang to attention in Morgan, like they had done when she was a teen and her waters broke.

'Even though he left his mark, he only stayed about a year, love, sorry,' said Sal.

Morgan's stomach dropped.

'I was gutted,' said Rob. 'He loved the outdoor gym, it inspired a real passion. I'd set it up as a venture for holidaymakers missing their weights, but locals started coming on a regular basis because he was really interested in helping people build their long-term fitness. In the short time he was here, real progress was made expanding the business.' Rob took another swig of water. 'One of my hardest workers ever, he left to go back up north when an offer from a prestigious, international gym came in, owned by a customer who had a holiday home here and wanted to go kayaking. The two of them got talking.' He sighed. 'Karma, eh? I poached him, then someone poached him from me.'

A shiver ran down Morgan's spine. She couldn't quite work out why, but the word gym unsettled her.

'This man in the photograph wasn't called Hugo, though,' chipped in Sal.

'What? But he never had a twin. Not that we knew of,' said Tiff.

Twin? Morgan almost laughed at Tiff's face. That would have nicely explained the mess at prom. The four of them had been secretly dating Hugo's double, a more good-hearted version of him.

Paige took a breath and stepped forwards.

'Felix. Felix Barron. That's his name,' said Rob.

'His mother was French,' added Sal before answering the reception's phone.

No.

Morgan wavered from one foot to the other.

This wasn't possible.

She wouldn't have married him.

She wouldn't have kept him secret, all this time they'd been rebonding.

'Why would he change his name?' asked Emily, looking confused.

'I've only come across one Felix before, a film producer,' said Tiff. 'Then Paige's husband, of course. Is he French too, Paige?'

Paige opened her mouth but no words came out.

'I'm sorry, but I can't give out any more information without contacting Felix first. It wouldn't be right,' said Rob. 'I've still got his number, somewhere.'

'It's okay,' Morgan found herself saying. 'I don't need the contact details any more. Sorry to trouble you.' She strode out of the building. Emily and Tiff rushed after her, Paige lagging far behind.

'Don't chicken out now,' called Emily. 'Come on, Morgan. We're doing this for Olly. Let's get Hugo's, I mean Felix's, phone number.'

'It's time we showed that con artist what we've made of our lives and that, despite his best efforts, the four of us have come together again,' said Tiff.

Morgan leant against a nearby railing. She bent over, about to black out. Immediately, Paige hurried over and Morgan shook her off. She stood up and smacked the railing, rubbing her knuckles, white-hot heat swelling within her. Morgan walked down the path that led to the sand and put her hands up to her ears as the others said her name. Finally, two hands pulled away hers. She opened her eyes to find Paige opposite her, Emily and Tiff looking confused.

'What's your husband's job again, Paige?' asked Morgan. Paige didn't reply. 'Shall I tell you?' she continued, voice shaking. 'He works for a gym company. Is it prestigious? International? Didn't you say something about charity work and him taking a group of kids to some centre in Gorton for windsurfing lessons? Christ, the clues were there all along.'

Slowly, Tiff turned to face Paige. 'You're shitting me, right...? Paige and Hugo? It's still going on? You went up the aisle with that bozo? Didn't think to tell us when we first met by the hazel tree at Dailsworth High a few weeks ago?'

'You *married* that bastard?' asked Emily.

Because the memory of him was a wound, a wound that ran deep, most of the damage lay hidden under the surface, but was still infected; a fragile wound Morgan had hoped would begin to mend now. What a joke. The road trip had been a waste of time.

'These last weeks, you could have saved me the stress of looking, Paige, knowing how much I wanted Olly to meet his dad... your husband. Not to mention, you've allowed Emily and Tiff to give up their precious time when they needn't have.' Her voice shook. Morgan folded her arms. 'Why con us like this? Is this payback? Why oh why would you marry the boy who broke up our friendship, who was a bully, who two-timed girls and strutted around as if he were cock o' the walk?'

'These last few days, it's no surprise you've been so quiet. Did you hope this trip would divert us, so that Morgan would never find out the truth?' asked Tiff. 'Is this because you can't have kids? You see Olly as a threat?'

Paige shrank back.

'Steady on, Tiff,' said Emily.

'Is it?' asked Morgan, tone shrill now. 'Christ, that's selfish.'

'Of course not!' said Paige. 'I would *never* stop Olly and Felix from meeting. I've been desperate to tell you! But I know you've got another reason for this trip, Morgan. Telling you all the truth, right at the start, would have meant we never came away, never had time to talk things through properly.'

'Don't blame your deception on me,' spat Morgan. 'I'm done. I'm going back to the B&B, packing and heading back to Manchester on my own. Message me Hu... Felix's contact details, Paige. When he gets back from Dubai, I will take it from there.' She looked at the three of them and tears filled her eyes. 'I so wanted us to be friends again, but some secrets are too big to get over. Emily lied about her mum. Tiff befriended Jasmine. Paige married our worst enemy. I'm not blameless, even though Felix had treated us so badly, I was clearly the only one to go so far as to actually sleep with him back then.' She breathed in and out. 'Don't contact me again, any of you. I mean it.'

'My pleasure,' said Tiff tightly. 'This was all one big mistake. We are different people now and there's clearly very little forgiveness between us.'

'We've each got our own problems,' said Emily. 'I for one don't need any more drama.'

'The Secret Gift Society is officially dissolved,' said Morgan and her voice caught. 'We never actually said that in 2004.'

'Let me explain; it'll make sense,' said Paige and pressed her palms together. 'When we met in New Chapter Café, a couple of weeks ago, and—'

'There's no point,' said Tiff. 'You've proved to us, Paige, that we are still capable of betrayal, even at our age when we are supposed to have learnt from our wrongs.'

Morgan delved into her rucksack and pulled out the notebook with closed cases written on the front. She opened it up and handful by handful, she tore out pages, waiting to feel better as they fluttered away on the sea breeze. She turned her back on the others and hailed a taxi. She got in on her own and slammed the door shut. The car pulled away.

29

PAIGE, EMILY, TIFF

Paige's knees buckled and she fell onto the sand as Emily walked along the beach, heading up to the northern headland. Tiff had followed Morgan back up the path, presumably to get a taxi herself. Time passed, she was unaware of how many minutes. A hand touched her shoulder. Morgan? Emily? Tiff?

'Are you okay?' asked Sal, the receptionist. She shook an embroidered handkerchief. 'One of you dropped this.'

Emily's. She never had liked tissues. Her mum used to tease her about it, saying she'd been born a century too late.

'Sounded like a bad argument.'

Paige couldn't speak.

'I'm afraid there's not much privacy on this beach,' Sal continued. 'What with the breeze, it's carried many an angry word over the years. Lovers' break-ups, the snappy words of tired parents, disgruntled cries from customers who can't master paddleboarding... I'm on my break. A nice hot drink, that's what you need.'

Numb, Paige followed her back up the path and into the building once more. Five minutes later, she sat in the staff room, behind the reception area, next to a pile of sports magazines.

'Thanks,' Paige muttered. 'I'm not sure the others would think I deserved this.'

Sal sat down opposite her and put her mug on the pile of magazines before placing her palms on her thighs. She leant forwards, lines around her eyes deepening. 'Felix is a good man. Kind, considerate, he made an impact during his relatively short time here. He often worked late and always helped out at charity events. Rob trusted him completely and within only a few weeks, he was allowed to lock up by himself. But I'm sure I don't need to tell you about his good qualities.'

'He works on youth community projects now. It's his passion.'

Sal offered Paige a tube of biscuits. She shook her head.

'We got talking once, at a Christmas party. He opened up about high school, about how he regretted so many things.' Sal chewed for a moment. 'We shouldn't be judged for a lifetime by the things we did in our youth. Paige, is it?'

She nodded.

'Paige, make your friends listen to what you have to say about the man Felix is now. If, after that, they're still full of anger then... you have to let go of them. I don't say that lightly. Female friendship is important, but not if it's stuck in a place of narrow-mindedness and resentment.' She sipped from her mug. 'Trust me. I had three close friends years ago. We'd hung out together since primary school, stayed living in the same town afterwards. We booked the trip of a lifetime... okay, only two weeks hiking in Wales...' She smiled. 'But still, it was all our budget could afford and we couldn't wait to get away from living with our parents. But a week before the trip, I landed the job of my dreams at the local swimming pool. I'd been unemployed for three months and it was an immediate start. I had to accept the offer but my friends couldn't forgive me. For weeks, I wrote apologies and phoned. Eventually, they softened but still made snide comments every time I mentioned work. That's not healthy friendship.'

'But we were so good together. High school would have been awful without Morgan, Emily and Tiff.'

'My friends were everything to me too. But we aren't needy young people any more, are we?' She looked Paige straight in the eye. 'You have a great husband. A job you enjoy?'

'Yes... yes, I do.'

'A successful one, I bet. Look, did you ever used to watch *Sex and the City*?'

'In my early teens, yes, with Mum.'

'Did you imagine that's what female friendship should be like? Out on the razz? Telling each other everything? Displaying unlimited loyalty and forgiveness? Always being there for each other, whatever, no conditions? Putting those relationships before all others?'

'The four of us used to joke about it. Morgan was Miranda, Tiff wanted to be Samantha, Emily was Charlotte, and that left me as Carrie – not a perfect match. I'd never wear a pink tutu skirt.' Her body shook less now. She took another mouthful of coffee.

'But that's not how it is for everyone – and that's okay. Friends come in all shapes and sizes – your partner, your mum, a colleague or neighbour, that person you chat to on Facebook, even your pet. It took me a while to realise the friendships that mattered most don't necessarily come from a school girl gang... or a cocktail bar.'

'Morgan, Emily and Tiff are good people, deep down, I know their values haven't changed.'

Sal picked up their mugs and took them to the sink. 'You're allowed to make mistakes, make amends and move on. That's healthy. If they still can't forgive you then *they've* probably changed more than you think.'

Paige left the activities centre with purpose in her stride, the brisk air drying her tears. Her phone bleeped. She took it out. Felix?

Hi Paige. Just got a text from Rob – I'm sure I've told you about him before, I worked at his water sports centre in Cornwall. He said four women turned up, calling me Hugo, claiming to know me from high school. Crazy, but it sounded like The Secret Gift Society. You're not there, right? Because even crazier, one of them apparently said I was the father of her kid. What the hell's going on?

Oh God, what had Paige been thinking?

* * *

Paige married Hugo? Emily kicked the sand with her boot, grains flying over washed-up seaweed. Her head throbbed, a migraine coming on, arguments always did that. How Paige must have been laughing at them, these last days. Yet she'd been so quiet. Emily stopped and looked out to sea. She understood Tiff's anger but her comment about Paige being threatened by Olly had been unkind. Paige said Felix had changed. Hard to accept. But then Emily was no longer that sweet, naïve girl who fell for her mother's scam. Glamorous Tiff looked unrecognisable and once-career-orientated Morgan had given up her teaching dreams to focus on being a mum.

Emily looked over her shoulder. Paige had gone.

What would Felix be like now? She'd hated her mum. He'd hated his dad. Parents shaped lives. Was his father one reason Felix had treated the four of them so badly? Paige had always been such an astute judge of character; was it possible that a man could have married Paige and fooled her for so long, day in, day out, into believing he was decent when he wasn't?

She carried on walking and a dog came into view, small, white and grey, with ruffled fur. The two elderly owners chatted to each other. Emily stopped the couple as they approached, pointed to their dog, said he was limping. Emily bent down.

'Let's have a look, little chap,' she murmured and lifted it up. Underneath, she saw a pine needle sticking out. Very gently, she removed it. The dog licked her hand. The owners thanked her for intervening. She got to her feet, breathed in salty air, missing Smudge all of a sudden. What had Paige meant about Morgan having another reason for going on this road trip? The four of them getting together again had simply thrown up more questions – and shown Emily how much she'd been living in the past.

However, as the couple walked away with the dog, she realised the trip had at least answered questions about herself. She stood a little taller, reached into her bag and took out something she'd hidden from the others, something she'd hidden from herself, pretending it was invisible. She walked up to the tide and took the lid off the hip flask and poured the vodka into the sea water, the threatening migraine disappearing. These last few months, during an especially bad day, a swig had helped keep her going until the evening's wine bottle. The therapist had warned this could escalate into an even bigger problem, and every time she took a mouthful, Smudge would cast a judgemental look, in the way only cats can.

She hadn't cared, but now Emily did because the possibility of a future she might love had opened up since meeting her old friends. Emily shook the hip flask until it was empty, put it back in her bag, took out her phone and texted Lewis.

* * *

Fumbling with the key, Tiff braced herself and entered the B&B almost on tiptoe, as if she were starring in a thriller. Thank God. No one was there. Quickly, Tiff packed, not wanting to see Paige again, not wanting to see the hurt on her face. How could Tiff have made that cruel comment about Olly? She wasn't still sixteen and raging with unpredictable hormones. It was nineteen years later. Tiff still focused on her bitterness about high school, and no one but her was to blame for that. Not moving forwards was a choice. She may have looked different now but the insecurities were the same. Yet so was her empathy – Paige must now have been feeling like shit. Morgan furious. As for Emily, Tiff had stumbled across her secret, had smelt it in their bedroom, seen the flask of silver in her friend's bag.

Christ, what a mess, best left behind.

Tiff sat down on the bed. Leaving that mess behind would mean running away again. That wasn't the action of a mature woman, but a person who lost themselves with an escort every time they needed to escape emotional turmoil, instead of facing it head on, like an adult.

Tiff took out her phone. Brought up Carter's number. Deleted it. Did the same with Marlon's.

No more running away.

No more blaming the past.

She pressed dial. Joe answered.

30

MORGAN

Have you found him at Fistral Beach, Mum?

Yes. Yes, I have. Kind of.

What do you mean?

It's complicated love. Let's talk when you get back.

I've been waiting eighteen years for this. Now I have to wait until Saturday?

I'm sorry. I don't mean to sound evasive but it's a lot to explain in a message. It's better if we chat face to face.

What's wrong? Is he… ill?

No. Nothing like that. It's all okay Olly. Don't worry. I'll tell you everything as soon as you're here. I'm sending a photo of him a few years ago. It was on the wall in the surf shop, in Fréjus. Love you xx

No reply.

That was last Wednesday night. It was now Saturday, Easter weekend. Neither Paige, Emily nor Tiff had contacted her since the four of them had left Newquay that day. She pursed her lips. Good riddance. Olly hadn't messaged again either. She'd cleaned, batch cooked, done laundry and weeded, but none of those things had helped. It was now late morning and she sat up the kitchen table. Her tea was cold. She'd only eaten half her toast.

Morgan had gone around to her parents yesterday, unable to face telling them about the trip; she simply said she'd taken a few days off work, fancied some time to herself. She stayed for dinner. Whilst Mum washed up and Dad dried, Morgan collapsed on the sofa. Dad came in and sat next to her. She was never too old to lay her head on his shoulder. The three of them sat in front of some game show. Morgan didn't shout out the answers to the maths problems, her parents exchanging glances. They were off to their caravan today for a week, but before she left, didn't forget to hand over Easter eggs for her and Olly. Morgan had forgotten to get theirs and burst into tears.

'That's it,' said her dad and led her back into the lounge. 'What's going on, lass? This isn't like you.'

'Is it Olly?' asked Mum.

If only they knew. Olly was eighteen and deserved to be told first. She'd caught a bug, that's all, she told them, but when she kissed her mum and dad goodbye last night, she could tell from their faces they didn't believe her.

The front door opened. Olly came in, rucksack on his back. He let it slip to the ground. Didn't give her hug and plonked himself down opposite. Vikram's dad had given him a lift home from the airport.

'Did you have a good time, love?' asked Morgan in as bright a voice as she could muster.

'Yep. You totally have to visit CERN someday. I'll tell you about it later.' He shook his head when she offered to make him a drink. 'You okay?' he muttered.

'I'm fine, love.'

'Tell me about Hugo, then. Tell me about my dad.'

Where to start. 'He's called Felix now. I don't know why. But... well, he's married to Paige. She didn't tell us until the end of the trip.'

Olly sat back in his chair. 'Fucking hell, that's messed up...'

How could she tell him off for swearing when she felt the same?

It poured out. How Paige had deceived the other three. How she claimed it wasn't because she felt threatened by the prospect of Felix having a grown-up son, when she and him may not be able to have children. She'd hinted that she thought Morgan had another reason for the trip, that's why she kept schtum, to give Morgan time to talk about it, but was her real motive to divert the other three's efforts? Wasn't she expecting them to have so much success in tracking down her husband? But then Paige had sent Morgan his number first thing Thursday. Morgan told Olly about how great it had been to feel as if they were putting their friendship back together, as if it were an old scrambled up Rubik's cube that finally, after much effort, got solved again. But then something unexpected scrambled it once more.

Olly got up and made himself a mug of tea, a fresh one for his mum, too. He sat down again and pulled off his hoodie. 'Will he want to get to know me, then? It's not like I'm a little baby he's going to get to name, and go through all that learning to walk and talk stuff with.'

Morgan wanted to make everything perfect, like she'd so often strived to do in the past; wanted to tell him Felix would love him to bits, that finally he'd have a dad who was there whenever he needed him. She scanned the tired face, the stubble on his chin, the trendy T-shirt he'd bought from Depop.

'All I can say is that Rob, the owner of that activities centre at Fistral Beach, spoke very highly of him, and said he was a decent man.'

Olly stirred his tea. 'So you haven't actually contacted Felix?'

'Oh, I've wanted to and spent a while focusing on the wording. The things I could tell him about my incredible son... but I figured *you'd* want to do this. I'll be there by your side, all the way, but he's your dad, not mine. I'll message you his number. He's back from Dubai today.'

Olly went over to Morgan. Crouched down and gave her a big hug.

'Thanks, Mum,' he said, in a muffled voice and went back to his chair. 'Have you told Gramps and Granny?'

'We could do that together. I'm not sure how they'll take it. Back in the day, they never liked Hugo – I mean Felix – or his dad. But their opinion doesn't matter, love. This is about you.'

'Is there no way you and your friends will make up? Did you tell them the other reason for the trip, then?'

'No. Everything blew apart before I could.' She explained about the other secrets – Emily's mum, Tiff and Jasmine.

'But you were teenagers back then! When I was sixteen, I hadn't told some of my best friends that I thought I was gay. Big things, little things, sometimes to cope, we have to hold it in for a while. Keep it private, until we can make sense of it ourselves. Or just to avoid the upset. Being my age can be hard enough. By the sounds of it, Emily and Tiff had their reasons. None of us are perfect.'

As a little boy, Olly would put a hot dog on a plate, give it nacho wings, raisin eyes, spaghetti antennae, and refuse to eat it. He also loved whoopee cushions. Since when had he become so wise? She told him about Prestige Fitness and how Felix helped with his company's charity projects – and how the surf shop owner in France suspected Felix had been running away from someone.

Olly finished his tea. 'It still hurts, Mum. I can't say it doesn't. You could have done this years ago. I'd have loved to have met my grandmother.' A muscle in his cheek twitched. 'But now is better than never. It's a start.'

She reached across the table and offered her hand. After a few seconds, he slid his into it.

'I'm going to call Vikram. I don't have to keep this a secret, right?'

'No. There's nothing to keep secret about you, Olly. If I wasn't so wary of heights, I'd climb to the top of one of those skyscrapers in Deansgate and shout that you make me the proudest mother in the whole of Manchester.'

Olly reached into his rucksack and pulled out a red, oblong bar. 'Good thing I brought back Swiss chocolate then.' His voice wavered as he pushed it over.

'Go on, scoot, ring your friend,' she said, in an equally unsteady voice. 'But I can't promise there'll be any of this left by the time you've finished.'

31

PAIGE

A key sounded in the lock. Overcome with the fear of a permanent wedge developing between her and Felix, Paige concentrated on the pan without turning around. Eggs Benedict, a favourite treat of his – second only to a bacon butty. She'd wanted to make something special for their first meal together in a week. She'd gone out early for the Saturday paper and to buy him a chocolate egg for tomorrow. Easter was the one time of year health-conscious Felix allowed himself to eat an excess of sugar. Paige stirred the Hollandaise sauce. She'd not been able to settle to read the weekend magazine. They'd had a brief phone call when she'd got back to the B&B last Wednesday, after the coffee with Sal, after his message came through about Rob having contacted him.

Why hadn't Paige told him Morgan had got in touch? That he was a father? That she was off to France with her old best friends? What else was she keeping from him? Didn't they tell each other everything?

Sal's voice ringing in her ears, she'd kept calm. They weren't teenagers any more. She apologised as best she could, explained the choices she'd made, said she loved him. Felix hadn't reciprocated, didn't even say goodbye before ringing off. She'd messaged the next day but got no reply. Paige had hardly slept since leaving Cornwall. She'd lost her friends again. Would she lose her husband?

The apartment door squeaked open. When she'd met Felix for the first time again, in her late twenties, her heart had ached as she'd listened, an ache that turned into a love that grew year by year, as Felix's confidence built and, through work, he'd helped youngsters struggling like he used to. He made her want to be a better person. He saw through the money, her posh accent, he kept Paige's secrets, like about the time she'd eaten a magic mushroom at university – and had teased her mercilessly that *that* was her biggest secret.

Oh, she'd get through if they ever split up. Marriage was a label. Like a designer jacket, with the fashion house's name cut out, it would still wear the same, still fit as well, like her daily life would without her gold band ring. She'd still go to work, pay her mortgage, see her parents and drink the odd cocktail. But even though her life would look full, without Felix, it would be hollow.

'Paige?'

She turned to face... his tired features, a mouth down-turned, skin dull, eyes that lit up when they met hers. Felix let go of his case and strode over.

'I'm a shit. Sorry I haven't messaged.' He held out his hand.

'I'm the one who should be apologising,' she croaked, relief rushing through her as they collapsed onto the sofa, arms around each other. 'How did your trip go?' she asked.

He perched on the edge of the sofa and held both her hands in his. 'Paige, I don't care about that. I've missed you. But also I've just found out I'm a father. Tell me everything about Olly. Is it Oliver?'

'Morgan didn't say.'

'Does he blame me for not being around?'

'All I know is, he's been desperate to meet you. He's going to study physics at university.'

'Gets his brains from his mother then,' said Felix and he gave a sad smile. 'I've played no part in shaping his life. It's... painful.'

'His looks are from you though. Olly's the absolute spit. Morgan told me a little. He's got a boyfriend called Vikram. Coming to terms with his sexuality was the final trigger for wanting to find you. It's an identity thing...'

'Really?' Felix tilted his head. 'Maybe I'll be able relate to him on that. My outside felt so unlike the inside at school, some days I had no idea who

I really was. It was the pits, as if I were a fake, covering up the truth. Poor Olly. If only I'd been around to offer him support.' He sighed. 'I've missed so much – his first tooth, his first day at nursery. I've not been there to help with homework or to listen if he's had a tough day at school, to pass on what I learnt, after everything I went through. I've never met him but it's as if I've already let Olly down. If only Morgan had told me back in 2004.'

'But you and your mum had already left England by the time she found out.'

'We had? Right. Yes. Of course.'

Paige squeezed his hands. 'You must be excited to meet him,' she said, forcing her voice to keep steady. 'Now you've got this amazing opportunity to make a difference. Oh, damn!' She jumped up and ran over to the hob. Smoke came out of the Hollandaise sauce pan. She turned the ring off, inwardly sighing. Yet another egg-fail. 'Might have to make bacon butties,' she said, in the best no-nonsense voice she could muster.

Felix got up and went into the kitchen. He leant against the marble-topped work top. 'I know what you're afraid of,' he said.

'Guilty as charged,' she replied and broke eye contact, 'I'm worried you've *not* come back with those amazing-looking pistachio and charcoal pastries from that travel programme we saw about the UAE that you promised me.'

He put his hands on her shoulders. 'Olly... it's a lot to take in. I... I am excited to meet him. It's scary too. What if I'm a disappointment? What if I'm the worst things he's imagined over the years because he must have thought me a right villain? But I want to make it work. Really, I do.'

Paige lifted up one of her hands, placed it on one of his. 'I'll do everything I can to help.'

He kissed her fingers. 'And I love you for it. But equally important to building a relationship with *my son*...' He let go of her and paced up and down. 'A son. I have a son. It's going to take some getting used to.' He rubbed a hand over his head and stopped walking, faced her again. 'Equally important is us building a family, having a child of our own as well, whatever it takes, Paige, remember? Don't get scared that I'll ever drop that goal.'

'You mean it?' She gulped.

'You and me... that's the most important thing in my life.'

They made bacon butties together, Felix putting on mustard, Paige ketchup, him choosing brown bread, Paige white. She didn't work out with weights, gagged at protein shakes, Felix got bored in art galleries and had only a functional interest in clothes, but the bond between them had only got stronger over the years. They ate on the sofa, something they never normally did, but then a lot of things were going to be different from now on. Paige gazed through the windows, onto the balcony and out to Manchester's skyline that, over time, had become taller and less green.

'About what you said earlier... whatever it takes... I talked to Morgan, Emily and Paige about wanting kids, how... it hasn't proved easy to get pregnant.'

Felix stopped eating.

'I'm going to see the doctor. Maybe be referred. Have some tests. I've been hiding from the fact we may have a problem. One thing this last week has shown me is that the truth always comes out eventually. So I'd like to take control and find it out for myself – for ourselves. Olly... he's proven the issue is with me.'

'Or there may be no issue,' Felix countered. 'It might be Mother Nature taking her time. But count me in. I'm coming to any appointment. I've worked my butt off at work. They'll give me the time off.'

A sense of hopefulness washed through her. She kissed him on the cheek. His aftershave smelt familiar, comforting.

'I'll make coffee,' she said, 'and then I want to hear about Dubai.'

'But first, you tell me about your trip and Morgan, Emily and Tiff.' He stopped for a moment. A pained expression crossed his face, one Paige had seen before; he wore it every time he thought back to Dailsworth High.

She went to get up but Felix's phone pinged. He looked at his screen, cheeks flushing.

'Olly Banks. Paige, he's contacted me.'

She shuffled up next to him and together, they read the text.

32

EMILY

Emily sat down in the garden centre. Easter Saturday and she was lucky to find a free table in the café, others filled with retired couples or families with young children. It was one of her and Lewis's favourite places to have coffee, so harmless, so tranquil, with its cheerful plants and gift section, the shelves of wholesome farm food. It provided such an uplifting, predictable atmosphere, the opposite to that in A&E or in an ambulance – and this one sold loaded meringue nests more suited to eagles than wrens in size. Emily's shoulders relaxed, her breathing eased, as she studied the menu – until a hand brushed her arm.

'Lewis.' Despite the years they'd been together, she always pictured him, in her head, in his green uniform. Today, he wore jeans and a sweatshirt. 'Thanks for coming. What can I get you?'

'My usual, please. But let me get them.'

'Don't be daft.' She joined the queue, taking her purse, leaving her handbag at the table, trusting Lewis to make sure no one took it. Trust with a man that had taken a long time to build.

Paige and Hugo. How could that be? Emily had seen Paige's face at the prom when he'd revealed all her secrets, the set jaw determined not to allow her to cry. That bastard had made fools of them all, played with their emotions, conned them into... conning each other. Rob's face popped into her mind and how warmly he'd spoken about the person Hugo – Felix – had become. Actually said he loved him.

Perhaps Felix was still a con artist.

She carried over the coffees – and two meringue nests.

'I like your hair,' he said.

'Thanks. I managed to get an appointment this morning. It needed tidying up.'

'And I haven't seen that jumper for a few years. Yellow always has suited you.'

Emily had knitted it several years ago, before the world became less sunny. She dug her fork into her meringue next and in between mouthfuls, told Lewis about her trip.

He sipped his coffee. 'I'm sorry it ended badly. Have you been in touch with any of them since you got back?'

'I wanted to. And I almost rang Tiff a couple of times. But what's the point?'

'You've mentioned them over the years, laughed about the cases you solved. I've sensed how much that group meant to you, and must do still now because you told them the truth about your mum, a truth you'd only told one person, me, until your French trip.'

This was true. Oh, years ago, when Hugo had fooled her into thinking she was in love, Emily had almost told him the truth as well, but she hadn't. Lewis was the one and only.

'I... I haven't told you everything.' Emily picked up her fork and played with a splodge of cream and berries until it turned runny. She could do this. 'How, the last few years, it's brought everything about her back. It's as if I've been taken for a mug again, like a stupid, naïve teenager, working my guts out and not being appreciated for it. That... that's at the heart, Lewis, of why I want to leave my job. I didn't tell you because it sounds pathetic. I'm a grown woman now, you probably think I should have got over it, but... when I think back, I still feel like that angry, devastated teenage girl.' Her eyes darted towards him.

'Oh, Ems... really? Right... I had no idea. Thanks. Thanks for trusting me with this.'

She bit her lip.

'I wish you'd told me before. I... I totally get it – why it's so hard for you to move on. What your mother did was utterly unforgiveable.'

Her shoulders relaxed. A lump grew in her throat. Of course Lewis would understand. 'I couldn't open up because voicing my feelings out loud would have brought back the shame, as if I'd let myself down. Many patients were lovely people, colleagues too. I've tried, really tried, to keep perspective, but every time a relative has shouted, every time a newspaper headline has criticised strikes... it's made me feel worthless all over again, like I'm an idiot for letting people take advantage of me.'

'You aren't worthless,' he said firmly, 'and I owe you a huge apology. I should have worked it out.'

'How could you if I clammed up? Perhaps the two of us should have just talked more.' She gave a tentative smile. 'Talking with Morgan, Paige and Tiff has given me new insight. I won't let Mum ruin my future.' She pushed away her plate. 'I've got a plan and intend to see it through.'

He studied her. 'You look good, Emily, as if the trip has relit your spark.' His voice wavered. 'One reason I left: I couldn't bear the thought that I was making you sad, saying the wrong things, hurting your feelings.' He took a moment. 'I'd do anything to make you happy, Ems. Even the hardest thing of all. Leaving.'

Oh, Lewis. They gazed at each other, an unfamiliar but not unpleasant shyness overcoming her as their legs touched under the table.

Since getting back to Manchester, Emily *had* felt more like the old her. These last few days, a strength had come back she'd never appreciated before the worldwide crisis hit. She'd tidied up takeout boxes, thrown away empty bottle of wine... and a few still full. She cleaned the house, did several loads of laundry, actually baked and for the first time, fully engaged with her therapy session. She hadn't had a single drink – hadn't wanted to. The prospect of a different future gave her the high her life had been missing.

'I just wish I could have helped more – that you didn't need to go to France to work things out.'

'How could you? I've not been a patient on a stretcher with a broken foot or collar bone; mental breaks are harder to spot, harder to fix. And you have helped Lewis, I can see that now. I really value having you in my life...'

'Emily, look...' His eyebrows knotted together.

'The divorce papers...' She gulped. 'If you really think it's best...'

'I don't know!' he blurted out. 'My head says yes but my heart shouts no.'

'Same here!' Emily took his hand, almost knocking over her coffee. 'We can work this out, can't we? Give things another go? Put off signing the papers. Give our marriage another shot?'

'Yes. Yes, we can. Maybe... maybe go on some dates? And if things go well... perhaps I could move back in?'

'Smudge will be over the moon. He's missed the way you scratch behind his ears.'

He lifted her hand and kissed the palm, then he blushed, let go.

'Also... I realise, now I *can* change career direction, and you've been instrumental in me reaching that decision too, Lewis.'

'But I've been telling you not to leave nursing. Whilst you were in France, Cornwall... I questioned myself over this. I've been so dead set on you not leaving the profession, one you excel at, I can see now that it's been unfair of me – a hundred times over now that I know recent years brought back bad feelings about your mum.' He stared at her curiously. 'You going off to France like that, being totally spontaneous, it's so unlike you.'

'What do you mean?'

'Oh come on, Emily. You've eaten the same thing for breakfast ever since we met.'

'Five blueberries and five strawberries on porridge, with a squirt of honey and dash of milk is a great start to the day.'

They grinned at each other in a way they hadn't for months.

'When you're married for so long, you assume you know everything about your partner, but you just heading off like that, with your old mates, having not seen them for so long, showed there are parts of you I don't know. Of course there are, I mean, that's normal, right? So who am I to say what's best for you?'

'But you did. Sort of.' Emily sat more upright, looking as if a surgeon had told her great news about a patient. 'I'm going to carry on using my nursing skills – but not with humans. You know how much I've always loved animals? Well, talking about Mum, openly, in France, took me back to before she got ill and what I wanted to do with my life until fate played a hand and taught me the skills to look after another person.' Her talking sped up, she could hardly contain he fizz in her stomach. 'I'd forgotten how much I wanted to be a veterinary nurse. So you were right after all. I'm simply diversifying.' Emily talked about one course she'd already looked into, how it would take a couple of years to qualify.

Lewis leant back in his chair. 'Blimey. I never saw that coming.' He grinned. 'Jesus, Emily. It's perfect.' He picked up his fork and dug into the meringue again. 'Looks like your working life is getting back on track, then. What about your friends... can you salvage any of those three friendships? Who was the least at fault for what happened?'

'All of us, none of us... We each had issues back in the day.'

Lewis finished the last mouthful. 'I treated a woman in her eighties earlier in the week. Nancy. She'd had a fall. Fractured her pelvis. It didn't stop her chatting. She even made us laugh. I checked in on her later, after my shift the next day. She was in fine spirits after a partial hip replacement. She wasn't worried about going home because of two friends who'd make sure she was okay. The three of them had been friends since school, stayed in Manchester and kept in touch – apart from the years they weren't talking, the sixties when they were in their twenties.'

'Why did they fall out?'

'At that time, one became a dope-smoking hippy, her other friend a staunch member of the women's liberation movement, whereas Nancy got married young and revelled in looking after her husband and home-making. On the surface, their common ground had disappeared and eventually this led to a big row, each calling the others patronising and judgemental. They didn't speak to each other for almost ten years.'

'How come they are still friends now?'

'She said she reckoned childhood friendship is unique. Special bonds are formed that cut through the nonsense of being an adult. They met up again when one of the others suffered a miscarriage. Nancy believes that when you become friends with someone as a child, you've seen the core of their personality that doesn't change. Whereas friends you make as adults never know the full picture, the backstory, they only meet the current version of you.' He sipped his coffee. 'Sorry, I'm going on. She was also a big

Man City fan. I stayed far longer than I intended with her. What I'm saying is... the friendships we make as kids, don't often come along later in life. In fact, when I got home last night, I reached out to Tommy Chapman on Facebook. We were best friends throughout school and lost touch when he worked as a holiday rep. We're meeting for a drink next week.'

They gave each other a tentative hug in the car park after arranging for him to come around one evening next week to help Emily research more veterinary nursing colleges in the area. As she drove home, Emily thought about Nancy. Whilst other people were probably going to question her choice of moving from treating humans to pets, she wouldn't need to explain to Morgan, Paige and Tiff. Years ago, come rain or shine, Tiff would accompany her when she'd sometimes walked next door's dog, knowing how much Emily loved doing it. And Paige would laugh about how her cat bolted straight for Emily whenever she'd visited because she always snuck in Dairylea cheese triangles for him, and Morgan had once helped her bury a dead magpie they'd found in the street, even saying a prayer over it despite being non-believers.

Emily had finally come home to her true self.

33

TIFF

Joe gave a wave as Tiff walked into the Corn Exchange. He stood outside Mowgli's. Saturday night and the building was bustling. She'd booked a table for seven, simply telling her parents she was meeting a friend. A friend that made her heart race in a way Carter and Marlon hadn't. Mum and Dad didn't need to know that. Carter looked like James Bond in a tux, Marlon like a rock star when he wore his leather trousers with a chain belt, but the flutters were superficial, whereas Joe sent blood rushing to deeper parts of her body.

And just like that, Tiff sounded like the scriptwriter of a B movie. During recent weeks, she'd done her best to ignore the growing sense of wanting to be with Joe. She found herself looking out of her window for him, jogging more often, and she made sure she looked her best when nipping out for milk or bread. All this despite one of Joe's most attractive qualities being how he acted as if he wouldn't care if she looked as scruffy as the local stray tabby he always talked to.

The waitress took them to their table, in a corner, dimly lit by fairy lights. Tiff breathed in the aroma of spices.

'How was your meeting with Max?' she asked once they'd sat down.

'First things first – I need a beer. Wine for you?'

She nodded before proceeding to point out her favourites on the menu – sticky chicken, the restaurant's amazing treacle fries, a special coleslaw, butter chicken, Himalayan cheese on toast. Joe insisted she choose the dishes and they share them.

'Tell me about your week, that's far more important than my day,' he said, after the waitress had delivered their drinks. 'Did you find this Hugo? What was it like meeting him after all this time? How did you and your friends get on?'

Tiff had given Joe the barest details before leaving London: that she and her friends hated this Hugo at school and that he'd caused a rift between them.

'He's called Felix now. I didn't get to meet him. My friends – old friends – and I got on okay, until a big argument at the end, so now we're back where we started. I won't get in touch with them again.'

'Do you want to talk about it?' he asked gently.

'I'd much rather hear about Max's new venture. Are you signing up?'

Don't. Don't come up and live in Manchester. We'll almost never see each other once I'm back in London.

There'd be no one to make her do a warm-up before running, no one to laugh at the eighties headband and leg warmers she liked wearing, or to pretend to be blinded by her favourite sparkly eye shadow. She didn't know anyone else who loved doing butterfly stroke in the pool, a way of swimming she'd had to learn for a bit part in a straight-to-DVD movie, or who also insisted on putting takeout pizza on plates and eating it with a knife and fork. Smooth Carter and Marlon kept their quirks hidden – they weren't paid to show their true personality – whereas Joe's were on display for all to see: how he sang as they jogged, old school rock like 'Under Pressure' by Queen, and he had a habit of smelling food before he ate it, drinks too, and books, even new running shoes.

They'd first met when she was out jogging; it used to be a rare thing for Tiff that only took place just before a new shoot. For motivation, a fellow actor had recommended an app to listen to, that made noises as if zombies were chasing you. Her earbuds lead had somehow worked its way out of the phone and a loud zombie moan sounded just as Joe passed. He'd given

Tiff the weirdest look and unable to stop laughing, she'd had to stop and explain.

Those dimples, twinkling eyes, the uneven mouth, the warm laughter that said Joe was joining in and not taking the piss... a shiver had run up and down her spine. She hadn't forgotten it because it still happened now.

Yet she had no clue as to whether Joe felt something too. Over in France, she'd pictured her and Joe on the beach, learning how to windsurf, both of them expending far too much energy teasing each other, holding hands as they walked into the sunset on the sand, carrying their sandals. With Carter and Marlon, she'd always dressed up in sexy dresses for dinner, frequented fancy bars, attended starry parties, all the things she'd done over the years to prove to herself that she was worthy. If Joe complimented her, it was about her even breathing after a run or her accomplished moves in the water. She'd come home from a cast event once, sparkling from head to foot. He'd been out for a late jog and sped over to say hello. He didn't comment on her diamante studded jacket, didn't ask for the gossip; instead, he spoke about how much he admired her ambition and professionalism, and took her arm when she yawned, insisting he make both of them a hot chocolate.

Unless all of this meant he didn't fancy her. Tiff took a glug of wine.

'Max's business sounds well planned,' replied Joe. 'He wants to run drama workshops, in the "Make you a star" vein. In fact, that's what he's called the venture. He's got on board a make-up artist and photographer to create a more fun atmosphere, make it more appealing to youngsters.'

'Right, that sounds interesting, albeit quite different for you to working in a school.'

'Sure does. Apparently, there's big money in it though; social-media-led parents are always looking for clubs like this for their kids, and with celebrities more accessible than ever these days, that's fed into older children on Instagram who want to access the glamorous lifestyle they see daily.'

'Then there are the parents like mine who, regardless of socials, want their kid to shine in a way they couldn't,' she said. 'They would have definitely sent me to a club with a name like Make You A Star.'

'Manchester is the place to do it too, with its history of creative adventurousness, with its vibrancy...' Joe said with enthusiasm. 'My train arrived early and I took a look around – the Northern Quarter, the Village, Deansgate. Talk about eclectic, and I loved the buskers in Market Street. But... I also came across rough sleepers. It's clear drug and drink problems aren't being tackled widely enough. So on a whim, I asked Max if he'd consider running mental health workshops as well. I've read up on some over the years, in scenarios like addiction clinics, and I'm in charge of wellbeing drama workshops at school where we explore emotional problems and coping mechanisms. The kids always say it's really useful.' He shrugged. 'But Max's main aim is to rake in money. He's tired of living on his teacher wage. He's always accepted he didn't have it in him to make it on the stage, but doesn't see why that should stop him earning big bucks. I don't blame him.'

'You've spoken of your frustration at how hard it is to get on the property ladder. I guess working for Max might help you with that.' Joe rented. His flat was much smaller than hers, yet he wanted to put down permanent roots.

'For sure. Visiting Manchester, loving the vibe, it's revealed there are other places in England I could be happy, where housing is much more affordable, so that's not a factor.'

The waitress delivered their food. Conversation stopped as Joe smelt the dishes and started eating, his face talking louder than words.

'Wow. I might have to come back to Manchester for this place alone.' Joe wiped his mouth. 'But not to work with Max. I think, for me, sticking with school teaching will be more rewarding.'

The treacle fries in Tiff's mouth suddenly tasted even sweeter.

'It must have been great growing up here,' he said.

'Fantastic shopping. You should visit Afflecks indoor market. Great coffee shops. My friends and I used to love the Christmas markets. But then the prom happened and it all got screwed.' She ate more butter chicken, drank more wine and then told Joe exactly what Hugo had done.

'For the first time...' Her voice wavered. 'A boy saw through my outside – the... the extra curves none of the other girls had, the clumsy manner. I used to pretend to the world – even to my friends – that I didn't care about my shape, but inside I longed to look like Kiera Knightly.'

Joe put down his knife and fork. Hesitated. Took out his phone. He scrolled through his photos and stopped at a woman, a little older than him with the same green eyes and kindly air.

'Alice?' asked Tiff. He'd talked about his older sister often. She lived in Essex where he'd grown up, was married with two children who always beat Joe at board games.

'Yes. She'd wanted to look like Kate Hudson. She'd ended up in hospital weighing less than six stone.'

'Oh Joe. I'm so sorry. You've never mentioned that before.'

'It's still painful to talk about everything she went through.' Joe didn't speak for a moment. 'I've never been so frightened than when the doctors said she'd suffered heart damage. She lacked confidence about how she looked but I dismissed that as a teenage thing, then it got so much worse.'

'Poor Alice. My problems were nothing like hers.'

'You can't rank sadness and low self-esteem. A friend of hers started using laxatives and that random factor was the beginning of Alice's downhill spiral. It taught me a lesson I'm grateful for – that looks are the last thing that matter. Yeah, I could try for a six-pack.' He picked up a treacle fry. 'But I'd rather have my takeout. I'm sorry this Hugo... Felix, whatever he's called, in the end made you even more insecure.'

This was new for Tiff. Opening up to the opposite sex. With Carter and Marlon, she kept conversations strictly on the surface. She and Joe talked about his sister and how Alice got into recovery. Tiff explained the pressures of her industry to look good, how it wasn't only on women these days. Whatever film genre they were in, male actor friends felt an expectation to have the body of a Marvel hero. Joe ordered another plate of cheese on toast at that point and Tiff couldn't help laughing. They moved on, again, to the wellbeing workshops Joe ran in school, and a flicker of something, deep down, ignited in Tiff, a spark that grew and grew as they finished their meal and ordered coffee.

'I could come into your school and help run workshops to do with body image,' said Tiff. 'I did one in a local theatre near me, a couple of years ago.

The kids were set challenges to improve their self-esteem, were asked to act out and interpret words such as "powerful" and "confident". The aim was to create a safe space where issues like eating disorders and body dysmorphia could be discussed.' Tiff couldn't stop talking, brainstorming about what each session could focus on.

'Tiff, this sounds brilliant,' said Joe and he asked her several questions about the concept before typing bullet points into his phone. 'Alice has often talked about how she'd like to share her experience too. She could be a visitor to the workshops.'

Across the table, Tiff smiled at Joe. She hadn't gone to the Ladies once whilst they'd eaten, to reapply her lipstick. She'd been too busy eating – as much as she wanted.

After paying the bill, they stood outside the Corn Exchange.

'Come over to mine for dinner after your Isle of Wight trip,' said Joe. 'We can put together a plan of these workshops, to pitch to the head.'

'Sounds like a date,' she said and then blushed. 'Not that I meant...'

Paige popped into her head: how she'd snatched Tiff's phone, locked herself in the loo and texted to Joe that Tiff would love to meet up with him.

No friends since 2004 had understood Tiff as well as The Secret Gift Society members.

She stepped forwards. 'No, actually, I *do* mean that, Joe. A date. You and me. Are you in?'

Joe looked as if one of his pupils had recited the whole of a Shakespearian play by heart. 'Wow. Yes, Tiff. A thousand times yes. Jeez, my charms need polishing. How many months has this taken?'

'How many jogs, more like?' she said and groaned.

They laughed and she slipped her hand into his. 'I... I need to take it slow. I haven't managed to shake off trust issues... since Hugo. Silly, really...'

He took her other hand. 'No, it's not. Things that happen when we're that young stick with us, as if bad events become part of our biology. But like we can heal an infection, we can heal old emotional wounds. It's just a matter of finding the right medicine.' He lifted her hand up and kissed the top of it. 'We've got all the time in the world. I can't promise I'll never hurt you. Relationships get messy. But I'll always try not to and I'll always be honest. Is that enough, Tiff?'

Head narrating her feelings like that B movie scriptwriter, Tiff leant forwards, every nerve tingling, and under the gaze of an approving moonlit sky, her lips touched his and her heart popped with desire.

34

MORGAN

Olly loped into the kitchen yawning in his black T-shirt and werewolf-print pyjama trousers. He went over to the Easter Egg on the kitchen table. 'Snickers? Another favourite. But it's Easter Monday today, not Sunday. What have I done to deserve two this year?'

'I can spoil my son, can't I?' Morgan pushed an empty bowl towards him and the cereal box. 'Juice?'

'Thanks, Mum.' He glanced at the window sill and the bunch of flowers, still in their wrap, standing in a vase of water. 'Are you going today, then, to that retired teacher's birthday party?'

'Still not sure,' she said and swiftly asked about his work hours.

'I'm on the afternoon shift, so can Vikram come over for an early lunch?'

'Of course.' She got up and poured him a juice. Sat back down again. Picked at her toast. Morgan went to say something but changed her mind.

The rings under his eyes darker than usual, Olly studied her. 'Thanks, Mum.'

'That's okay. Vikram's a nice lad.'

'No... for not grilling me yesterday – after my phone call.'

'Oh. Well, I figured you'd need time to digest it.' It hadn't been easy. In the end, she'd gone out for a walk. When Olly used to come home from primary school, she'd tease out details of his day over biscuits, loving listening to excited talk about playtime and his favourite lessons. Or they'd have a cuddle if someone had been mean or his free school dinner had been 'yucky'. Those open conversations very much depended on his hormones as he progressed through high school, and these days, she strived to respect his privacy, despite her maternal sense of wanting to protect him.

Olly scooped up a mouthful of cereal and carried on until his dish stood empty. After downing his juice, he leant on the table with his elbows. 'It was weird, talking to him after so many years of not knowing if he was even alive. I've imagined so many conversations, but when it came to it, I had no idea what to say.'

'As if you were in some parallel universe?'

'Yeah, one where you'd eat chocolate eggs for breakfast instead of those from chickens.' He reached for his egg and gave a small smile as Morgan shot him a disapproving look. Olly folded his arms. 'He didn't sound like I'd always expected; his Manchester accent wasn't very strong. He asked about school. Asked about university. It was... awkward.'

'Bound to be, love.'

'He even asked about Vikram. Totally embarrassing.'

Morgan sat a little straighter. This was new, another person being treated like she was. For some reason, Olly humoured his gran's questions about his boyfriend, but if Morgan asked anything, it was written off as cringeworthy.

'Felix told me about his job. Asked if I was into the gym. We haven't got anything in common.'

'How did the call end?'

'He said it would be cool if the three of us could meet up. At his, or ours, or in a café. He said he was really happy we'd spoken. That he wanted to be a part of my life.'

'What did you say?'

'*Maybe*. Then I said goodbye and hung up.'

'Do you want to get to know him?'

Olly took his elbows off the table and leant back. 'What if he's disappointed, Mum? What if I am? What if it fizzles out? What if... he hurts you again?'

Oh, Olly. Sweet, caring, Olly who deserved so much. She gave him all of herself. But as he got older, he wouldn't always want Mum around, not like when he was little and the two of them lived in such a happy world of books and crafting, of park walks and baking together, of feel-good movies and having friends to tea. As he'd moved through the teenage years, other people had become important: mates at school, that physics teacher he'd stay behind with after class to talk about nanowires and quantum dots, that young woman who worked at the garden centre and loved fantasy movies as much as him.

A dad might become one of those other people who mattered as he continued to become less reliant on Morgan.

'That's a lot of what ifs. What ifs hold you back in life unless you turn them around – what if the two of you get on great? What if you build a solid relationship?' She gave him a sharp look. 'For the record, it would be impossible for any father to be disappointed in my Olly Banks.'

'But what if you still hate him?' Olly muttered.

Morgan broke off the corner of her slice of toast and chewed on it for a second. 'I don't have all the answers, Olly, but I'm prepared to hear his story. Paige got together with him again as a grown woman. She runs her own business, has responsibilities, and has worked hard to achieve her goals. I'm hoping that means that she's savvier than the teenager who was taken in – like the rest of us – and that he's changed.'

What Felix had done at school had been coldblooded. It wasn't like stealing someone's lunch box or even cheating on a girlfriend. He'd spent weeks conning four girls into falling for him. Then humiliated them in front of the whole school...

However, since having Olly and gaining a different perspective on the school playground, her view had altered on bullies. Each had a story that explained their behaviour. Like the one in Olly's class, at primary school. She made mean comments about other kids who didn't have as nice school stationary or trainers. Turned out her parents had split up, a bad divorce, and her dad showered her with gifts, in a clumsy attempt to keep her happy. Occasionally, over the years, when she was less angry about the prom and about the gap growing between her and Olly over his dad, Morgan had wondered what Hugo's story had been. Or rather Felix's. His new name would take some getting used to.

Morgan reached for the jam and slathered more on the remaining piece of toast. She ate a large mouthful. 'In any case, Olly... I trust you.'

Olly met her eye.

'I trust you to make the right decision about your father. It doesn't matter if I'm not keen. You're one of the most intelligent, generous people I know. If you want to meet him, you'll give Felix a fair hearing – and you won't let him pull a fast one, either. You'll see him for the man he is now.' She put a hand on his shoulder. 'Follow your heart, love. I'll be here if you need me. We can meet him together, for the first time, if you prefer. Whatever suits.' She kissed him on the head, went over to the sink and turned the taps on.

Olly stood up to go. He turned around at the kitchen door. 'I had to be really brave, ringing Felix yesterday. I almost chickened out.'

'I'm proud of you – whatever the outcome.'

'Perhaps I take after you, Mum. You're one of the bravest people I know. By my age, you had a two-year-old kid, you were looking out for me, making sure I had everything I needed, putting yourself second, getting a job you've never really liked much. That takes guts.'

Morgan gripped the washing-up sponge tightly.

'And it's time for you to be brave again. You've got two hours until one o'clock. Get yourself showered, Mum. Put on those nice grey jeans you bought. I'm thinking last chances don't come along very often.'

Morgan turned just in time to catch the back of Olly's head as he disappeared out of the kitchen and went upstairs. Here he was, taking charge of the situation. In that moment, not going to uni, not getting a degree, none of that mattered because everything up to this point had led to her being lucky enough to know such an amazing young man, an amazing adult.

Her – and Felix's – wonderful son.

35

MORGAN

Morgan walked down Greenacre Lane, carrying the bunch of flowers and a box of homemade fudge. She'd experimented with a new recipe, yesterday, just in case she went: crème brûlée flavour. Olly had given her a thumbs-up through the window as she reached the end of their drive. Morgan turned up her collar, braced the fresh spring wind and hoped the trek would clear her head. Didn't work. Shoulders tight, as if she was sat at her till and a long queue had formed, she stood before the front door, raised her hand to ring the bell, changed her mind. A face appeared at the window, curious eyes behind gold frames, a brown pixie cut especially blow dried. The door opened.

'Bienvenue, ma pucette! So pleased you came. Are those flowers for me? You are so generous.'

'Happy Birthday!' Morgan passed her the box of fudge. Mlle Vachon may not have worn designer clothes, but she'd always smelt expensive, Parisian, and Morgan breathed in a heady, sweet scent.

'Are your friends coming?' she asked.

Morgan's shoulders relaxed. They weren't here. Good. Sad. 'I don't know,' she said brightly and wiped her feet before following Mlle Vachon through the narrow hallway, lined with Impressionist prints, and into her lounge. 'Now, how about you introduce me to that travel agent boyfriend of yours?'

Mlle Vachon stared at her for a moment and then smiled. 'What would you like to drink? I have my favourite Pastis, but it's not to everyone's taste. There is wine, beer or soft drinks. Or George will be happy to make coffee.'

Two couples around Mlle Vachon's age sat with plates full of food, talking about the upcoming celebrations for King Charles's coronation in May. Another younger couple said hello and prompted their small girl, who sat cross-legged on the carpet, drawing, to do so too. Three women in their sixties chatted about a film they wanted to see. Jazz music played in the background. Mlle Vachon introduced Morgan to her friends and neighbours. It was an open-plan lounge and dining room and Mlle Vachon led Morgan to the back where cold food was set out on a large oval table. It included a sliced baguette alongside a plate of cured meats and a colourful cheese board. To the left was a hatch that went through to the kitchen. On it sat glasses and drinks bottles. In the kitchen stood a short, bald man, holding a tea towel in front of his checked waistcoat.

'George, this is Morgan, who I told you about,' said Mlle Vachon.

His wrinkles deepened and he came over to the hatch. He flipped the tea towel over his shoulder. 'Lovely to meet you. What's your poison?'

The doorbell rang and Mlle Vachon hurried away. As he poured out her glass of orange juice, Morgan asked George about his years working in travel. She mentioned her recent trip to the south of France.

'The Riviera never goes out of fashion,' he said. 'In fact, Remy and I hope to holiday in St Tropez this year.'

Remy. How lovely. Morgan never knew that was Mlle Vachon's name. Whereas the house was familiar, as the girls had visited once. Mlle Vachon had been off school after a minor operation, and they'd hated the temporary teacher that replaced her and made them conjugate verbs ad nauseam. They'd popped around with a get well card, even writing in French inside. The room was as cluttered, and the girls had loved it. Mlle Vachon had given them a free rein to look at her trinkets, like the collection of small, copper kettles in front of the fireplace and the little music boxes still on the unit next to the television. One played 'La Vie en Rose' and Morgan had closed her eyes, drinking the *chocolat chaud* Mlle Vachon made them, pretending she was in a café in Paris. The armchairs were more modern now, she had blinds instead of curtains, and a metal uplighter instead of the old-fashioned lampshade, yet the place had kept its distinct, striking character with the same colour palette, gemstone themed with ruby reds, sapphire blues and emerald greens. On top of a unit to the right of a hatch was a large glass tank, containing two goldfish. She'd let the girls feed her old fish, Gauguin.

A woman came towards the hatch. 'Morgan,' said a calm voice.

'Emily... you came?'

Mlle Vachon shot them a curious look before lifting up a plate of mini onion tarts and handing them around.

George asked Emily what she'd like to drink and then the two women moved to the side, standing by the French window.

'I wasn't sure you'd come,' said Morgan.

'Me neither. It was a last-minute decision.' Emily wore a smart blouse tucked into navy jeans and her hair had been cut and styled. It was now several inches shorter than in Cornwall. 'But Mlle Vachon was always good to us. I brought her a tin of English biscuits, do you remember – she used to dish them out in class, after a test? Digestives, shortbread, malted milk, she'd say the French couldn't beat our biscuits and fish and chips.' Emily thanked George for the lemonade and he went off as the doorbell rang again. She looked out of the window. 'Despite how things ended... I'm glad you found Hugo. Felix,' she said, tightly.

'Thank you for coming on the trip.' Morgan hated the formality between them.

'Right. Better mingle.' Emily went into the lounge, just as Tiff walked in. They glanced at each other before Emily accepted an onion tart from Mlle Vachon and sat down beside the women still chatting about the cinema. Tiff handed a shiny, helium balloon to Mlle Vachon, along with a bottle of champagne. She directed Tiff towards the hatch and George gave her a glass of wine. Tiff then walked over to Morgan, still by the window.

'Good of you to come,' said Morgan politely. 'You must have a lot of packing to do before leaving for the Isle of Wight on Wednesday.'

'Yes, all the essentials. Toiletries. Clothes. Night light.'

'You still don't like the dark when you sleep on your own?'

Tiff shrugged and glanced over Morgan's shoulder, into the garden. 'Do you think Paige will come?'

'I doubt it.'

'She shouldn't have deceived us but... I went too far, accusing her of seeing Olly as a threat.'

Morgan exhaled. 'We probably all said a lot of things we didn't mean.' She picked up an olive and ate it. Today wasn't about her, it wasn't about The Secret Gift Society; it was about their beloved Miss Moo Moo. She went over to her. 'Is there anything I can do to help?' she asked Mlle Vachon. 'Are those mini croque-monsieurs I saw? They look amazing. You made them that time we came around to visit.'

Mlle Vachon beamed. 'Although I hope you won't be disappointed with my cake. I may still like French savoury bits but it takes a lot to beat a good old plain Victoria sponge.' Her voice softened. 'How was your trip, *pucette*? Any luck in finding Hugo?'

Morgan faltered. 'You'd better sit down.'

Mlle Vachon scanned the room and checked on her guests who were laughing, eating, tapping their feet to the music, Emily and Tiff on opposite sides of the room. '*Bon*, follow me.' She led her into the kitchen. George winked and left. They sat at a tiny table pushed against the wall.

'So... yes, we did,' said Morgan. 'It was quite a road trip that led us from here to France to Cornwall.' She explained how he and Sylvie had moved into the grandparents' house, and about his job in the French surf shop, then the one at the activity centre in Fistral. 'He's called Felix now.'

'What?' Mlle Vachon had been quiet until that point. 'He's changed his name? Why? When? And according to this surf shop owner, he was running away from someone?'

'There's more to come. He's married to Paige. He's been living here, in Manchester, for several years.'

Mlle Vachon's eyes widened, bigger than ever, behind the glass lenses. 'Hugo... I mean... Felix, and Paige, they are together? After everything that happened?' She shook her head. 'Why did she agree to this trip, then? Why not tell you in England?'

Morgan shrugged.

Mlle Vachon sat muttering to herself in French, shaking her head. 'Felix... he is okay?'

'I presume so,' Morgan replied in a short tone. She looked sheepish. 'Sorry, but his welfare is the least of my worries. All I want is for this to work out for Olly, with minimal upset.' Yet Morgan couldn't help wondering why Paige hadn't come. Perhaps she and Felix had fallen out?

'I understand, I do, but he was one of my best friend's sons. Hugo... Felix, was a good boy deep down.'

Paige was good, deep down, Morgan knew that in her heart, and despite all the lies, despite the hurt, she didn't wish her ill.

'But you saw the way he was at school, pupils and teachers blinded by his charisma. Surely you weren't as well?'

'He had a... difficult home life, Morgan. Oh, I am not excusing what he did. He treated the four of you abominably. But us humans, we have two voices inside: one skilful, well-meaning, the other not so. Circumstances can make us befriend the wrong one. Felix, he...' She sighed and patted Morgan's hand. 'How *is* Olly? How are you holding up, *pucette*?'

'Olly has phoned Felix and is still in shock. Me? I don't know.' Her voice trembled. 'The four of us had a big row in Cornwall. Other secrets had come out, just as we were getting on again.'

'Remy, time for the cake!' called George.

Mlle Vachon got up and held out her hand. 'Moping won't do. Come on. Help me cut it. We have guests, plates and George's sweet tooth waiting.'

Morgan ate the Victoria sandwich whilst Emily and Tiff avoided eye contact. The three of them offered to help wash up once everyone had gone. Morgan kept looking at the clock. Paige really had kept away. Emily went into the dining room to crouch down and study Mlle Vachon's fish, Monet and Matisse. Morgan dried the last plate just as a rapping on the front door resonated through the house. Mlle Vachon disappeared and came back, minutes later, holding a gift bag. Morgan's stomach flipped.

'Are you sure I'm not too late?' asked Paige as she came into view.

Mlle Vachon looked at the four of them. 'It's never too late for cake.'

36

MORGAN

'Thanks for a lovely birthday, *mon cher*,' said Mlle Vachon to George as she fetched his coat. 'See you for lunch tomorrow? We can eat leftovers, then go for a walk if the weather holds.'

George waved at Morgan and her friends. He winked at Mlle Vachon and kissed her on the cheeks. She saw him into the hallway and they spoke in low voices for a few minutes. The front door closed and Mlle Vachon reappeared.

'*Bon*... let's sit at the table.'

'George is lovely,' said Paige, fiddling with her watch strap. 'How did you meet him? How long have you been seeing each other? His accent isn't Mancunian; where does he come from?'

Mlle Vachon indicated for them to sit opposite each other, two either side, her at the end.

Her lips twitched into a smile. 'My pupils haven't changed much. I still see through distractor technique, young Paige. You and your classmates would try all sorts on me back in the day if a test was due. Like the time... yes, in your Year Eleven, out of the blue you told me about a law that the French National Assembly had just voted to pass, banning religious clothing and items from schools – you'd overheard your parents talking. I remember because a classroom discussion ensued. I indulged you because it was a controversial, important subject. Still is.' She ran a hand over the tablecloth, free from crumbs now. 'On the surface, a lot has changed since 2004, on a public, global and personal level. I've got arthritis, often I'm still in bed when school bell time comes around, I have trouble finding the right words in French, let alone English...' She formed a fist. 'But the more fundamental things are the same, such as religious discord, discrimination, such as the basics of our personalities. In here...' She thumped her chest. 'I'm still the person I was back then.' She gazed at the four faces. 'I couldn't help you, that night of the prom; you were full of hormones, teenage angst, anger, humiliation, disbelief, hurt. But you are grown women now. Fine ones, I can see, at that.'

Morgan, Paige, Emily and Tiff exchanged sheepish glances.

'I know about Paige marrying Hu... Felix, but Morgan mentioned there were other secrets too.'

Silence tightened the air between them. Morgan's heart pounded in her ears; it was as if she were back at school and waiting outside the head's office. Very occasionally, she caused mischief, tipping Jasmine's rucksack upside down or bunking off a lesson to smoke with Paige in the toilets.

'We all hid things from each other,' said Morgan. 'Not only was I the only one to... get intimate with Felix; I actually *did* care how boys saw me and feared I was going to end up with no one.'

'I never told the girls that people looked at my clothes and belongings and made certain judgements, and I hated it,' said Paige.

'The others had no idea I was actually unhappy with my appearance, or the looks and comments from others,' said Tiff.

'Each of us wore a mask,' said Emily. 'Mine was to hide stuff about my mum.'

'Tell me, *pucette*,' said Mlle Vachon softly.

Emily explained the truth about her mother's illness and 'death'. 'When Mum realised I'd found her out, she called me a nosey little bitch, too clever for my own good. She warned me men didn't like clever women and that I'd end up on my own if I wasn't careful.'

Morgan had heard French swearwords before, but never from Mlle Vachon.

Mlle Vachon took off her glasses and rubbed her eyes. Put them back on. 'Go on, *chérie.*'

'Mum had always laughed at my modest dress sense, and put my big, comfy knickers on her head once, threatening to show the neighbours. She took me shopping, bought me more fashionable stuff, but then went mad when I wouldn't wear the short skirts. Mum sneered and said a lorry driver wouldn't have been interested in her if she'd been an intellectual.' Emily looked out at the garden. 'Thing is, Dad is really intelligent. There's not much he doesn't know about English wildlife...'

Emily spoke as if she found it hard to stop, and Morgan understood. Mlle Vachon always did have a knack of extracting the truth.

'When I told my younger brother Mum had left, he blamed me at first, before he understood the whole truth,' Emily continued. 'He said I hadn't looked after her well enough. She'd actually told him I was Dad's favourite. In some weird way, I reckon she was jealous of me.'

'Oh Emily,' said Mlle Vachon. 'I wish I'd known.' She paused. 'Being treated by your mum like that must have been impossible to talk about, almost as if you'd have been making it up.'

Vigorously, Emily nodded her head. 'Out loud, it sounded so unbelievable... as if I was just being dramatic, or looking for attention, or even worse...' She swallowed. 'As if there must be something deeply wrong with me if my mother behaved like that.'

Morgan caught Mlle Vachon's eye as she gave her, Paige and Tiff pointed looks. She began to understand why Emily had found it so hard to open up.

'I did manage to tell Felix some of this stuff though, because of the common ground between us, his dad treating him as badly. He was... so understanding. The colour drained out of his face. He said my mum and his dad sounded like a perfect match. When he was younger, his father would tease him for crying, tell him he needed to toughen up. He gave me a really long hug and said I could talk about it to him any time.' Emily caught Paige's eye. 'I never told him about Mum not really dying, but he knew all the bad stuff she did to me and didn't mention any of that at the prom, even though he was clearly doing everything he could to hurt us that evening. At first, I thought it was because he'd been speaking the truth about his dad and he was worried I'd tell everyone. But as I matured, as I looked back, I decided perhaps he did have a shred of decency in him.'

'Have you ever worked out what was at the root of your mum's behaviour?' asked Morgan.

'Me and Dad have talked about it over the years. With my brother too. After the shock of her deception had passed, the three of us became really close. Still are. She'd never said much about her childhood and we didn't visit my grandparents often. When we did, the atmosphere was always frosty. Once I asked why we didn't see more of her family and she simply said they were a bunch of tossers.' She shot Mlle Vachon an apologetic look. 'She had a brother too. Younger as well. Her parents were made up and spoilt him rotten, gave him all the chances, sent him to private school, encouraged him to go to university. Mum was dyslexic and they'd call her stupid.' A tear trickled down her cheek. 'I loved her so much when I was little. She didn't need to do any crazy stuff to get the attention of a girl who thought her mummy was the cleverest, prettiest person on the planet.' Her voice cracked for a second. 'Turns out, my love, along with Dad's and my brother's, wasn't enough.'

'You've been so strong,' muttered Tiff.

'*So* strong,' said Morgan.

'You really have,' added Paige.

It was getting dark outside. '*Chocolats chauds?*' suggested Mlle Vachon gently.

Morgan got up to help her. When the two of them came back into the room with the hot chocolates, the others had closed the blinds and switched on the lights.

'Right,' said Mlle Vachon, 'what other secrets are keeping you four apart?'

Tiff rubbed the back of her neck and opened up about befriending Jasmine.

'You know she is head now?' asked Mlle Vachon.

'She hasn't changed,' said Paige.

'If nothing else, you have to admire her determination, her ambition,' said Mlle Vachon. 'That girl stood out in no way academically and yet here she is, at the helm of one of the best high schools in the district.'

Tiff sipped her drink. 'I've no excuse for befriending Jasmine despite the way she had – and continued – to treat my best friends. It started off as just helping her with English, but soon I couldn't resist becoming friends with one of the populars. So shallow. If I could go back, would I do it again? No. But I can't change the past. All I can do is ask for forgiveness.'

'Honesty is a quality to be admired as well,' said Mlle Vachon. 'What Tiff has said is very real. Sometimes good people do bad things. We can't take them back. All we can do is learn and move on. I suspect you did, Tiff?' Mlle Vachon prodded.

'Oh yes, for sure.' Tiff looked at Morgan, Paige and Emily. 'Once I'd left school, started my career, gained confidence, however fun Jasmine was, even though I saw a different side of her, I realised what a betrayal it had been. On my first proper job, I had a bit part. The lead actor was vile to work with, a real diva. He counted the number of lines his co-star had and demanded the same number. One day, he made the runner cry; we'd become friends and I found her sobbing in the toilets. I went back on set and he was full of charm, asked if I wanted to go for drink after the day's filming. Despite not liking him, what a chance that would have been to pick his brains and network. But I said no straightaway and took the runner out for coffee instead.'

'But Jasmine had bullied us for years,' said Morgan. 'How could you overlook that?'

'I don't know, I really don't – yet is it so different to each of us ignoring what a bastard Felix had been?' asked Tiff.

Mlle Vachon sipped her hot chocolate. 'No one reaches my age without regrets. Show me an older person who's gained their wisdom through leading a mistake-free life, and I'll show you a liar. Mistakes hurt us. Shape us. Act as a mirror to show us the person we truly aspire to be.' She put down her mug. 'When I was seventeen, I slept with a friend's boyfriend.'

The other four sat up.

'Without explaining, I backed off from the friendship. Hurt her, proba- bly. I took the coward's way out and... ghosted her, youngsters would say now, instead of confessing. However, I've forgiven myself. It took a while. He was funny. Good-looking. I was lonely and had secretly been jealous of my friend. We had drinks at a party, she was out of town with her parents. I instigated what happened. He and I never spoke again.'

Wow. Mlle Vachon had always looked so... wholesome.

'Does this episode make me a terrible person? No. It makes me human. Have I ever cheated on a friend again? You bet your life I haven't.' She sat down again and adjusted her glasses. 'Talking like this doesn't mean any of you forget what has happened. It's about accepting each other's flaws. It's about... growing. Perhaps since being back together, you have started to get some perspective on where your teenage heads were at.' She turned to Paige. 'But you have married Felix as an adult. You have a current story to tell.' Mlle Vachon stretched. '*Bon*. Despite all that cake, my stomach rumbles. Let us take a break and have a light tea, yes?'

Chatting about the weather, the Easter weekend, Mlle Vachon's French club at the library, they put out the remaining baguette, cheese and cold meats, crisps and a plate of crudités. Mlle Vachon fetched a bottle of red wine. Morgan declined and didn't understand why Paige raised her eyebrows at that. They picked at the food, apart from Paige, who ate nothing at all. Eventually, silence fell.

'I used to chuckle that you four called me Miss Moo Moo,' said Mlle Vachon. 'I went out with a retired farmer once. He told me that cows are very social animals; they form friendships within the herd, and produce more milk if named and treated like individuals by humans. Friends have seen me through my life, especially as I've never married, never had children. I've gone through periods on my own, with no partner and when friends have been busy, periods that have been lonely – not in terms of filling the day with activity but... emotionally. Those times emphasised my friends' value, despite fallouts we might have had. Sometimes saying, "I'm sorry" or, "I miss you" feels like the hardest thing but trust me, it's not.'

Paige took another mouthful of her drink before pushing back her chair and taking a deep breath.

'Felix and I discussed me coming here today,' she said. 'He agreed I could share his story – said it was right.' She fiddled with the expensive watch again. Mlle Vachon rubbed Paige's arm as she began talking...

37

HUGO

Gripping the banister with every step, Garth stomped downstairs. Garth, that's what Hugo had started to call his dad, in his head. You had to earn the name father. Garth stumbled down the last step and swore loudly. Hugo and his mum sat in the kitchen, it was a Sunday morning. As a treat, they were having bacon butties. They looked at each other – which was new. It was only a small gesture but an acknowledgement that was never voiced, never discussed. When he was little, in front of Hugo, Sylvie would pretend nothing was wrong. But as her son got older, the charade became harder to carry off, although she still stuck to the story that his dad was a good man – he worked very hard, needed understanding, that without him, they'd have nothing.

Hugo believed the opposite. That without him, they'd have everything. Like calm. Laughter. The cat he and Mum had always wanted. His dad said any pet would take away too much of busy Sylvie's attention, saying he was only thinking of her. They'd have excitement about the right things as well, like enjoying takeout as a pair or going to the cinema together – not about Dad working late or catching flu and having to stay in bed, away from them.

Garth staggered into the kitchen and collapsed, filling a chair, hair greasy, unshaven, pyjamas smelling of beer, looking nothing like the sociable, smart version of himself who went to the pub. Garth gave a loud burp and Sylvie winced.

'Still recovering from that meal you made Friday night,' he said and gave her a pointed look.

Sylvie poured him a cup of tea. 'I'm off to the shops in a minute,' she said, in a tone as artificially bright as the Blackpool illuminations that Hugo had always wanted to visit. Garth had never let him and Mum go, said slot machines were a waste of money, even though a couple of times a week, he went to the bookies. 'So what do you fancy for your tea, love?'

'None of that foreign muck we had on Friday. I wouldn't feed a dog cold rice wrapped up in seaweed.'

'I liked the sushi, Mum,' said Hugo in a measured tone as she got up to make her husband's bacon butty. Hugo reached for the ketchup but Garth gripped his wrist, keeping one eye on Sylvie, making sure she didn't see. He squeezed so tightly but Hugo refused to flinch, despite knowing there would be a sore, red mark later. He'd have to hide it with his watch – or, if he met his mates, spout the elaborate lie created over several years, that he belonged to a boxing club and the bruises came from there. The elaborate lie he'd told his mum was that they did martial arts at school. Mum wasn't well; she often got sad, and took tablets. Hugo worried about burdening her further. Sylvie turned around and just in time, Garth let go. She put his breakfast in front of him.

'You disagreeing with me, lad, with your la di da ways?' asked Garth. 'Don't you forget who's helped you get this far – *me* grafting, day in, day out, putting those fancy shoes on your feet that you wore to the prom last night.'

Mum was the one who'd got up early this morning to do her first cleaning shift of the day, just before Hugo did his paper round. Garth was happy for her to work seven days a week whilst he worked when he felt like it, picking and choosing plumbing jobs.

'Given you every opportunity, I have, to be a somebody, when I never had that chance. You'd better remember that when you're older and living in some fancy pad in London. Your mum deserves the best, that's what I'm thinking of.'

'Leave him, Garth,' said Sylvie quietly.

Garth turned to her very slowly. She stared at her mug of tea, sat very still.

'Did you say something?' he asked.

'No. It was nothing,' she mumbled.

'I don't like your hair tied back like that,' he said. 'It makes you look ten years older.'

Her eyes glistened.

'I only say it, Sylvie, because I love you, want you to look your best.'

'Thank you,' she said and gave a small smile, pulled out the bobble. Hair with early greys tumbled across her shoulders.

'There's my girl.'

Stomach on fire, jaw stiffened, Hugo willed his dad to piss off, to leave Mum and him to chat and enjoy just an hour of the weekend alone. Instead, Sylvie got up from the table and five minutes later came back, grabbed the shopping bags and squeezed Hugo's shoulder gently before she opened the back door and left.

'Eat up lad,' said Garth. 'I work hard to put food on this table.'

Hugo hadn't started his roll yet; he had no appetite. Not after the prom. Not after the way he'd hurt those girls. Garth squirted brown sauce over his bacon, lifted up the roll and took a large bite. Sauce dripped down his bristly chin and landed on his pyjama shirt. He wiped his mouth with his sleeve. 'So you couldn't even get voted prom king last night? That, after losing the football captaincy? You said it wasn't your fault, what happened with Coach, but you were stupid to get caught seeing that other girl. Mind, it wasn't the worst crime in the world. Coach needs his head testing if he's going to lose players over girls, and he needs to stop sucking up to the headmaster. Nothing worse than a brown noser. I hope you got revenge on those girls who dropped you in it, like I told you to. No son of mine gets done over. Not if he's a man.'

'What, a man like you?'

'Too right.'

Hugo gave a wry smile.

'What's so funny?' Garth put his palms on the table and leant forwards.

'You.'

Garth's cheeks flushed but Hugo didn't care. He wasn't afraid of his father any more, not after yesterday's prom. He'd had enough. Yes, Hugo had got his revenge, in the aftermath of Garth punching him in the chest for getting dropped from the football team. But neither of those things were the actions of a man.

'You, a man who bullies his wife? Who hits his son?'

Garth blinked for several seconds and then roared, lunged forwards and grabbed Hugo's shirt collar, knocking over his mug of tea. Hugo's heart pounded *ba boom, ba boom*, like it used to when he was little and Dad would clip his ear when Mum wasn't around, or shout at him if he made too much noise playing, or if he cried when he fell over, telling him it was for his own good, that people expected boys to be strong. Hugo would take the crying to his room, sobbing into the pillow, telling himself he was a bad son, and that one day, he'd make his father proud. Sure enough, he excelled at sport. A muscular body and generous height helped, although still, his father never once said he was proud. Hugo learnt how to become popular, too, by actively behaving the opposite way to how his dad behaved towards him, flattering people, making them feel special – yet with an underlying hard edge. His fists would fly first if anyone disrespected him. It didn't happen often.

Because Hugo's biggest aim in his life was not to end up like his father.

He took in the flaring nostrils, the cold eyes and ugly expression, he smelt the bad breath: things that used to give him nightmares. Hugo pictured the hurt faces, the tears, of Morgan, Paige, Emily and Tiff – the only four pupils to have ever seen a glimpse of the true him. Their rock bottom became his.

He was angry at Garth but oh so angry at himself because last night confirmed what Hugo had feared for a while.

The worst had happened.

Hugo *had* turned into his dad.

It stopped now. It wasn't too late to change. His remorse over last night told him that. Firmly, he pulled his father's hand off his collar, his athleti-cism giving him the advantage. Garth stood up and threw a punch. Hugo veered sideways before standing up taller, stronger. Now *he* took Garth's collar, dragged him to the wall, pushed him up against it, held him there, his grip not loosened by his father's struggles, tight enough to keep him trapped, but not bruised.

'You ever fucking touch me again and you'll regret it,' said Hugo, very clearly, his nose practically on his father's.

'Don't you dare speak to...'

'It's over.'

Garth broke free and threw another punch, saliva dripping from the corner of his mouth. Hugo caught his arm. 'Play nice and I won't tell Mum. I'll go to sixth form college, then uni. I'll leave you two alone.'

Hugo had no reservations about lying, not when it was to protect his mother. A plan had built in his mind, over recent weeks, as the deception with The Secret Gift Society got out of hand, as he became fond of the four members he was on a path to destroy. He was going to have an honest conversation with Mum and was going to ask her friend, Mlle Vachon, if they could visit one afternoon. Hugo could tell by the way the French teacher looked at him at school that she knew he wore a mask. If anyone could help, it was her. Once, he'd heard Mlle Vachon and his mum talking; he'd been thirteen and was starting to see his dad through different eyes. Mlle Vachon asked Mum if she was happy and Mum talked about how lucky she was to have a husband so devoted to her, who took control of the money. He said he was better at maths and didn't want her to worry about that. Also he was such a good judge of character and could spot bad friends of hers a mile off before they had a chance to hurt her, pressing her to drop them.

Mlle Vachon had replied. 'Control isn't love, it's a form of management. Of governing. Of ruling over. Of no equality. It is everything a relationship shouldn't be.'

Mum simply replied that Mlle Vachon didn't understand, that their relationship wasn't like that. Even if it was, she could never say anything, Hugo might get taken away by social services. Mum had given a nervous laugh.

Hugo had felt guilty at the small voice in his head that said he longed to be taken away from his dad. But he could never leave Mum. As it was, he existed in a cloud of guilt that he wasn't able to stop Garth from making her life so miserable.

But fuck that, now he was sixteen. He wasn't a kid any more. Now Hugo could work full-time, have legal sex, drink alcohol out with a meal, ride a moped, he could join the army, do so many things. That included standing up to a coward – and helping his mum leave him. He would stand side by side with Mlle Vachon; his mum might listen to the two of them together.

'Wait 'til I tell your mother about this,' spat Garth.

Hugo let of his father's arm and smiled. 'But you won't, will you? Because you worry I'll tell her the truth. Then there's the small matter of the police.'

Garth stepped away. 'What do you mean?'

'You never thought this day would come when I couldn't put up with your shit any more? The number of people, teachers too, who've seen my bruises at school. The police would never find the imaginary boxing club I talk about to cover you, proving your guilt. You think next door hasn't heard your shouting? Theses terraced walls are paper thin. I can tell by Mrs Taylor's sympathetic looks that she's listened to your gaslighting word for word, especially after you've been drinking. That'll be why her husband won't have anything to do with you.' Hugo gulped and tears came out of nowhere, running down his face.

Garth burst out laughing. 'Oh, look at Mummy's boy. This is all bluff. Christ, you're going to get a hiding.'

He moved forwards. Hugo did as well. Garth looked confused.

'Yes. I'm my mother's son. Thank God. Human. Sensitive. Loving. What's fucking weird is you *laughing* in a situation like this.' Hugo's voice shook. 'I loved you once, Garth, but you should have had my back instead of punching it every time I wasn't looking. It was your job to keep me safe, to help me build my confidence. Instead, I've spent my childhood tiptoeing around. We could have been best mates. You wouldn't have cared if I hadn't been football captain, or hadn't been voted prom king. You'd have simply been proud of me for being me, and helped me navigate this mad world. *That's* why I'm crying because I finally accept it will never happen. You're a monster who's torn me down instead of building me up. You're a whiny, needy little child at heart. I have no father.'

Hugo wiped his eyes and gave Garth a hard look before walking into the kitchen to clear up the spilt tea and wash up. He tipped Garth's roll into the bin. Garth went to protest but one raised eyebrow from Hugo and he skulked upstairs.

38

MORGAN

Morgan passed around a packet of tissues. Mlle Vachon blew her nose.

Poor Hugo.

Poor Felix.

A lump formed in Morgan's throat. Their geography teacher used to pretend to punch people who were talking. Everyone hated him. He threw a fist at Hugo once, missing his head by a mile, but Hugo had ducked. The whole class laughed. Morgan had never seen Hugo look so pale. Of course, he'd recovered quickly, got to his feet, put up both his fists, did a funny boxer's dance. The teacher sent him outside for disrupting the lesson.

'Felix saved his mother,' said Mlle Vachon. 'I could never make her see sense on my own. It broke my heart.'

'He's still genuinely remorseful about the prom, about everything,' said Paige in a quiet voice.

'Was Garth the person he was running away from when he left France?' asked Emily.

'Yes. His dad got wind of Sylvie's death. Felix guessed he was looking for money. Felix inherited his grandparents' house, just as his mum had, after her death. He wasn't afraid of Garth but once and for all, didn't want to see him ever again, reckoned he'd always be turning up, trying to blag favours, money, and preventing Felix from leaving the past behind. So he came back to England as quickly as he could and changed his name by deed poll. Felix was always his first name, after Sylvie's beloved grandfather. Garth hated it but it was the only thing she ever insisted on. As a compromise, Garth chose Hugo as a middle name and that's what he was known by. Barron was Sylvie's maiden name.' Paige sipped her wine. 'He's never told me much about the detail of the relationships he had with you three. He's... loyal like that.'

'In a screwed-up way,' said Tiff.

'His life was screwed up,' said Paige, simply. 'He was caught up in the abusive world of his father. Felix feared that everything he'd worked for, to please his dad, to keep peace, to try to repair his dysfunctional family, had come crumbling down because of us finding out about him seeing Sophie.'

'That's one thing I don't understand...' said Mlle Vachon. 'The Hugo I knew wasn't a two-timer.'

'Mlle Vachon, with due respect, he four-timed us!' said Tiff.

'But that was part of a plan, non?' replied Mlle Vachon. 'He genuinely cared for Amelia. I'd seen the way they were together.'

'He's thought about it a lot over the years, had counselling,' said Paige. 'Amelia's dad was a headmaster – upstanding, principled. Sophie's was a detective, putting wrongs right. Looking back, Felix believes he was searching for a replacement father figure he could look up to.'

Amelia once said to Morgan that it was weird how Hugo would often spend more time talking to her dad, when he went around.

'I'm sorry about Felix's dad... and your mum, Emily. The pressure your parents put on you, Tiff. I was very lucky with mine,' said Morgan.

'Me too,' said Paige.

'Hugo – Felix – told me his dad was ill, like my mum. I assumed he meant physically, but now I can see he meant that his dad had a drink problem and no doubt other mental health issues...' said Emily and she shook herself. 'I need a walk, to clear my head. I can't take this in. I'm actually sorry for the person who treated me like a fool, who stole my first kiss and threw it back in my face.'

They all got to their feet.

'Go, *mes chéries*, I am tired now, but Paige, please, you'll give Felix my contact details?'

Paige gave her a hug. 'He said he wanted to get in touch with you again. Thank you, Mlle Vachon. Thanks for helping us talk this through like... like adults.'

'I say it again: what fine adults the four of you have become,' she said and dabbed her eyes.

'It doesn't always feel like it,' said Tiff, in a small voice.

'I often think I'm doing the mum thing wrong,' muttered Morgan.

'Me too, for a different reason,' said Paige.

'My life hasn't turned out as I expected,' mumbled Emily.

'That's why friends are so important,' said Mlle Vachon, quietly. 'Sylvie and I helped each other. Garth was her weakness but in other areas, she was as strong as they came and often talked sense into me on the days I doubted myself and worried I'd let down the school or a pupil.'

The four old friends looked at each other.

'Having said that...' Mlle Vachon folded her arms under her chest. 'Never forget that the most important friendship is the one you have with yourself. A good friend is kind, patient, respectful, and if the voice in your head is not those things then you need to ignore it.'

Morgan shivered as they stood under the crescent moon and waved to Mlle Vachon as she peeked through her lounge blinds. They walked down Greenacre Lane. At the end, a small path led to the right.

'I haven't been to Greenacre Park for years,' said Morgan. 'I wonder if it's still got those four swings in a row.'

It did. The women sat down and swung higher and higher, to the point that a little Olly would have shouted he'd touched the sky.

Olly. He was Morgan's whole universe. However, the last few weeks had shown her that for both their sakes, it was time to open her heart to others. Den had got the closest but, even then, a barrier had always been in place, not letting him fully into the life she and Olly shared, a life she'd always protected.

'Woo hoo!' shrieked Tiff.

Paige joined in. Then Emily. Next Morgan.

'Shut up!' hollered a voice from a nearby house. 'My kids are trying to sleep.'

The women looked at each other and started laughing. They got off the swings and dropped onto a bench. Emily announced her plans to become a veterinary nurse. Morgan said she was determined to go to university. Paige talked about how it was time to stop putting off getting fertility tests. With a little encouragement, Tiff opened up about Joe, said they'd kissed, and like in the old days, the others wanted the details.

'I can't wait to meet him,' blurted out Emily, 'if you want me to, Tiff.'

'That would be... good. And I'd love to meet Olly. I could give him some autographed photos for his friends.' Tiff grinned.

'I'm hoping to meet him too, if that's what Olly wants,' said Paige. 'He sounds like a wonderful young man.'

'So we're going to stay in contact. Does that mean the four of us are...' Morgan couldn't say it.

'Friends again?' said Paige. 'I hope so.'

'Me too,' said Emily.

'Definitely,' said Tiff.

Morgan could hardly breathe. 'You know, the word "algebra" comes from the Arabic word *al-jabr* that means *the reunion of broken parts...*'

'Now we've put our friendship back together again,' said Emily. 'Stronger than before, right?'

The others nodded.

'Sorry for what I said about you feeling threatened,' said Tiff to Paige.

'Yes, sorry for doubting you,' said Morgan.

'It's okay,' said Paige. 'You'd had a huge shock.'

'What I still don't get, Paige,' said Emily, 'is why you didn't tell us about Felix when we first met up, outside Dailsworth High. I'm glad you didn't,' she hastily added, 'otherwise we probably wouldn't have got to know each other again. But why didn't you take the easy option? In Cornwall, you mentioned something about Morgan having another reason for the trip we went on.'

Paige looked along the bench, past Emily and Tiff. 'Morgan?'

Morgan's eyebrows knitted together. She bit the inside of her cheeks. It was easier to pretend that the other reason didn't exist. She only talked about it now and again with Olly.

'When we met up in that New Chapter Café, you got upset, Morgan. I followed you to the toilets, remember?' said Paige. 'I sensed there was something you weren't telling us, why you wanted The Secret Gift Society to get back together. I asked you straight but you didn't reply.'

Morgan's face flushed.

'Little things over the last week have concerned me, like you not drinking in the pizzeria in France and Mlle Vachon's today, and the backache you've mentioned, both fed into my worst fears, from what I saw written on that letter in your handbag.'

That explained why Paige had quizzed everyone about illnesses they'd had in the café near the surf shop in France. She must have been hoping Morgan would open up.

'You left your handbag outside the toilets at New Chapter Café,' continued Paige. 'I'd taken it back to the table for you. One word in particular from the letter jumped out. I didn't mean to see it and—'

'Morgan?' said Emily.

Tiff leant forwards.

'I'm okay. Honestly,' she said. 'I just... something bad happened, before Christmas, and straightaway, despite the years apart, I wanted to be with the best friends I'd ever had.' She took a deep breath. 'One night I ended up in A&E with acute indigestion. Olly was away and I was low after a crap day at work, so I treated myself to a movie night with pizza, garlic bread, and ice cream and I lay down whilst eating – the worst thing for heartburn. But the pain was so severe, I was on my knees, and I rang for an ambulance because I thought I was having a heart attack. I was so embarrassed at the hospital...'

'Go on,' said Paige, gently.

'But when I took off my shirt for the ECG test, the doctor turned his attention to a mole behind my shoulder. I'd never seen it. He didn't like the look of it and sent me for tests. It was a stage two melanoma. Cancer.'

'That's the word I saw on the letter,' said Paige, her voice wavering.

'It's a frightening word, right? I was in shock for a couple of weeks.' Morgan exhaled. 'I reckon I got it due to those countless weekends I helped out my granddad with his gardening business when I was at school. He paid well and I loved being outdoors. I never applied sunscreen, not even in the summer. Nor did he, and several years ago, he had a few skin cancers cut out.'

'Oh Morgan. I'm so sorry,' said Emily.

'Have you had it removed?' asked Tiff.

'Yes. In January. They didn't hang about. The operation was a success, they cut out the mole and the skin around it, and got rid of all the cancer cells.' She turned to face her friends fully. 'That letter was about a check-up I've got next month. It had only arrived the day we met. My mind was focused on meeting you guys and I must have absent-mindedly put the letter in my bag so that Olly didn't see it. I'm going to have these check-ups every three to six months for the next five years.' She swallowed. 'If you three are in my life, it's as if my head, inside, isn't so dark, I could ring you or we could go out and get pissed.' She gave a small smile. 'Or maybe not that. I'm on a health kick.'

'Thank God. Oh Morgan, this all sounds positive...' said Paige and grabbed her hand. 'I've been so worried.'

Morgan held on tightly.

'Does Olly know yet?' asked Emily.

'He does now. But I'd kept it secret until the day before we went to France. I... hadn't wanted him to worry. The operation was a day case. I pretended I was at work. Then I took a few days off and they put me on light duties when I returned. I'd told Mum and Dad. They were really supportive. Dropped meals off for us, for a while... Olly and I weren't talking much so he didn't really notice anything much different.' Morgan touched her shoulder. 'The whole thing gave me an extra push to find Olly's dad, in case, one day...'

'Now none of that,' said Emily, firmly. 'The prognosis is excellent for stage two melanoma.'

'I know. I've seen the figures.' Statistics Morgan could work with. 'But you can't help thinking the worst.'

'I'd feel the same,' said Tiff, 'but those thoughts aren't facts and come from the voice in your head being affected by the negativity bias we're all born with: to suspect the worst so that we're on guard and survive longer.' Her cheeks blushed. 'I read an article about it once when I was suffering from stage fright.'

Emily held Morgan's free hand and Tiff held Emily's and Paige's.

'We used to say our oath and help other people, but we never really used our gifts to sort out our own problems, did we?' said Morgan.

'Perhaps there's something in what Miss Moo Moo said,' mumbled Emily, 'about the most important friend being yourself.'

'Well, I'm almost worldwide famous so that makes sense,' said Tiff, with a gleam in her eye. 'Used to mixing with the likes of Keanu Reeves, not Manchester hoi polloi. Best to keep to myself for a good time.'

'Regardless of any career change, I won't forget my geriatric care training,' said Emily, face beaming. 'I'm the friend I'll need for a comfortable old age.'

'I'm the coupon queen and can smell out a supermarket bargain,' said Morgan. 'I can't think of a friend I'd rather have in the current climate.'

'I can read an enemy like an open book,' said Paige, mouth upturned, 'so in case adulthood gets like high school again, I'll prioritise me. Talking of which...' She rummaged in her handbag and pulled out a sheaf of torn pages. 'I picked these up on the beach, in Cornwall. Our closed cases.'

Morgan reached out, feeling as if she'd been handed a winning lottery ticket. 'I'll stick them back in the notebook. I'm so glad I didn't throw it out.' She pressed the papers to her chest.

The women linked arms and huddled together as the evening chill set in. Morgan's phone bleeped and she read the message. Her shoulders started bobbing up and down as laughter produced tears in her eyes.

'It's Jasmine. She must have got my number from Olly's old records.' Morgan wiped her eye and stood up. Importantly, she cleared her throat.

'Hello Morgan, I'm asking this out of desperation, obviously. Is The Secret Gift Society still operating? I don't wish to get the police involved at this stage – I have the Dailsworth High's reputation to consider – but we have a phone thief in our midst. I've had several angry parents in to see me. The school's own investigations haven't been productive. Would you and the other members consider taking this case on, for old time's sake? I'd be... most grateful. Yours, Jasmine White, Headteacher.'

Morgan, Paige, Emily and Tiff looked at each other and the man in the house hollered again as their raucous laughs filled the park.

39

MORGAN

Morgan stood outside the hospital. It was the day of her cancer check-up: the appointment the letter in her handbag had talked about. That carefree night swinging in Greenacre Park felt like years, not weeks, ago. Her scar had healed really well during the four months since the operation. She'd tried not to become obsessive about checking her body for new moles after each shower, twisting in the mirror, lifting up her arms and feet. She pulled her anorak tight as the spring breeze blew against her neck as if trying to shake her out of the spiral she'd fallen into for a few moments. It happened now and again.

'Ready?' asked Paige.

'You'd better be,' said Tiff, 'it's almost as cold out here as on the Isle of Wight.'

'Apparently, this hospital's canteen serves excellent coffee,' said Emily.

'Thanks for taking the day off, you three,' said Morgan. 'I really appreciate it. Well, Paige at least...' She smiled.

'I'll have you know I've signed a temporary contract to work at a small medical clinic until my veterinary nursing course starts in September,' said Emily.

Morgan punched Emily's arm playfully, stomach fizzing at the prospect of the coming autumn when... she'd be starting university, like Olly. Felix wanted to cover Olly's accommodation costs whilst he was there, and any other bills, his son only had to ask. This freed up Morgan's savings to pay for her own university expenses. She'd turned down his suggestion at first, used to being independent. However, Olly had insisted, said it was his decision.

'It'll be great, us both students at the same time,' he'd said.

'Does this mean I can visit and go "out out" with you and your mates?'

'Mum. Please never call it that again,' he groaned.

A man in a wheelchair passed the four women and went through the hospital's doors that opened automatically.

'You can't blame me for taking it easy after three weeks' backbreaking filming,' said Tiff.

'What, eating delicious film set catering? I saw a programme about it once,' said Morgan, a twinkle in her eye.

'As well as romancing Joe,' added Emily.

'He came over to sightsee for a weekend whilst I filmed; we hardly saw each other!' Tiff protested.

Morgan looked at Paige and they both shook their heads in an affectionate manner. Morgan was glad Paige had finally seen her doctor. She and Felix had been referred. Within a few weeks, they'd find out if there was really a problem. Paige and Felix had also invited Morgan and Olly over for lunch. Yes, it was awkward. Once or twice, Morgan had snapped. But as Felix talked, slowly the heart palpitations steadied. Felix was good with Olly. Didn't push. Didn't shy away from the fact he'd fucked up in the past. In light of everything new she'd learned about Felix, Morgan reckoned he had a gift too – resilience.

Morgan gazed past Emily's shoulder into the distance, and three figures stopping outside a café. Mlle Vachon's arm was linked with Felix's. He had his arm around Olly's shoulders. Olly turned around and stared. He gave a wave in the air. Morgan waved back, then he and the other two went in, disappearing from view. Morgan, Paige, Emily and Tiff would meet them there after the appointment.

Morgan looked at her friends, one by one. 'I nearly forgot.' She delved into her rucksack and pulled out four boxes, kept one for herself and handed out the other three. They opened them up and held the silver necklaces in the air, each of them bearing a tree. Sunshine glinted off them.

'These are like the leaf necklaces we bought from Afflecks for our fourteenth birthdays,' exclaimed Tiff.

'Except we've each grown a few branches since then,' said Morgan.

The others gave her a hug and then helped each other put them on.

'Right. Let's do this,' said Morgan. 'The sooner I'm in, the sooner I can put Olly's mind at ease.'

'And your own,' Paige murmured. 'You don't have to pretend with us.'

They entered the reception area and Morgan breathed in the smell of disinfectant. Many hospitals in China didn't have a fourth floor, where her appointment was today, because in Cantonese-speaking countries, the word four sounded like the word death. But in English, it reminded her of more positive words, such as fortitude. Formidable. Forgiveness.

They said friends were the family you choose, but to Morgan, it was more elemental than that. The Secret Gift Society had sounded like an adventure novel, fantasy even, but not one of the four flew, had super strength or could shape-shift like molten metal. That didn't mean an indescribable force, a bit of magic, like that of the hazel tree, hadn't held them together. Oh, they'd been placed in the same tutor group back in Year Seven, but over twenty other pupils had been in it too. Mother Nature didn't disclose all her tricks, and for once, logical Morgan didn't need an explanation as to why she and the other three had been drawn together then, and again now, why they'd never been able to forget each other.

Logic. Kindness. Empathy. A sixth sense. Everyone had a gift unique to themselves, Mother Nature made sure of that. But it was up to each person to find out what theirs was, and then to use it for the good of others – and themselves.

'You look great,' whispered Emily.

'I'd be scared in your position,' said Tiff, 'but we're by your side.'

Paige squeezed Morgan's arm. 'I've a feeling everything is going to turn out fine.'

Morgan looked at her friends, did the maths and smiled. Yes, it all added up.

ACKNOWLEDGMENTS

First off, huge thanks to my innovative, hardworking, approachable publisher, Boldwood Books. The whole team is positive and enthusiastic, whilst remaining transparent and realistic, something I very much appreciate as an author. Thanks to the amazing design team who've not given up on trying to find just the right * * *look* * * for what I write. With *Lost Luggage, The Memory of You* and now *When We Were Friends*, they've smashed it. Thanks to Nia for her Amazon and pricing expertise, to Claire Fenby and Jenna Houston for their marketing know-how, to Candida Bradford, Ben Wilson and the rest of the team, including Amanda Ridout at the helm.

A special mention to my editor, Isobel Akenhead. It can be tricky being handed to an editor who hasn't signed you, but Isobel has never made me feel anything less than valued and her enthusiasm shouts from the page with her edits. Isobel's wonderful sense of humour is the icing on the cake.

Huge thanks to my agent, Clare Wallace, at the Darley Anderson Agency. This one's for you, Clare.

Several things inspired this story of friendship, and one was a group of girls I used to hang out with at high school. We called ourselves RAGS, an acronym made up of the first letters of our names. Thanks to Rachel and the other members for their friendship back then. I have fond memories of the time we spent together.

For Netflix fans, *The Umbrella Academy* also inspired this story and the concept of people having magical gifts. Whilst in that TV series, the gifts are superhero-style, I became fascinated with the idea of having a gift that was considered ordinary, was invisible to the naked eye, yet could bring about big change.

Martin, Immy and Jay, you three are my superheroes, day in, day out.

Thanks to all the bloggers who've supported this story. A shout-out to Rachel Gilbey and her associates. You are all so generous with your time. It's hugely appreciated.

I have to mention The Friendly Book Community on Facebook. Thanks for your continued support and the banter!

To use the other meaning of the word gift, you, readers, are one for me. This is my nineteenth book and some of you have been by my side all the while, others have joined me later. To every one of you, thanks for the feedback and excitement over each new story. Those things keep me at my desk.

Lastly, a word to those of you who have often felt on the outside and aren't really sure why. I say to you that friendship isn't always like we see on *Sex and the City*. Your best friend might be family, a pet, your partner, someone you only talk to online. There are no rules. Whatever suits you best. Friendship is about being comfortable and not having to put on an act.

ABOUT THE AUTHOR

Samantha Tonge is the bestselling and award-winning author of multi-generational women's fiction. She lives in Manchester with her family.

Sign up to Samantha Tonge's mailing list for news, competitions and updates on future books.

Visit Samantha's website: http://samanthatonge.co.uk/

Follow Samantha on social media here:

facebook.com/SamanthaTongeAuthor
twitter.com/SamTongeWriter
instagram.com/samanthatongeauthor

ALSO BY SAMANTHA TONGE

Under One Roof

Lost Luggage

The Memory of You

When We Were Friends

Boldwood

Boldwood Books is an award-winning fiction publishing company seeking out the best stories from around the world.

Find out more at www.boldwoodbooks.com

Join our reader community for brilliant books, competitions and offers!

Follow us
@BoldwoodBooks
@TheBoldBookClub

Sign up to our weekly deals newsletter

https://bit.ly/BoldwoodBNewsletter

Milton Keynes UK
Ingram Content Group UK Ltd.
UKHW041106250923
429337UK00002B/19

9 781804 154366